Starflight to Destiny

Books by Patrick Dearen

The End of Nowhere
Haunted Border
Apache Lament
Dead Man's Boot
The Big Drift
Starflight to Destiny
To Hell or the Pecos
Perseverance
When the Sky Rained Dust
The Hidden Treasure of the Chisos
On the Pecos Trail
Comanche Peace Pipe
When Cowboys Die
The Illegal Man
Starflight to Eternity

Nonfiction
Bitter Waters: The Struggles of the Pecos River
Devils River: Treacherous Twin to the Pecos, 1535-1900
Lone Star Lost
Saddling Up Anyway: The Dangerous Lives of Old-Time Cowboys
Halff of Texas
The Last of the Old-Time Cowboys
A Cowboy of the Pecos
Crossing Rio Pecos
Portraits of the Pecos Frontier
Castle Gap and the Pecos Frontier, Revisited

Starflight to Destiny

Patrick Dearen

SPEAKING VOLUMES, LLC
NAPLES, FLORIDA
2022

Starflight to Destiny

ISBN 978-1-64540-834-5

For my son, Wesley Dearen

Chapter One

"I could've had it. It was there in the dark, spinning, waiting. Something powerful, intelligent, waiting for me to let it out. I could've had it all, but I don't even know what it is!"

Skaggs had muttered incoherently ever since Blake Sharrel had looked back through the boulder field to see him slump to the base of an outcrop. Now Blake stood over him, listening to the desert wind howl like a Rhythian hellhound and watching the chalky swirls powder the craggy face with what seemed certain to be a death mask.

Ohilo's twin suns were a fire against Blake's skull as he knelt beside the old man. Blake's breaths came in spurts as if he tried to breathe inside a starship fuel chamber, but Skaggs's gasps were pitiful and broken by frightful coughs that specked his white beard with blood. From his torso oozed life, dark and thick.

For an hour now, the two had tried to shake their pursuers in this maze of boulders, but there was no escaping the fierce suns that swelled Blake's tongue. Three hours before, in a choking gulp, he had downed their last water, and now he faced a vagabond's death at the hands of nature, or a criminal's death at the electromagnetic crack of a Banning semi-automatic.

Either way, he thought, it wouldn't have mattered much if it had been anybody but the United Star Systems chasing them.

"Two days and still after us," rasped Blake, glancing over his shoulder. "Something's not right, just not right, I tell you. They wouldn't keep after us this way for stealing next to nothing."

Skaggs groaned from deep inside and a spasm racked his body. His eyes suddenly were great ovals of white with pinpoints of black, and he stretched an arm to the sky, the muscles tensed and fingers quivering, as if straining for something beyond reach.

"The Leijan!" he shrieked. "You're waiting for somebody to come back!"

Blake slapped a hand to the Banning at his hip and checked the dust that whipped through the boulders. "*Quiet.* You'll have them on top of us!"

When Blake turned again to those crazed eyes, he felt a strange cold grip his neck. He shuddered, clutching his throat and gasping for air, and his eyes fixed on the quaking muscles in Skaggs's uplifted arm. He followed the tatters of the shirt from shoulder to elbow, saw the dust clinging to the forearm and the blood caking the wrist, watched the quivering hand and bony fingers reaching out toward . . .

Blake started, his gaze frozen. He convulsed and tried to draw away, but his body refused, as if it were no longer his to command.

Beyond the old man's fingers lay the twin suns, and somehow Skaggs seemed to touch them. No, it was something far beyond which seemed to claim that hand, something intelligent and strong in the reaches of the galaxy, a thing so evil that inexpressible fear surged through Blake.

His vision blackened, his lungs crying for oxygen. He implored the thing to ease its grip, give him air, set him free. Skaggs's outstretched fingers quaked violently and he cried out, splattering blood on Blake's chest. The chill at Blake's throat became scorching desert heat, and then he was wallowing in Skaggs's blood and swallowing air. He lay there long moments, his lungs heaving and the dust grinding against his face. He struggled to his elbow and looked into Skaggs's eyes, and they suddenly seemed to hold more than insanity. It was as if they had looked upon things not to be seen, things man never was intended to know.

"Lee-juhnnn," mumbled Skaggs. "Calling. It's calling. Leijan's secret can't . . . no . . . please . . . can't die with me."

Blake dragged himself up with the aid of the outcrop and studied the desert. He was scared. Scared of that inexplicable sensation of an alien presence, scared of those troops, scared of the thirst in his throat. He glanced at the blood-streaked leather pouch on the ground. That's why he was here, for a lousy two hundred credits. Let's do a job on the starflight payroll shipment from Earth when it docks in spaceport, the stranger who called himself Skaggs had told him that night in the sleazy palace of delights. There's a million credits on board, maybe two. Enough, Blake had realized, to strike another blow in his personal war against the United Star Systems, the U.S.S.

But the two of them had gotten away with next to nothing, except a U.S S. company on their tails and an energy bolt wound at the muzzle of a Banning. Blake had spotted the troops only an hour before, pursuing as relentlessly as ever through unyielding waste and searing heat. But why should they care that much about a couple of underachieving thieves?

He watched the specks of blood pit the dust as another coughing fit racked Skaggs. Blake couldn't understand the sensations he had felt moments before, but he had more important worries right now. The troops had to be getting close. Grasping the satchel, he shook it in Skaggs's face.

"Why's this so important?" he whispered. "Or is it something else they want? You maybe?"

Skaggs coughed violently and pressed his hand against his wound. "Guards . . . retina match . . . saw me . . . recognized . . . had to . . . saw me."

"What are you saying?"

Skaggs weakly parted his scraggly beard and found a measure of coherence. "Take away beard, twenty-five years."

Through the bloody and dusty whiskers, Blake saw the scar, deep and jagged from chin to ear. Frowning, he drew back, pricked with the memory of a thousand wanted posters dotting walls in colonial outposts throughout the United Star Systems.

"Lasky. *N. G. Lasky*." He shuddered, unable to reconcile the impression he had held of the petty thief before him with the person most wanted in the U.S.S. the past three decades. "I thought you were dead. Everybody does but the U.S.S. You know the kind of price they've got on your head? Where you been all these years?"

"Through all hell."

Blake sank inside. "You too," he said quietly. And for a moment he was back on Rhythia, a young U.S.S. officer watching his superiors unleash the sharp-fanged hellhounds on the only woman he had ever loved.

Skaggs-Lasky clutched his arm. "The Leijan's secret. It won't let it die with me. Power beyond my wildest . . . The things I've seen . . . nobody else . . . closer."

Blake suddenly realized he could leave the old man to the troops and flee without pursuit; only the desert would then stand between him and safety. He could even get away with the booty, minor though it was. But that abrupt memory of her, and the mental agony he had borne all those years because of her forbidden worship of the Leijan—that legendary force promising such power—wouldn't let him turn away. No matter that the troops pressed close, he had to listen, had to try to understand what had made her do what she had.

He dropped to the old man's side. "The Leijan. What's it all about?"

Those haunted eyes again seemed riveted into great mysteries, and as Skaggs-Lasky spoke, it was with the sudden strength of one possessed. The succeeding few minutes found images beyond understanding racing through Blake, filling him with awe and strange fear. Then came a sudden movement beyond the nearby boulders, bringing him whirling with a hand on his Banning. There was a shout, a command, and a blue bolt of energy whizzed by his ear to explode against the outcrop. He spun to the old man, his hands fierce on his shoulders.

"Where is it?" he demanded. "Tell me where the Leijan is!"

He pressed an ear close to the trembling lips of the man convulsing before him, and in the seconds before the troops stormed in to send Blake fleeing, Skaggs-Lasky whispered in his dying breaths the location of the fabled power known as the Leijan.

***

Of all places to escape the long arm of the U.S.S., the slums and sleazy palaces of delight in the Black Market sectors of outpost cities such as Ohilo's capital offered the greatest haven. Here, a man could blend with a sea of lemstel addicts, dregs, dropouts from society. It was here Blake took refuge, with only two hundred credits in his pocket but a multitude of thoughts haunting him.

On this night in Shahnina's Palace of All Possible Delights, he sat oblivious to the frivolity, staring through swirling leche smoke at his distorted image in a flagon of lemstel. Already the intoxicants had dulled his senses, yet they only intensified his memories of Lyra, the dreams of two persons bonded forever by love.

Forever.

It was a long time sometimes, too long for someone lacking the commitment to see it through, to back up words with a lifetime of sharing, of caressing, of holding the other tightly and vowing to be always at the other's side to face together the madness life offered.

"Together," he muttered, a caustic laugh sticking in his throat. He held out the flagon to the empty bench across the stone table. "Here's to togetherness. Here's to you, you whore." The lemstel was fiery in his throat, the bitterness fiery in his mind.

The liquid ran down his chin as he withdrew the flagon, and then he slammed it to the table to slosh foam.

Skaggs-Lasky. It's your fault, you and all your lies. She was gone and I didn't care anymore. I didn't care and now you've brought it all back, made me crawl through hell like all those other years.

Fingers suddenly ran through his hair. He smelled an Ohiloan perfume that had been known to send men mad, and he turned to see dark, flowing tresses braided with gold ornaments. He followed those strands up past a clinging, silvery garment and found the puffy face of a lemstel addict.

"You," she said. She nodded to the golden hanging beads that cloaked a doorway. "The rooms, come."

He seized her wrist and slung her arm away. "Get away from me."

She ran the back of her hand along his cheek. "The lemstel, it makes you forget, but you must remember."

Blake burst to his feet, the bench grating against stone floor and toppling. He clutched her elbow and backhanded her across the mouth. "I said get away!"

Raucous laughter erupted. Falling away, the woman sobbed quietly and slunk back into shadows thick with smoke.

Rent by conscience, Blake stood with lowered head until her moans died in the din of hoarse grunts and girlish squeals. From nearby, the coarse laughter continued.

"You sure put that piece of trash in her place," came slurred, gravelly words.

Blake lifted his head to the table beyond, where a burly figure sat facing him; the man's eyes were bloodshot and he guzzled lemstel from a flagon at his tangled red beard. Lyra's face filled Blake's mind for the hundredth time that night, and suddenly he felt as much hatred for himself as he did bitterness toward her.

"You talking to me?" he asked.

The man withdrew the flagon to leave foam hugging his beard. He pointed, flagon in hand, across the room. "She ain't fit to wipe my filthy boots on."

Again came Lyra's face, this time coupled with an ache in the back of the hand that had struck. "Figure she's still better than red-bearded scum." He reached for his flagon and drank long and hard, ignoring the screech that told him the man had scooted back his bench and stood.

Blake offered only a glance as the man took a step toward him, the close-set eyes glaring. He stood half a head taller than Blake, and his massive shoulders and the scar tissue about his eyes evidenced a powerful man who had seen his share of fights.

"Look at me, you—" The stranger's words ended with the vilest of epithets.

Unflinching, Blake wiped his mouth with the side of the hand that held the flagon. Finding those red-streaked eyes, he flung the vessel's contents full into the matted beard.

The man seemed so stunned by Blake's impudence that he just stood there a moment, clawing at his burning orbs. Then rage set him lunging forward. "I'll tear you apart!"

Knuckles drove into Blake's cheek, his temple, his midriff, snapping his head back, gashing his eye, sucking the air from his lungs. He doubled over, the blows still raining, and dropped to his knee and a hand. Then a boot swept toward his eyes out of a dreamy, shadowy world that no longer held pain and he collapsed.

Throughout, Blake never lifted an arm to defend himself.

He was only vaguely aware when two men dragged him into a grimy hall past the beads, and even less so when hands rummaged through his pockets. He lay there writhing and moaning, Lasky's words haunting him in semi-consciousness. His mind reeled with abstract concepts and images that were at once legends and truth, dreams and reality. Where did one end and another begin? How could a man ever know?

He opened his eyes to see Lyra's face as she drew near, her fingers clutching a damp cloth. No, it was another who knelt above, bathing his wounds, a woman with golden ornaments in her hair, a cut on her lip.

"Don't, don't," he groaned, his own voice distant in his ears. "Can't go on. Just let me die."

"Shhh," she whispered, dabbing his face. "You will not die. Great things are destined for you."

He stared at her through a haze, and this time he did not push her away, even as she dragged him to a cramped and dank room thick with the odor of sweat and urine. Through a fog, he saw a blanket settle over him, and though he believed them alone, he heard as if from afar the woman imploring the help of another. Then nightmare and delusion gripped him, as they had each night since Lasky had whispered such secrets.

Blake opened his eyes to morning sunlight filtering through tattered velvet curtains that shimmered to the whistle of wind. He lay on the floor, a blanket tucked about him, and as he stretched, his lower rib and kidney ached. He groaned and found a knot at his temple, a scab in his eyebrow.

"You are alive. Did I not tell you so?"

He looked to see the woman with gold-braided hair sitting on a bed. Her lip was cut and swollen, because of his own hand. He turned away.

"Why'd you help me?" His voice was lifeless, drained of all hope or caring.

"You want to die, Blake Sharrel. You want to die because you hate yourself, because you hate what you have become."

He came to his elbow and faced her once more. "How you know me?"

"You are known throughout the palaces of delight as one who nurtures bitterness like a vineyard, bitterness toward the U.S.S., toward every woman. You come to a place where women are cheap, thinking you can mistreat them and no one will care. But there is one who still cares, and that one is you."

Blake edged up, the soreness crippling him. "Why don't you shut up."

"You must remember what you were," she said as she stood. "You have a destiny, Blake Sharrel."

He was on his feet now, gingerly, blanket in hand. "The only destiny I have is to knock you across this room if you don't shut up."

"You do not hate me. It is only yourself you hate. You pick a fight and then do not defend yourself, because of her."

Blake stiffened. "Who are you?"

She lowered her head as if studying the filthy bed. "You see what I am now." She raised her eyes. "But it was not always this way. When I was young, I saw things, heard voices that few have heard since ancient times. Some say I was a prophetess."

Blake laughed caustically. "This is some place for one."

"Heed my words, Blake Sharrel. I have not seen who she was, what she did to you, but I called on the One Who Sustains during the night and saw another yet to come. In her hand is a key, and in your mind a strange story, and together you will stand as mighty servants so all may be fulfilled."

"You crazy fool." He flung the blanket into her face and headed for the door.

"Cover my mouth, Blake Sharrel, but you cannot silence the One Who Sustains."

Then Blake was through the door and fleeing down the hall, three words pursuing him relentlessly: "Remember your destiny!"

Chapter Two

Rhonda Gregory stooped at the entrance of the grotto in the Valley of the Skull and watched the dust hang in the shaft of light inside as a hand-held laser slowly disintegrated rock. The air was musty, and the shadows held an unease that left her yearning for the receding warmth of day. She rested her knee on the narrow ledge, and at her heel fell two hundred meters of precipice, all the way to the badlands on the canyon floor.

She shuddered, trying to drive away the cold coming from inside, and watched her father's sweaty hand scan rock with laser. He worked with the care of a practiced archaeologist, but also with near-obsession, and Rhonda touched the mound of rubble before her and fought back the emotion.

"Dad, you've got to come down, rest awhile."

The laser hummed as its ray continued to dance. Nostrils inhaled, exhaled. And that silent, inexplicable cold still penetrated like a quiet wind across a glacier.

She crawled inside, her flowing chestnut hair brushing the jagged overhang. "Let's go down, let me fix you something to eat."

The whisper of the laser persisted. She reached for her illuminator, and its beam found his face and she began to tremble. The wide eyes were as unresponsive as the grotto's walls, and down his etched features ran rivulets of sweat and dirt.

She crawled through the low passage to his side; he turned at her touch and his eyes came alive. "Rhonda, I . . . I think it's *here*." He motioned to the laser-scarred wall before them. "Do you know what it would mean uncovering the holy of holies, right where they worshipped the thing?"

She turned to the wall and ran quivering fingers along its coarseness, studying it with a trained eye. It was gritty, and when she looked at her fingers, there was only dust that seemed to emit a crypt-like cold.

"Oh, Dad," she half-sobbed, brushing back his sweaty hair. "You've been working too hard. Let's go down, rest a little. Tomorrow'll be a fresh day. You'll feel better."

"No, it's here. I know it's here. A little more and I'll find it." He turned to splash rock with laser. "The Leijan. I'll find you. I'll find the answer if I have to crawl through hell!"

She left his side, her face flooded with emotion. When she sought the jagged crevasse of light defining the grotto opening, it was as though icy hands clutched her from behind. Her mouth grew dry, and even though she too was an archaeologist, a person of science, she became intensely afraid.

What was it that made her feel this way? How could these walls possibly hold anything worth fearing so? She tried to rationalize it as worry about her father, but this was the kind of terror that crept down her spine and sent her clawing at the ground until the oppressive Brazeille Two sun beat down from above.

She collapsed, exhausted, by the crate of explosives on the ledge and remembered a little girl, always at her father's side as he dug relentlessly in the desolate gullies and buttes of a remote archaeological outpost. She saw again his eyes growing increasingly obsessed, listened once more to her mother plead with him not to work so hard, tell him that, in time, the answers would come.

She remembered that same girl, starting away each year for colonial school in the adjoining star cluster, looking back for a final glimpse of home and always seeing her father wave from a new dig, just he alone amid sun-baked crags. And upon term's end, the first image that burned itself into her mind from the descending shuttle was always of her father standing steadfast in the wasteland that was his life. Each time his face would be more lined, his eyes more haggard. Then his words and gait began to lose their vigor, his tired eyes reflecting the strain of a man doomed to but fitful sleep, all signs of deterioration wrought by a brutal, frustrating life on an otherwise uninhabited planet on the fringe of unexplored space.

Rhonda had been home from the university that summer her mother had fallen ill. With meager medical supplies, her father had tended her the best he could, and those desperate times had been the only occasions Rhonda had ever seen him away from the digs during daylight. With the supply shuttle not due for months, he had contacted the nearest U.S.S. star base and begged for aid. But while the life of a commissioned archaeologist was important to the U.S.S., that of a family member was like dirt flying from a dig, and she had died in his arms. And then there truly had been nothing left for him to live for except to find answers to tomorrow by digging for the Leijan's secrets in the Valley of the Skull.

Now, as Rhonda lay tasting the sweat trickling down her face, she realized he too was dying, at the hand of the fixation that had summoned him across the United Star Systems so many years before.

Back inside the interstellar-age Quonset hut that served as home and laboratory, Rhonda sat alone beside an open window and studied until the shadows of the far canyon wall crept close. For the thousandth time she reviewed the computer data, seeking clues to this great, inexplicable sinkhole that constituted the lone blemish on a wasteland world without other noteworthy features. To look upon it from orbit was to feel a distinct unease, for the orifice too closely resembled the face-first imprint of a human skull, complete with eye sockets ever staring. The computer monitor, however, spoke only in cold, hard facts:

ARCHAEOLOGICAL INVESTIGATION, VALLEY OF THE SKULL

Chief Archaeologist: Gerald Gregory, duration 41 solar years.

Assisting Archaeologist: Rhonda Gregory, duration 8 solar years.

Supervisor: S.H. Langdon, Secretary of Archaeology for Science Cabinet, United Star Systems. Newly assigned.

Site Location: Brazeille Two, uninhabited planet.

Discovered: 337 solar years ago.

Duration of Dig: 337 solar years.

Importance: Site of intelligent life, now presumed extinct.

Relevance to Leijan: Earliest-known place of Leijan worship, artifact-dated 7,000 solar years in past.

Rhonda's head spun. How could any of this be, when Earth had developed interstellar travel a mere six centuries ago? Only then had man begun to seed a galaxy seemingly void of other intelligent life, yet there was no denying the archaeological evidence of onetime human habitation and Leijan worship on this outpost world.

Rhonda continued to scroll. The facts about the Leijan, like those of the Valley, served only to raise questions without answer:

Nature: Device or substance. Worshipped by underground cultists for almost a solar millennium.

Origin: Unknown. Clues shrouded in folklore.

Properties: Incredible force.

Potential: If harnessed, unlimited power. A threat to the security of the government.

Location: Unknown.

Recommendation: Continue archaeological investigation in Valley of Skull. Reduce threat of unauthorized seizure by limiting team to two persons.

Addendum: Leijan worshippers banished to planetary colony Vi-olesha Two 532 solar years ago. No contact since. Entry into Violesha planetary system forbidden. Leijan worship elsewhere a capital offense.

Rhonda proceeded to review the geologic evidence of a cataclysm that had wiped out all life in the Valley almost a thousand years ago. Most disturbing was the astounding coincidence about it all, for the catastrophe seemed to have occurred at the exact moment Earth's leaders had spontaneously laid down arms to avert nuclear holocaust and preserve mankind's existence. Only then had Leijanism, a religion with rites apparently identical to those once practiced in the Valley, sprung up on Earth.

The historical facts that sped across Rhonda's monitor told the rest of the story. Peace had spawned the United Earth System, predecessor to the United Star Systems. The government's iron fist had rendered war a thing of the past. Only Leijanism had triggered opposition, evolving as it had into a fanatical cult so esoteric as to confound all but its practition-ers. Eventually the cult's penchant for mutilation and human sacrifice had led to its banishment to an isolated planetary system. Subsequently, U.S.S. explorers had stumbled upon the Valley of the Skull, where battle-scarred inscriptions in rock hinted at great secrets in the holy of holies, wherever that might be.

Rhonda closed her eyes to the whirring monitor.

Questions.

Questions without answers.

She was deep in reflection when her father, his face exuding awe as he clutched something minuscule, staggered through the door and collapsed.

"Dad!"

She upended her chair in the rush to kneel close. His mouth was drawn and twitching and his bloodshot eyes stared blankly.

"What's wrong?" she asked. "Tell me what's wrong!"

His wide orbs slowly focused on hers, and in them she read a strange fear. He grasped her arm, and she felt the tremor that gripped him.

"The holy of holies!" he babbled excitedly. "In the grotto, Rhonda. It's in the *grotto*."

He came to an elbow, his white hair a disorderly shock, and extended the minute object with quaking fingers. It fit comfortably in her palm, a dark, metallic three-pointed star that somehow seemed to emit a strange warmth as she listened to his ravings.

"A chamber, the things I saw when I broke through. Skulls, lining the walls and ceiling, black, nearly too black to see. Cold, like icy hands grabbing at you all the way, a dozen meters, right up to an altar of skulls. Skulls everywhere." He stretched a quivering hand to the artifact in her palm. "This, just lying on it, underscored by etchings, Greek like so much else in the Valley, thousands of light years from where it ought to be. I can't understand, not any of it!"

"Oh Dad, calm down!" she pleaded, wiping his sweat-beaded face. "Just lay there, rest a minute. Please, you're scaring me."

"The etchings, they told about a star that shined bright in the morning only to fall into total dark and end up worthless, about somebody locking it away a thousand years and somebody else letting it go *with a key shaped like a star*. What can it all mean?"

She didn't know, but concern for her father explained only a measure of her surging fear.

It was only after she persuaded him to take a sedative and helped him to a couch for long-denied rest that he finally spoke with greater composure. As the twin moons crawled across the windows, bathing them in twilight, they talked far into the night, the star-key on a table before them an ever-present reminder of the mysteries they faced.

At one point, Gregory's voice dropped to a whisper, and even though they were the lone inhabitants of a world, he glanced over his shoulder.

"You know why I'm here, Rhonda, why I've done this all these years. You've never asked me, and I've never said, but you know."

"It was never for the U.S.S., was it, Dad? You know something about this place. You suspect something. You think it's our only chance, don't you. That man's future, his hope for a future, somehow is tied in with all this."

Gregory leaned forward to massage tired eyes. "Twenty-seven. That's all I was when I first dragged your mother here. Just a girl, facing a hard life, but so supportive of anything I wanted. Three years, I told her, just three years and I'll have the field experience to go back to the university and have everybody's respect. Oh boy, the plans we had, a nice home in a good neighborhood with a swing in front, a garden in back, and a house-full of kids in-between.

"I owed her better than this. I owed you better. But then I started chasing mysteries in this awful place and they just grabbed hold of me and wouldn't let go, still won't let go." He motioned to the artifact. "So what's this thing's role in all of this?"

"A key?" quizzed Rhonda. "Is this it, Dad? Is this what the etchings were talking about?"

His raspy words grew quieter, slower, wearier. "We don't even know what the Leijan is, so how can we make sense of something said to be a way to let it loose?"

"Let loose a thousand years from when, Dad?" Rhonda briefly studied the reflection of moonlight in the object. "Was there any frame of reference? And set free from where? The holy of holies? The Valley of the Skull?"

As he shook his head, Rhonda noted how he had aged in just the past few hours.

"Maybe the answers are still in the grotto," he said. "Maybe they're on the Leijan colony, Violesha Two. You know how many centuries they've gone without outside contact? Wouldn't their traditions still be pure? If we could just get there, talk to them. Maybe we could sift out the legends, get hundreds of years closer to what those first cultists on Earth knew." A sigh of near-resignation left him sagging in his seat. "Maybe there's not any answers. Maybe it was just coincidence all those things happened at the same time. The catastrophe here, the end of the war, the Leijan cult starting up on Earth."

Rhonda placed a reassuring hand on his arm. "There was life here, Dad, Earth people. We know it. And yet there couldn't've been, not that far back when nobody'd developed space flight yet. Think about it. Seven thousand years ago we were supposed to still be riding donkeys, and yet somehow we came all this way.

"We've either got to accept that, or believe that one time there was another form of intelligent life in the galaxy and it was here, and that even separated by thousands of light years, both of those humanoid groups developed identical cults completely independent of each another."

She shook her head. "No matter which one we believe, it's going to grate on all we know as scientists." She took the star-key and again felt its strange warmth. "It's all got to be interrelated, and if we can't find the answers here, then all we can do is live with it, or get to Violesha Two somehow."

Gregory's chest expanded and he stood. His knees seemed weak, and he had to support himself with the wall, yet his voice gained new strength. "Day after tomorrow that new secretary of archaeology will be here. Langdon, isn't it? The Science Branch makes out like it's not totalitarian like the Military, but they're worse in their own way. They strand us here six months at a time and then send somebody to check up on us, afraid we'll find out something we can use against them. If we only could. They ban organized religion and seize every scrap of sacred writing, then turn around and make the U.S.S. itself a religion to bow down to and never question." His voice dropped. "The government's everything and people like your mother are nothing."

He nodded to the star-key. "We've got to keep quiet. You hear me, Rhonda? We've got to keep quiet. Anybody they see as a threat to their power, they'll crush."

He glanced at the window, beyond which the distant grotto lay hidden in shadows. "Answers, up there maybe. Tomorrow I've got to find out, seal the grotto. The rest is up to you, studying the artifact, making sense of it. Just a day, that's all we've got, a day."

She stared at the mysterious object in her hand and wondered if there were some things better left untouched.

Chapter Three

Long before day broke over the Valley of the Skull, Rhonda's father retreated to the grotto while she initiated tests on the artifact. As the day wore on, she was astounded to learn that it was composed of a hitherto unknown element, a significant discovery even aside from its possible bearing on the Leijan. By late afternoon she turned her attention to age-determination; under ideal conditions, tests could date an artifact to within hours. But it was an involved process, the final stage consisting of long minutes of submersion in chemicals monitored by computer.

It was during this anxious wait that she stepped out on the veranda and looked up-canyon. She could barely discern the grotto's entrance, a small oval of black high against the vermilion gorge wall.

A pinpoint of light suddenly exploded into sight far above the canyon rim and she started, the hot wind somehow chilling her. That steady burn in the sky could be only one thing, atmospheric friction against a craft shuttling a crew from an orbiting ship.

No. Langdon couldn't come today, not twelve hours early.

She lowered her gaze to the grotto. "Dad!" He was there, in the holy of holies, still digging for the answers, and now it was too late to seal that chamber.

With only minutes remaining before the craft would streak down-canyon, she rushed back into the lab, her mind reeling with all that she had to do. With tongs she clasped the star-key and reached to detach the computer. Her eye suddenly caught the readout on the monitor and she froze, stunned. Regaining her composure, she deleted the information from the computer banks, and then swept aside all evidence of an age-determination test.

Except for the artifact itself.

She seized it and whirled about in frantic search of a hiding place immune to discovery. It slipped from her fingers and clanged against the floor at her heel. The heel. If she just had time to pry it loose, gouge a hollow, hide it inside.

But she didn't *have* time. Slipping the artifact into a zippered pocket, she burst out into the blazing heat and made for the trail zigzagging up to the grotto.

It took her long, anxious minutes to fight through the badlands and ascend to the dig, and by the time she reached the crate of explosives on the ledge before it, she already could hear the roar of starship engines from far up-canyon.

"Dad!" she called into the shadows. "Langdon's here, the U.S.S. They're already here!"

Reflected light swept across jagged stone, and then a disc of brightness swayed before her and a moment of dreadful silence preceded a desperate cry. "They can't be. Oh Rhonda, not yet, not today!"

The light came nearer, and then her father was in the twilight, gesturing back with a trembling hand. "I can see it. I can look right through an eye socket and see it. In that awful altar of skulls."

"Oh Dad," she said, taking his frigid arm. "Get out in the sun. You're freezing."

"A tablet, is that what it is? The etchings on it, can it be interstellar coordinates, a Greek calendar? The answers right there and I can't make it out, can't break through. I've got to have more time. The skulls, too hard and cold. Now it's too late. What are we going to do?"

She embraced him. "Pray," she said, and then they staggered recklessly down the trail as rubble tumbled to the depths.

As they reached the final switchback, Rhonda felt a tremor through her boots. She turned to see the falling sun momentarily eclipsed as a silvery craft with friction-blackened underbelly thundered past to sweep its shadow along the cliff. Though she and her father had slowed to a walk, she knew that they hadn't gone unnoticed, and that the trail behind led only to the holy of holies.

By the time they gained the alkali flats fronting the lab, the ship already had settled to the ground amid a storm of dust spawned by retro-rockets, and a crewman in the uniform of the U.S.S. stood in the hatch. Rhonda brushed at her hair and hoped the harried lines in her father's streaming face were not as apparent as she feared. But how could they possibly act as if nothing was unusual?

They reached the craft's shadow to see the crewman yield the ladder to a stoop-shouldered man with thin, gray-flecked hair. His beady eyes were close-set and his chin receded, and as he climbed down, the decided thickness at his midsection grew pronounced. His appearance was incongruous with the fit and trim image the U.S.S. demanded, but the khaki uniform with yellow stripes at the sides bore the insignia of the Science Branch, not the Military. Even so, a holster at his belt bulged with a standard-issue military Banning.

He turned to them and Rhonda saw her father's lips tremble in awkward silence, forcing her to take the initiative.

"I'm . . ." Why couldn't she control the tremor in her voice? ". . . Rhonda Gregory. This is my father, Doctor Gregory."

The man's eyes swept over her; despite his wedding band, he seemed to pay her rounded charms special attention. Or was she just self-conscious?

"Secretary Langdon. From the Science Cabinet." He looked at her father and extended a hand.

Gregory's fingers twitched as sweat poured down his brow. Again his lips formed unvoiced words. And Langdon's hand hung in open space, ready for the handshake that never came.

Rhonda shuddered and reached for Langdon's hand. "It's nice meeting you," she said, smiling nervously as he turned to the touch. "My father's under the weather today. You know how this heat is. You're early, aren't you? We weren't expecting you till tomorrow."

Again, Langdon studied her. "Arrival date was changed. I'm sure you were notified."

"Anyway, we're glad you're here. It gets pretty lonely out here sometimes with just the two of us."

Langdon's eyes wandered again up and down her clinging flight suit and he smirked, validating Rhonda's first instincts. "Maybe I can be of service in that respect." He glanced at the three men who had climbed down behind him. "This is Captain Pierce, his crew." The former, bearing the stern countenance and close-cropped hair of the military, was a burly man with deeply browned face and a pilot's wings at his collar.

Rhonda nodded politely. "We put in a request for supplies. Were they delivered to you?"

Langdon addressed the ranking officer. "Take care of matters, will you?" Then he turned to her father. "That high dig you were coming down from? Any promise?"

The only reply was the howl of the wind, and Rhonda hoped Langdon didn't read the same things in her father's eyes as she.

The sun had plummeted over the far ridge of the Valley by the time the three of them took seats on the veranda. Minutes before, Rhonda had given her father a sedative, so that now his hands were steady. Still, he fumbled nervously with the report in his lap as he looked at Langdon, who sat against the backdrop of silhouetted spires.

"I want to apologize for seeming so rude earlier," Gregory said with an old man's voice that now seemed older. "This heat, I get a little disoriented sometimes."

"Show me what you've got."

Gregory's fingers seemed frozen to the folder, and Langdon gestured toward it. "Your report. You've got it, don't you?"

"Yes, I . . ." He extended it with a hand suddenly unsteady. "I'm afraid there's not-not much new."

Rhonda cringed as Langdon focused on the records of each day's digs, tests, observations, and conclusions. She knew her father faithfully had documented the early days of the dig in the grotto; at the time, his professionalism had outweighed any concerns for personal safety. But now those very notations loomed immense, for they had not had time to strike them.

"This unusual marking you found in the north sector. You uncovered a number of items near it, Gregory?"

"Nothing that . . . hasn't been found all through the Valley. Human bone fragments, a cranium, particles of gold and silver that could've been tooth fillings."

"You did age tests?"

"In the back section. Right at a . . . at a thousand years."

Langdon looked up, his interest obviously piqued. "That takes them right up to the cataclysm."

Rhonda saw her father swallow hard.

For long, quiet minutes, Langdon read on. Throughout, Rhonda sat stiffly, as if a pin had pulled free from an atom-splitter grenade and an explosion were imminent.

Finally the supervisor lowered the papers and studied her father's face. "That marking in the north sector. What made you think it was a directional clue, led you to calculate the point high on the cliff?"

Beads of sweat popped out on Gregory's brow. He shifted uneasily, started to speak, but then coughed into his fist. Rhonda felt the atom-splitter readying to detonate.

"That's my fault, I'm afraid, Dr. Langdon," she interjected. "Call it woman's intuition. Unfortunately, I was wrong."

His eyes caught hers. "You spent months up there, blasting a trail, excavating. All that on a hunch?"

She turned a hand over in a shrug. "Regardless of what prompted it, it's been fruitless. Historically, the valley floor's yielded the only worthwhile finds."

Langdon's eyes narrowed. "I may be new to this position, but don't patronize me. Intuition? I've got no patience for digs that don't further the purpose of the search."

"So what is the purpose? My father and I are driven by a quest for scientific knowledge, not totalitarian needs."

"You're out of line!" Langdon's features went dark with anger. "You talk like that and the U.S.S. will . . ." He breathed sharply. "My younger daughter's still a teenager, rebellious as the day is long, but even she knows when to curb her tongue. Now tomorrow you're taking me to that marker, and after that, to that high dig if I'm inclined. Is that clear?"

In sudden dread, Rhonda stood and bit her lip to forestall the words she wanted to say. "Perfectly." And without inquiring if the briefing had ended, she wheeled and walked away, conscious of the star-key in her pocket and the urgency it required.

***

In secrecy that night, Rhonda concealed the artifact in her boot heel, just as she had contemplated. Still, she felt anything but secure a few hours later as day broke on a barren and rugged gully in the Valley of the Skull. Between close-set bluffs of rock, she and Langdon hiked side-by-side behind Gregory and two U.S.S. guards.

"I want to know something," said Langdon, breaking the rhythmic sound of boots crunching gravel.

She looked up to find his eyes passing a little too carefully up and down her frame. He grinned, as if realizing her thoughts.

"You admit getting lonely out here. Easy to see why. You picked the remotest habitable planet in the colonies. Why do that, anyway, be here on a job meant for a man?"

Rhonda's anger flared. Even now, there were those bent on subjugating women. "I've done all right for myself. If you looked at my file, then you know I was first in my class. Besides, I'm here to help my father. This is his life's work."

Without subtlety, Langdon continued to study her curves; he seemed to enjoy the fact that she was aware. He laughed quietly. "We're both intelligent adults. You and I know the needs of a man and woman." He took her upper arm, stopping her in mid-stride. "I can see you've got it all, Miss Gregory. We'll be back at the lab by evening. Hadn't you better take advantage of the situation while you can?"

Rhonda jerked her arm free and glared. "The plumber back home. You suppose he used that same line on your wife?"

"You little—"

"In her case," she interrupted, looking him up and down with contempt, "maybe I can understand if she was tempted."

Without waiting for Langdon's reaction, Rhonda turned and marched after the others.

Mid-morning found the group at the rim of a stairstepping dig bordered by serrated overhangs. A gritty wind powdered Rhonda's boots and created a haze in the four-meter excavation, which confined a shrouded boulder that angled up to crest at a meter or so. Rhonda's mind spun as she considered the implications of that marker hidden by a veneer of sand, but most of all, she feared for her father's life and her own.

Placing a steadying hand on his arm, she descended with him, and Langdon followed at their heels.

Gregory touched the boulder with his boot. "Here," he mumbled. "The rock that set us doing all the fruitless work on the cliff."

Langdon found a brush in his daypack and knelt to sweep the surface. Over his shoulder, Rhonda watched the bristles revealing stroke-by-stroke a linear scratch that became an arrow, underscored by one Hebrew character after another until a complete inscription was unmistakable.

Though she had studied the marker before, she felt the hair rise on her nape as Langdon shrank from it. His mouth went agape and the brush trembled in his hand.

"*Kadosh kahadashim,*" he muttered. "The holy of holies!"

"We . . . we thought it was Hebrew too at first," Gregory said hoarsely. "But now we . . . we think it's just a freak of nature, a natural cracking when the rock was subjected to a . . . to a rapid change in temperature."

Oh Dad, thought Rhonda. *Why couldn't you be a better liar?*

Without honoring Gregory with even a glance, Langdon sprawled before the boulder. Rhonda knelt at his back, sighting with him along the arrow and past the excavation's rim, all the way to the towering battlement and black grotto. In the cliff face just above that dig loomed a striking erosion pattern comprising wavy, triple lines, like "S's" stretching toward fang-like ends.

"The sign of the Leijan!" whispered an awe-struck Langdon.

When he stood to stare at the rocky heights, it was with the countenance of one who suddenly found himself on the brink of a great mystery solved. Rhonda rose with him, the distant erosion pattern disappearing as always, and she knew that the archaeology secretary would sprawl to the boulder a second time even before he did so. This time, she let him sight down the arrow alone, knowing that he would again find in the cliff a stunning etching that no other angle in the Valley of the Skull would reveal.

Now, Langdon rose not to stare at the grotto, but to spin to a hovering guard at excavation's rim.

"I want more troops on the ground. Double-time it back, have Captain Pierce bring in another shuttle from the orbiter. I want him to contact his superiors, isolate this solar system, have the Science Cabinet rendezvous here ASAP."

"Sir, what kind of reason should I give?"

"I'm secretary of archaeology. That's the only explanation he needs!"

Rhonda watched swirls of sand dance between the guard's legs as he marched away. "It's completely unprecedented, uncalled for," she argued, turning back to Langdon.

Langdon's fleshy face went red. "A maze of markers all over the Valley. Hint after hint about a holy of holies. A dozen generations baffled. Now this, the most definitive directional clue in all these centuries, pointing straight to the first Leijan sign ever found outside the colonies, right where you've been digging."

Gregory's cheek twitched. "It's a freak of nature, just a freak of nature."

Langdon gave him a penetrating stare. "You've found it, haven't you? *Kadosh Kahadashim*, the holy of holies."

"An empty lead, I assure you," spoke up Rhonda, trying to convey calm assurance. "You're an archaeologist. You know how many promising leads turn out to be nothing."

Langdon turned his suspicious eyes on her. "This some kind of game to you? You know the penalty for withholding findings? Try life terms in a penal mine."

For anxious moments the wind gusted violently. Gregory's twitch grew worse. The star-key seemed to push up through Rhonda's boot and burn her heel. She glared at Langdon and suddenly hated him, hated him because of the U.S.S. insignia at his shoulder, because he stood for the government that had let her mother die. As her mind quickened with a sudden plan, she forced a slight laugh.

"You must have a better imagination than we do, Doctor, if you think you've seen the sign of the Leijan somewhere. Why don't you give us a chance, hold off bringing in all those busy people till you check the grotto for yourself? Isn't your credibility on the line, maybe even your place on the Science Cabinet? Come on, let me show you."

Langdon studied her for long seconds, evidently analyzing her comments. He glanced at the distant fortification and its dark opening, and then turned to the U.S.S. guard. "That'll be all, Corporal. You can go back and place yourself at Captain Pierce's disposal."

"Sorry, sir, one of us is to stay with you long as you're in the field."

"You'll take *my* orders. This is for the eyes of the Science Branch only. Is that clear?"

The guard shifted uneasily. "Yes, sir," he said, wheeling and departing.

Watching him disappear around a bend, Rhonda found a ray of hope. Langdon had taken the bait, but how could she and her father act upon it?

When she turned, she found Langdon glaring.

"Last chance to make it easy on yourselves," he snapped. "Anything different you want to tell me before we go up there?"

Rhonda hadn't found an opportunity to clue her father in, and he had a quick answer.

"Yes. Go to—"

The back of Langdon's hand quick against Gregory's mouth prevented him from finishing. Frail and hurt, the only person Rhonda had in all the galaxy stumbled back and collapsed.

"You had no right!" she exclaimed, glaring at Langdon as she rushed to her father.

"You think the U.S.S. needs *him* anymore?" The secretary slung a hand toward the cliff. "Get him on his feet. Let's go!"

***

Rhonda never had felt so weary, so hopeless, as when they stopped with heaving lungs beside the crate of explosives at the grotto. She glanced at the Valley of the Skull falling away to the side: the grotesque spires and myriad buttes, the snaking gullies and bone-white flats, all imprisoned coffin-like by a great rock battlement whose red-hued strata stretched left and right to fade in distant haze. When she looked again to the grotto, she found the kneeling Langdon framed by the jagged entrance, and suddenly she pictured his skull crushed against those rocks far below.

Then flashback overwhelmed her; she was a girl living a lonely, hard life in a world where she might wander forever and find only her parents, and her mother was quoting from memory: *You will not kill.* It came from ancient Hebrew and Greek writings outlawed by the U.S.S., and though Rhonda had faced the government's atheistic curriculum throughout her schooling, a mother's unwavering faith had led her, too, to acknowledge silently a Creator who sustained not only the universe, but her life. And she grappled with her thoughts of violence.

"The air, so cold," muttered Langdon, stretching his hand toward the hard shadows. "It doesn't make sense."

"Inside," she tempted, "you'll find a lot of things that don't. Things you never dreamed of."

Langdon spun. They were the first words she had spoken to him since he had raised the ugly welt on Gregory's cheek. "So there's more here than meets the eye, is there? You're too late. I don't need *you* to help me figure that out." Behind the light of an illuminator, he crawled inside.

The dark slowly swallowed him until his boot heels alone were in sunlight, and then there were only Rhonda and Gregory, and a musty, frigid draft that filled her with awe. The eyes of father and daughter met in a union of fear and desperation before the skull-sized rock at their feet seized Rhonda's attention. She looked again at Gregory, finding his silent, trembling lips, and knew what she had to do.

Grasping the rock, she crawled after Langdon.

Well inside, Langdon stopped, and Rhonda stopped with him. "The current, the way it rushes," he said, splashing a ray of light across the wall where she had last seen her father working. "There. An opening." He scrambled ahead with the collective anticipation of a dozen generations of U.S.S. scientists and flung himself prone before the squeeze way, completely oblivious to Rhonda even as she slunk nearer. "The cold, it's pouring right out."

He thrust his light inside and Rhonda positioned herself above him, watching as if from afar as her hands brought the rock to her shoulder, and on up until it scraped the ceiling.

"There," he uttered. "On the wall, the floor, it looks like—"

"Skulls," said Rhonda, and she crashed the rock down on Langdon's again and again.

Chapter Four

As Langdon sank, the ray of his illuminator grew still against myriad black skulls, frozen in eternal grimaces in the holy of holies. Rhonda shrank from the horrid sight, and from the rock wet with blood. She forced herself to remove the Banning from Langdon's holster, and then scurried frantically for daylight, her mind filled with terror at the sudden sensation that something incredibly evil stalked her.

She found her father sitting on the ledge, his face buried in his hand as he wept uncontrollably.

Rhonda stood, her conscience pierced by an image of a rebellious teenager who needed the guidance of a father, even Langdon. "I think I killed him, Dad."

Gregory didn't look up. "Oh Rhonda, what are we going to do? What in Heaven's name are we going to do?"

"Whatever we have to," she said, and helped him to his feet. She turned to the grotto. "The explosives. We've got to seal the grotto, keep the U.S.S. from finding anything. Can you do it?"

"It's too late. I've forgotten, don't know . . ."

She placed gentle hands on his shoulders and shook him. "Dad, you've got to. Don't you see? We can't let them find what's in there, find Langdon's body. I've watched you set explosives, but you know I've never done it. Oh, Dad, you've got to help us, for Mother's sake!"

She prayed that her plea would touch the hatred he had borne ever since she had died, and suddenly his eyes were alert, his words coherent. "They let her die, Rhonda, just let her die. We'll blow every rock!"

Together they worked from the crate of explosives, stringing primer cord through gelatin, stacking the cylinders like cordwood through the mountain, delicately attaching a blaster cap that, from its position on the ledge, would be subject to remote detonation. Within minutes, Rhonda was stumbling down-trail after her father, all senses fixed on the flats below.

At trail's base, he whirled, detonator in hand. "Here. I'll do it from here."

She stayed his arm. "We've got to buy ourselves time. The guards can't suspect anything yet."

The lines in his face froze as he processed her words, and then he concealed the detonator on his person and they pushed on toward the lab.

As the two of them struggled through boulder fields and across deep rifts, they formulated a bold, desperate plan. It was risky, but what other hope did they have, when a shuttle and troops would swoop out of the sky any moment?

Behind an outcrop hiding flats and the ship, they paused long enough for Rhonda to pull out her shirttail and slip the Banning inside her belt. She had studied weaponry history at the university and spent time at a shooting range, but now she might be called upon to use a Banning against a human being. And the blood of a father was still fresh on her hands.

Gregory's fingers suddenly were tender on her arm. "If we don't make it, if *I* don't make it, just know that I love you."

Her chin quivered as she embraced him. "Oh Dad, me too. More than anything."

He withdrew to look at her from arm's length, and fierce determination darkened his features. "For your mother's sake, for the sake of every decent person, *don't let them have it.*"

Together they walked into the open.

In the craft's shadow, they stopped at the ladder against the blackened heat shields of the fuselage, and Rhonda grasped a rung at eye level and looked up. "Captain! Captain Pierce! There's been an accident."

Within seconds the officer's burly form filled the open hatch. "What's the trouble?" His voice was hoarse and the words staccato-like, as though he were conditioned to barking out commands.

"It's Doctor Langdon. He's up in the canyon, about a thousand meters. He had an awful fall and twisted his leg. I think it's fractured."

Pierce glanced up-canyon. "Neither one of you stayed with him? He could go into shock."

Rhonda squeezed the rung to steady her nerves." You can reprimand us later if you like. The important thing right now is to get him some help. He's just past the double spires, in the shade of an undercut ledge in the wash."

There ensued the longest seconds Rhonda had ever known, the most penetrating scowl she had ever faced. Did the quiver in her voice, the desperation in her eyes, betray her? Any second, a shuttle would thunder into the gorge and it would be too late, for her, for her father, maybe for all decent men.

Still, she couldn't help but wonder if this man might also have children back home.

Finally Pierce turned to the ship's interior. "On the double! Langdon's hurt. Get the first aid kit, the litter. You're goin' after him."

Another minute and the two crewmen, bearing a collapsed litter and emergency pack, were running across the flat for the spires pointed out by their commander. Rhonda watched until they disappeared around the outcrop, and then looked at Pierce, who had descended and now stood beside her. For a moment she saw him not as a U.S.S. officer, but as just another dad, perhaps, obligated to a deep-space mission that kept him from some little boy in need. Then the holster at his hip creaked as he turned to the ladder, and Rhonda slipped her hand inside her shirttail and found the Banning.

Just as he seized an overhead rung, she shoved it into his ribs.

"What the—"

"Be smart so you can go home, Captain." Unbuckling his holster, she unsheathed his weapon and handed it to her father. "Start climbing. We'll be right up after you."

Pierce's neck reddened. "You'll pay for this."

Rhonda followed him up, keeping enough distance so he couldn't kick her in the face. At the hatch, she paused, but remained attentive to the officer who trembled with rage. "Can you do it from down there, Dad?"

"Outcrop's in the way. I'm coming up!"

***

A twitch at his ring finger.

The first thing to pierce Langdon's fog, it was identical to what his older daughter had experienced at the onset of neurodegenerative disease all those years ago. But there was also a creeping cold and a frightening gloom, and he instinctively rolled away to face a shaft of daylight. Its warmth was a salve to his shivering frame, and he dragged himself toward it, his numbed senses fighting to escape their bonds.

Langdon's dream world persisted even as he gained the ledge, but it was a dream in which he recognized a burning sun and cylindrical explosives and, most vividly, a blasting cap ready for detonation. A part of him that was still somewhere else whispered in his ear, urging him closer. There was something it wanted him to do, and when he hesitated, his shadow self picked up his hand and forced his fingers to free tiny wires.

***

"My word, Rhonda, it won't detonate!"

From inside the ship, Rhonda looked at her father, framed in the hatch, and saw a sudden pinpoint of light high in the sky over his shoulder. "Over the cliffs. Oh Dad, it's a shuttle. We've got to go. Get in, close the hatch."

Gregory turned to the sudden nova. "No!" He raised a fist to it. "I swear on her grave you won't get it."

Before Rhonda could take his arm, he was down the ladder and stumbling across the flat.

"Dad! Come back!"

"Go!" He gave a half-look over his shoulder. "You can't wait. You've got to go now!"

The last she saw of him he was staggering half-crazed with desperation toward the trail to the grotto.

She whirled to find Pierce had taken a step toward her, his body coiled like a cat ready to spring. "Don't make me do it!" she said, brandishing the weapon. "Get the engines going. You're taking us up."

***

With his shadow self leading the way, Langdon began to crawl.

He crept as far as he could down-trail through skull-baking heat until he gained the shelter of a narrow, dark overhang. He lay there, his head swimming, his vision fading in and out as a wispy figure he recognized as Gregory stumbled up past him.

In a dream that wouldn't end, Langdon heard voices challenge Gregory from far below and watched a pair of guards mount the trail in perplexed pursuit.

***

As a cursing Pierce rushed about at Banning point to complete the pre-flight tasks, Rhonda heard the building thunder that could only mean that the shuttle had entered the gorge. If her father could just hide in the canyon somewhere. If he could hide for just a little while, then maybe . . .

No. She had to go now. She followed Pierce into the cramped forward deck and strapped herself in before lights flashing on a control panel partially plastered with photos: a smiling bride with red bouquet, a crib-bound baby with rattle, an elderly woman with Pierce's eyes. At eye-level, the red hues of the gorge spilled in through a transparent shield across the craft's nose.

She waved the Banning skyward. "Take us up."

He flicked a series of switches, and the drone of the engines became a deep rumble in the bowels of the ship. It intensified until the vibration battered Rhonda's legs through the deck, and then the ship rose reluctantly to hang horizontally just above the level of the lab roof. A sudden jerk with the force of several G's threw her against the seat. Her head swam with the surge of blood to the back of her cranium. Her breast ached with the sensation that her heart pushed against the rear of her chest cavity. Looking up, she saw the saw-like ridge of the barrier cliff plunging toward her.

It fell until it completely filled the shield to bathe the deck in eerie red twilight, and then suddenly veered away to Pierce's banking maneuver. As the craft leveled out, Rhonda found the cliff at her side as they ascended up-canyon to the blast of nuclear thrusters.

***

A sonic boom quaked the overhang and showered Langdon with rubble. He still lived in a valley of shadows, but as he inched forward on his stomach, the secreted half of him recognized the silver-black fuselage of a ship sweeping by. Simultaneously, the glint of sunlight from the opposite direction warned of a second craft on a collision course with the first.

Then the cry of guards rose up from below and a warning shot from a Banning shattered rock forty meters up-trail, throwing a kneeling figure to the ledge outside the grotto. Langdon watched a lacerated hand stretch out, the fingers straining, and his shadow self whispered that Gregory reattached tiny wires that the two parts of him had separated.

***

As the ascending craft screamed past the grotto, Rhonda checked the larboard porthole and glimpsed her father, a pathetic little figure far below on a ledge that hung in limbo between summit crags and canyon floor. She stretched out her hand, his name on her lips, and then gasped as a sudden, ineffable brightness became dust and a legion of hurtling boulders. The shock wave rocked the ship, and at the pilot's terrified expletive, she turned and found the charred metal of the incoming shuttle eclipsing the sky.

"We're gonna hit!" exclaimed Pierce.

Rhonda's world swam and her safety belt knifed into her skin as Pierce banked toward a mitre-shaped peak. The oncoming ship was so close that she could read the terror in its pilot's face. A quick grinding of metal wrenched the controls from Pierce's hands as a wing clipped the fuselage. For a horrifying moment, there was only the peak dead ahead. Then Pierce regained the stick and pulled it toward him, slamming Rhonda back in her seat and rocketing the craft skyward to miss the summit by meters. From behind came thunder, audible even above nuclear thrusters, and Rhonda fought the force of many G's to turn to the extreme lower porthole and see utter maelstrom.

Far below, jagged metal that once had been a shuttle flew out from a scintillating orange fireball clinging to the cliff.

Chapter Five

Rhonda stared through the porthole at the encompassing blackness jeweled with stars, and grief for her father choked her.

No. She couldn't dwell on it, for what already had happened was set in stone. But the future still loomed unlived, its scenes unwritten, and her life was open to myriad directions.

Still, she wondered how she could go on. She was without anyone, a fugitive burdened with great secrets. Her father had given his life so she alone could possess them, but every answer she held was clouded by dark mysteries.

Furthermore, she had no idea where to flee to escape the U.S.S. Strangely, her own safety didn't seem that important. For ever since the star-key had touched her hand, she had felt as if a spell had been cast on her. It filled her with wispy images, fleeting apparitions, a silent voice that seemed to summon her from afar.

Fear and hopelessness shrouded her, yet from the recesses of her mind surfaced memories. From her deathbed her mother was whispering, her voice pained, yet at peace. She was telling again of her faith in One who guides the aimless and gives hope to the hopeless, the Great Designer whom man would know by what He brings to pass.

With sudden strength, Rhonda shook off the fear and grief and turned to Pierce at the controls. "Set a course for Violesha Two," she ordered with a wave of the Banning.

"That's the Leijan colony. Forbidden territory."

"I know what it is. Just do it."

"It'd take months in this flyer. It's not designed for extended flight."

"It's capable of it."

Pierce nodded to the Banning. "Yeah? And are you capable of stayin' awake and holdin' that thing on me the whole time?"

"I'll set the ship on automatic and lock you in the storage bay."

"What about food, water? We've got enough for a week, two at most."

"We'll stop at a colony for supplies."

Pierce looked at her with disgust. "You think you got it all figured out, don't you? Well, let me give you one more thing to think about. You see how the ship handled in the atmosphere with that damaged wing? Odds are, first time we try to re-enter, we'll spin out of control and crash."

"Lay in that course."

But as Rhonda stared again into the silent, mysterious heavens, she couldn't help but wonder if a violent end was what the Creator intended to bring to pass.

***

Blake lay in a flophouse room reeking with human waste and reached for the bottle on the floor. The filthy canvas cot creaked underneath him, and the chilled night air sweeping through the window above carried sounds of wickedness from across the alley. For a week he had lain here, staring at the twin suns by day and the stars by night, rising only to urinate in the corner and gnaw on the jerked hindquarter of an Ohiloan hare. Then the bottle always had re-claimed him, to assuage his torment and guilt, confusion and fear.

He had known no other existence since he had fled the haggard woman's words down alleys of iniquity to the flophouse that was home. He had bolted the door, yet the words came even now, through senses clouded by lemstel.

I don't want a destiny, he said silently as he drank again and stared through the window. *I just want to die.*

He focused on the stars whose light had hurtled outward millennia before he had been born, all to reach his eyes at this moment. How insignificant he was by comparison. How petty his troubles, his bitterness, his hopelessness. Did anyone in all that vastness care but him? So what was the use? Why go on, when he was just a meaningless, infinitesimal speck, powerless to change a single thing in all the universe?

He took another swig, drowning deeper his life, and when he looked again at the sky, he started, as though pricked by a blade. The clouds of starlight somehow seemed to swim, wisps of light moving against a black dome. He lowered the bottle and sat up. *Drunk,* he thought, closing his eyes, *stone drunk.* But when he opened them again, the image was still there, a whirling starry mass, its brilliance reaching down from infinity like a wispy hand with index finger straining to touch his own. And suddenly, he no longer seemed alone.

He came to his knees and stretched out his hand to the sky, seeking that mysterious presence that seemed so far away, yet so close. He had to have it, let it encompass him, as though he had lived his entire life just for this one moment. Vivid images swept through his mind; he tottered on the brink of a great, black gulf, and from far above stretched down a hand. It came closer, until he could feel its warmth over the cold of the abyss. All he had to do to be spared was take it, close fingers on fingers, flesh on flesh. He flinched at sudden demands he heard only in his mind, something about who could go, who *would* go.

No, he said silently. *I don't want you. I don't want a destiny.*

He grew lightheaded and everything went black, and the next thing he knew, he was staring at a sky lighted by early dawn. He shook himself, unable to understand what he had experienced or to reconcile the seemingly abrupt transition from night to day, when several hours obviously had elapsed. He lay back, his arm across his eyes, and then rolled over and reached for the bottle.

Lemstel. If it couldn't make him forget reality, maybe it could help him forget his dreams.

Drinking long and deep, he glanced up to see what appeared to be a meteor blazing across the dawning sky.

***

Rhonda tightened the safety belt that secured her to the violently quaking seat and prayed as the craft plummeted out-of-control down through the atmosphere of Ohilo.

Exterior panels heated red-hot by friction ripped free of the hull and became fireballs streaming past the porthole. Through them Rhonda glimpsed the great, flesh-colored land mass spinning ever closer. The roar of wind exceeded even the blast of retrorockets, and the savage vibrations told of stresses that threatened the craft's structural integrity.

"Can't take much more!" said Pierce, fighting the controls.

Rhonda's head spun and she felt herself drifting away. She yelled out, struggling to shake it off. She had to live, because of her father's sacrifice, because all decent men might somehow depend on her. And yet the very framework of the ship groaned as if ready to break apart.

In her last instant of consciousness, she took in Pierce's desperate curses, her sudden nausea, the intensifying fire of the streamers through the porthole. And then there was oblivion.

She opened her eyes to see drift-sand obscuring all but the uppermost section of the cracked forward shield and to find Pierce's head slumped. They had crash-landed, and it had been severe, judging by the warped metal at her face and the daylight spilling in through a crack in the hull.

She unbuckled herself and, standing, found the Banning on the deck. Pierce's headrest was bloody from a gash at his hairline, and a section of the instrument panel had torn free and ripped through his shoulder. He groaned and stirred, but she made no move to render aid. He was her enemy, and were the situation reversed, he and all who wore the insignia of the U.S.S. would no more help her than they would a Rhythian snake.

She started out of the forward deck, but got only as far as the inner hatch before turning to face those who stared at her from the control panel: a bride, a child, a mother.

The blood of one man was on her hands already, a stain she would carry forever, no matter how justified her act might have been. If she left Pierce this way, she would confirm that she was unworthy of the faith she secretly claimed.

She went to him and stifled the bleeding in his shoulder with direct pressure. Placing the Banning on the empty seat, she tore a strip from her shirttail and set to bandaging his head. Suddenly a hand grasped her wrist, and in alarm she looked into his opened eyes.

"Your game's over, you slut," he said hoarsely.

She looked over her shoulder for the Banning, but Pierce was quicker. His hand lashed out and seized it.

"Let go of me!" she cried, twisting free.

Pierce reached for her again, but the safety belt restrained him. He fumbled with the release, and in those moments, Rhonda darted out of the deck. She gained the sealed outer hatch and worked madly to spill daylight inside, but the apparatus was stubborn, foreign to her. She turned to see Pierce staggering after her, cursing and brandishing the Banning. The lock suddenly gave, the hatch swung out, and the rays of double suns reflecting from dunes burst in on her a mere moment before she jumped.

From where she lay in sand that half-buried the ship, she looked up past charred heat shields to find the groggy man steadying himself with the hatch. In the time it took him to lift his weapon, her hand found sand and flung it into his face. He yelled and instinctively brought his support hand to his eyes. Half-blind and reeling, he clutched vainly at the hatch and, with a cry, toppled headlong to her feet.

He lay there very still, blood from his reopened wound contrasting with ground as white as his bride's gown. The only evidence that he still lived was the stirring of sand granules at his nostrils. Rhonda pried the Banning from his hand and quickly withdrew; this time she would not assume that he no longer posed a threat. She gained a wing partially buried in the sands and walked it to its end, where she squinted at a choppy sea of sand dunes stretching waterless in all directions, the whiteness broken only by blade-like shadows at their narrow crests.

Oh Dad, she said silently, feeling the suns bake her skull. *All you did, and for this. For me to end up here with the key to some awful thing I'm not even sure what is and have no idea where to find.*

She retreated to the shade of the fuselage, found Pierce still unconscious, and engaged the ladder by means of the outer control. Gaining the hatch, she took stock of provisions: two liters of water and three cans of rations. The craft obviously was mangled beyond repair, even the communications system, though she had no one in all the colonies to contact. She knew this planet to be inhabited; it was that fact, coupled with their depleted supplies, that had forced them here. Yet Ohilo was also known for deserts that sometimes stretched thousands of kilometers between outposts. And even if by miracle she could reach a city, what good would it do? She lived now only to reach the forbidden colony of the Leijan on Violesha Two, yet the very craft she had hoped would take her there lay crushed.

She poured a little water down Pierce late in the evening as the shadows of the craft crawled outward. Sundown found her sitting on the wing, staring at the suns sinking side-by-side into clouds of deepest indigo. A chill surprisingly crept into the air, but the heat radiating from the sand and metal left her comfortable. Soon the stars popped out, shimmering in a haze. She had to take some kind of positive action, but in Heaven's name, what could it be? She touched the heel of the boot folded under her, remembered the age test readout, and closed her eyes.

If I only had the faith Mother had, she said to herself. *If I could just see things the way she did, have the same kind of assurance.*

When she lifted her gaze again, she saw a soft, red glow spreading across the western horizon, the lights of a city.

Chapter Six

Brimming with new hope, Rhonda strapped on a water canteen inside the cabin and donned a flight jacket stuffed with rations. Descending to Pierce, she cautiously covered him with a blanket and poured water between his cracked lips. Withdrawing a little, she nudged him in the leg with her boot and watched him stir by the light of her illuminator.

"Captain, I'm leaving you some food, water. You understand me? Food and water. I don't know why I'm doing this, but I'm leaving you some."

She knew why. In a far-off grotto, she had crushed the skull of a man created by God. His life to give, and only His to take.

Throughout the night, Rhonda struggled through the sands toward the western glow as the two moons hurtled through the sky in rapid orbit that saw the smaller overtake the larger. Rhonda, too, knew she was in a race, for dawn would bring double suns and incredible heat. Her pace seemed frightfully slow, her boots disappearing with every step across dunes that rose and fell ten meters. A wind crept under her jacket collar, chilling and dehydrating her. She drank sparingly, knowing the day would bring a greater need for water, and consumed a food canister only when her knees gave out and her spirits fell.

Dawn found her atop a dune and studying the buildings of a slum-ridden city on the fringe of the sands. She was so weak she could hardly lift her legs, but her mental exhaustion was worse, for she had barely slept in days. During the first couple of hours away from the ship, she had concentrated well enough to formulate a plan, but now her tired mind struggled to recall it.

In the slums of the colonies, she knew, operated an aggregate of thieves, murderers, and contraband runners known as the Black Market.

Its members were a dangerous lot, stopping at nothing to satisfy their greed. But with the right bargaining tool, perhaps her knowledge of a downed U.S.S. shuttle with invaluable parts, she might strike a deal that could gain her passage to the Leijan colony. It was a risky venture that could end in death, or worse. But did she have any choice?

On the city's outskirts she stopped where drift sand stood high against the wall of a roofless ruin. She brushed past a leaning door that hung precariously from a creaking hinge, and found rubble inside. Glancing skyward, she visualized the course of the suns and retreated to the shadows of a fallen inner door angling against a corner. She sat to drink water and eat her last rations, and then curled up with her jacket as a pillow and lapsed into sleep with true hope finally inside her.

Stirring only briefly during the day, she awoke refreshed to find that the suns already had sunk below the ruin's west wall. Soon, shadows would creep across the city, and the slums would come alive with immorality and illegal activity, exactly what she hoped to find.

Shedding canteen and belt, she headed for the city proper.

***

As Rhonda entered Shahnina's Palace of All Possible Delights, leaving behind a sudden sandstorm and wicked lightning, she pressed a reassuring hand against the Banning in her jacket pocket. In the ruins she had dreamed of the barbaric act she had committed in the grotto, and she had awakened in a cold sweat. She had sworn never again to place herself in a situation in which she might have to harm another, yet she now faced hard, cruel men whose eyes betrayed their desire.

She went to the bar, and a score of bloodshot eyes followed. The bartender, obese and grinning, stood with folded arms as he watched a girl dance on the dais. Rhonda laid a hand on the bar's edge. "Pardon me, I need to find somebody."

He turned, his eyes obviously roaming her. He picked at teeth stained yellow by leche weed butts and nodded to the tables. "Lots of credits flowing. You'll stay busy enough."

Rhonda felt a rush of blood to her face. "I want to negotiate a trade." She glanced around and leaned closer. "Something valuable for discreet passage to Violesha Two."

The man's eyes narrowed, and he seemed to focus on her shoulder. Ronda looked too, finding a Science Branch insignia, and shuddered as she realized she wore the jacket of a man killed by her own hand. But that wasn't the half of it. By thoughtlessly wearing U.S.S. apparel into a Black Market sector, she had opened the door for needless suspicion.

"You don't think," she said, "I'd come in alone if I was one of them, do you?"

"I don't know. Would you?"

She shifted nervously; somehow, she had to speak the language he understood. "I got it off a dead man. After I killed him."

The man's cheek twitched. "What you got to trade?"

"I'll tell that to somebody that can help me."

He seized her wrist. "Don't get smart with me, you wench."

She slipped her free hand inside her jacket pocket and glared at him. "I'd be careful. Awfully careful."

The man studied her hand giving bulk to the jacket. For the briefest of moments he hesitated, but pride lost out to fear and he withdrew his arm.

Rhonda's knees quivered. "So you taking me to somebody that wants to do business, or do I go somewhere else?"

The man glanced at the hanging beads in a doorway beside the bar. "Stay where you are."

She watched him disappear beyond the gold beads shimmering in the firelight, and then faced the tables where unkempt men clutched squealing prostitutes and quaffed lemstel. The smoke of leche weed, a mind-altering drug rolled into cigarette form, swirled through the room and singed her nostrils. At the university, she had heard of such dens of wickedness, and now that she saw for herself, she couldn't understand why anyone would choose such a place.

But maybe choice was no more an option for some of these individuals than it was for her.

***

The lemstel had ruled Blake for a long while now, holding him at bay in his wretched room; not even hunger had lured him elsewhere. But finally something happened that sent him stumbling out the flophouse door and into the dark. He had downed the last of the fiery intoxicant.

It brought him again to Shahnina's Palace of All Possible Delights, in his pocket a few credits he had kept in an empty lemstel bottle. As a cat-like woman, her lithe body gyrating in rhythm to drums, danced in the flickering light of firebrands on the wall, Blake sat tearing meat from a bone and quaffing lemstel. Several hours of unconsciousness had preceded this flagon, so that he now saw and thought clearly. He dwelled on the strange woman who had set him on his spree, and he was glad she was not among those who brazenly roamed the male clientele. Her words had sounded a discordant note too deep inside him.

Yet, hadn't he returned to this very palace, when a half-dozen others lay within a few blocks? Why was he letting her talk of destiny affect him so?

He had seen his reflection in a window as he had entered: a stubble-faced shell of a man, no longer able to stand erect, with tattered clothes reeking with urine and sweat. Is this what he had become? A degenerate imprisoned by lemstel and lacking the will to break out, all because of what Lyra had done six years before?

He brought the flagon to his mouth and drank deeply, hoping to dull his mind again to the point where he wouldn't care.

He lowered it to look at the door and see a slender, auburn-haired woman, strikingly set apart by a U.S.S. flight jacket, enter and study the unruly crowd. He couldn't see her face fully, but the firelight dancing on her shoulders and hips strangely captivated him, though the room held many other women whose charms were more amply revealed. For a moment he looked upon her as he had once looked upon every woman, as a human being struggling through life just as he, as much in need of caring and love. Then Lyra's face filled his mind, and empathy became bitterness, and bitterness lemstel fiery in his throat.

Lyra. She had possessed all the qualities he had always wanted in a woman: sensitivity, beauty, enthusiasm. She had met him with a laughing smile under the snow-capped peaks of the Academy, taken his soul with a touch and caress, filled him with hope through her promise that her love would go on forever. Then she had died before the fangs, a scream of hatred for him on her lips, and all the tender moments, all the sharing and caring they had known for two years, suddenly had become a lie. An utter, abominable lie.

He lifted flagon to lips, tasting the bitterness, but his eyes focused beyond the foam. At the bar, the auburn-haired woman stood alone.

He started, the lemstel hanging in his throat. He lowered the mug, absorbed in her finely chiseled features: the clear, well-spaced eyes; the long, silky hair and prominent cheekbones; the full, moist lips and rounded chin; the complexion darkened by sunlight. Mentally he super-imposed Lyra's face over hers, and the resemblance around the eyes was frightening.

No. A chill enveloped him. *I don't want to see you, not anybody that even looks like you.*

But when he closed his eyes, he could still see Lyra, still see the eyes of the woman at the bar, and he knew that the memory would haunt him until it wrenched the last ounce of hope and caring from his soul.

When he looked again, it was to see the bartender spreading wide the golden beads and licking his lips as he watched the woman's rounded hips precede him through.

A strange spell tugged at Blake, screaming for him to follow this woman with Lyra's eyes and a demeanor that exuded hope. He had never before felt such a compulsion that seemed to come from both inside and afar, one that filled him with mad desire to find in her eyes memories of what he had once been.

He scooted back his bench, the legs grating on the floor as he began to rise.

No. He would sooner crawl through the pits of death than follow the whore.

He sank into his seat, reaching for his lemstel and blessed oblivion, and then turned to a hand on his shoulder.

She stood above him, her mouth bearing the scar of a cut and her eyes penetrating his very being, the woman with gold-braided hair who called herself a prophetess.

"Your destiny," she whispered, and nodded to the doorway.

Blake rose and yielded to the voiceless summons from beyond the dangling beads that swam golden in the firelight.

Chapter Seven

Rhonda didn't like the look on the bartender's face as he spread the hanging beads and bid her enter a long, shadowy hallway. As she took a step, and then another, she was ill at ease, envisioning him seizing her from behind. She turned as the beads fell back in place to obscure the firelight.

"You lead the way," she insisted.

The bartender shrugged and brushed past, preceding her to the third door on the left. He rapped twice and pushed the door in with a creak. He grinned at Rhonda and motioned inside.

Reassuring herself that the Banning still bulged in her pocket, she entered a room reeking with leche weed and illuminated by a firebrand beside tattered purple curtains. Below the flame, a burly, broad-shouldered man, his tangled red beard matted with filth, sat behind an ornately carved desk and puffed on a leche cigarette. The smoke curled upward, seeking a cracked window pane.

"You lookin' to be a whore, or what?" he snarled, staring shamelessly at her charms. "One like you oughta bring a lotta credits, 'less I keep you for myself."

The door closed behind her and Rhonda glanced around to see that the bartender had followed.

"Are you in a position of authority?" she asked the bearded man. "The Black Market?"

He scowled. "I'll do the askin'." He took a deep drag. "He says you killed a man for that jacket. Where?"

"Brazeille Two."

"Lyin' wench. Nothin' there but the Valley of the Skull."

"It has a dead man in it now." Again, it was language they could understand.

Red Beard leaned back and surveyed her between puffs. "Jackets like that ain't easy to come by." He took in her rounded charms again. "Whatta you got?"

"A U.S.S. shuttle craft. It's not flyable, but I think the parts would be worth bargaining for."

Red Beard straightened. "Where is it?"

This time it was Rhonda who refused to answer. "I need passage to Violesha Two."

Studying her, he rose to obscure the firebrand's light. "The Valley of the Skull and Violesha Two," he mused. "Last time I heard the legend, both of 'em were mixed up somehow with the Leijan."

"As long as you get your shuttle, what do you care?"

"Plenty, if the Leijan holds the kind of power they say it does."

Rhonda forced a quiet laugh. "Don't tell me you really believe those stories."

"We'll believe anything that'll put us ahead," interjected the bartender at her shoulder.

Rhonda glanced at him, but it was Red Beard she addressed. "Then you ought to jump at the chance to get a shuttle. So Violesha Two. Is it worth passage there?"

Red Beard shook his head. "That colony's been off-limits for centuries."

"Why do you think I came to you? If commercial flights went there, I'd book one." She breathed sharply and turned to leave, only to find the bartender's hand on her upper arm.

"Oh, we can get you there, all right," spoke up the bartender, "providin' you're straight up with us about that shuttle."

Rhonda turned and took a step toward Red Beard so that the bartender had to release his hold. "How soon?"

"Leave in a couple of days maybe, if we got reason to," said the bearded man. "I figure you tellin' me where that shuttle is oughta be reason enough. So where is it?"

***

Just outside the door, Blake stood listening to the gruff voice of the red-bearded man who had beaten him so severely. If anyone knew the hearts of Black Marketers, it was Blake. For six years he had lived among them, drunk their lemstel, and smoked their leche weed. He had engaged in numerous illegal activities at their behest: hijackings, lemstel-running, break-ins. The Black Market was the sole powerful enemy of the U.S.S., no matter how weak by comparison. That had been enough to lure him into league with its members, who often consummated a deal by slitting a few throats. And so, as he stood listening to Red Beard's promise, he knew it was a lie. He wasn't sure why it should have bothered him so, but nevertheless he rued the inevitable outcome of this scene.

All he knew was that the woman had set three words bouncing around in his head like loose bearings.

Lasky.

Leijan.

Destiny.

***

"How can I be sure I can trust you?" asked Rhonda after long hesitation.

55

Red Beard laughed, revealing jagged teeth. "You can't."

"Then I'll tell you about the shuttle when we're en route to Violesha Two."

"You'll tell me now, or you won't ever be en route."

Rhonda still balked, trapped by her dilemma. What honor could these dregs of the colonies have? Yet how could she ever gain passage to Violesha Two without trusting them? She had to take a chance, even the slimmest of chances.

Red Beard slung a hand in her direction. "Get this lyin' wench outa here," he told the bartender. "She ain't got nothin' we want, except maybe what's under her clothes."

The bartender shoved her toward the door.

"Wait," said Rhonda. "Okay. Out in the desert, due east, the distance a person can walk in a night. It's half-buried in the dunes. This sandstorm might cover it completely if you don't get to it soon."

"Its crew? Where are they?"

"There was just the pilot. He was injured, unconscious when I left him. He may be dead by now."

Tugging at his beard, the burly man came around to stand before her. "Violesha Two, huh? What is it you expect to do there?"

Fear enveloped her, for she saw that the bartender had edged to her back. "I'm an archaeologist, just doing research to back up a find."

Red Beard raised an eyebrow and grinned. "You're quite a find yourself," he said, drawing so near that his foul breath was in her face.

Rhonda stepped back, only to find the bartender at her shoulder blades. She wheeled and read it in his eyes, and then she thrust her hand in her jacket and spun back to Red Beard.

"Grab her!" he said.

Rhonda's fingers closed on the grip at the same moment the bartender pinioned her from behind and she involuntarily squeezed the trigger.

Red Beard lunged as an energy bolt whizzed by his ear and shattered the window, unleashing a storm of sand and rain. Then his hands were on her wrist, prying the weapon from her grasp.

She fought like a trapped hellhound, kicking and biting, but a sudden blow from the back of a hand buckled her knees and cowed her into submission on the floor. She lay there, tasting the blood, and followed grimy boots up to legs and torso and tangled beard.

Red Beard laughed sadistically. "I always did like 'em with spunk. With this one, I get spunk and a shuttle and a whole lot more."

Then they were upon her, muttering vulgarly, their hands rough and violating.

***

Blake had often turned a blind eye to this brand of Black Market iniquity, and even willingly had accepted a self-made lie that no such violations of womanhood ever took place. But somehow, as he stood listening to the woman's futile cries and the men's obscenities, it pricked a nerve deep inside. Her talk of the Valley of the Skull and Violesha Two, the correlation with what Lasky had told him, and those eyes . . . They reflected what he once had been, the caring person who had known how to live, who had seen wonder and meaning in every day. That man would have bashed in their filthy, vermin-ridden skulls.

He cursed himself silently, remembering and yearning, and as he visualized the scene inside, he suddenly redirected all his invectives to that red-bearded animal.

Throwing his shoulder into the door, he splintered the jamb and burst in with a fierce cry.

The sand rushed in with vigor at the sudden draft. On the floor, arms and legs tangled in desperate struggle, one set of hands fighting to subdue the bleeding woman and another to disrobe her. The bartender swore as she sank her teeth in his wrist, and then Blake seized him by the neck and dragged him away. Another oath died in the bartender's throat as Blake drove his skull into the wall, marking it with a bloody trace as the man slid to the floor. Coming about, Blake saw the upward swing of a Banning in time to catch Red Beard's wrist with a boot and fling the weapon across the room.

Shaking his hand in pain, the marketer scrambled to his feet as the woman turned to claw at the floor. As his gaze met Blake's, a smug smile parted the filthy whiskers.

"Well looka here, will you? Whatsamatter? Didn't get enough?"

Blake stood unflinching. "All I'm taking."

The marketer, his reflexes obviously dulled by leche weed, made a bull-like rush, but Blake easily sidestepped the charge and drove a vicious fist into his kidney. The man groaned and came up with a backhanded forearm that caught Blake in the shoulder. The blow left Red Beard's cheek unguarded, and Blake unleashed a savage hook against his ear. It staggered the man, but then he was upright again, lunging and throwing a barrage of punches.

Weak or not, Blake still had the instincts of a person Academy-trained in hand-to-hand combat. He ducked under roundhouse rights and lefts and delivered a short, crisp punch to the soft belly. As the marketer doubled over, Blake drove a brutal knee up into his chin. The man's head snapped back and his eyes rolled up into their sockets, and then he sank to his knees and fell face-first.

Blake gave him a final merciless kick and retrieved the Banning. Only then did he turn to the woman on the floor. He studied the blood at her mouth and the half-open blouse, and then looked at her stirring attackers. He faced her again and tossed the Banning so that it clanged to the floor at her side.

"Kill them."

She looked at him, lines filling her face, and then at the two men who had tried to commit such an unpardonable sin against her. Taking the Banning, she stood and stared down at them. For a moment, intense hatred seemed to mask her features, but she bit her lip and the weapon went limp in her fingers.

"No," she said quietly.

Blake's cheek twitched. Crossing the room, he tore the weapon from her grasp. "Then I will," he said, almost matter-of-factly.

With suddenness, he squeezed off two energy bolts that cracked like lightning and the men ceased to squirm.

Blake clutched the gasping woman's arm as the stench of burned flesh rose up. "Let's get out of here," he snapped.

Together they fled through the broken window and out into the howling storm.

Chapter Eight

A block away, as they turned down a dark alley flowing with mucky water, the woman hesitated in the pouring rain. "How could you just murder them that way? You killed them and just *walked away.*"

Blake stopped and looked at her in stunned silence. Through the shadows, he again noted the familiarity about her eyes. "Maybe you are just a whore," he said, and continued through the run-off.

He knew that she followed, but as they sloshed through a maze of empty streets, Blake never looked back. At the entrance to the flophouse, he turned to find her drenched and shivering in the gloomy alley. Lightning cracked, momentarily allowing their eyes to merge as the far wall seized their shadows.

"Get away from me," he snapped, and turned to the step.

"Thank you for what you did," she said above the patter of rain.

Blake paused and faced her. It had been a long time since he had heard such words; in the slums, gratitude was as foreign as loyalty. Nevertheless, he was disgusted that he had risked his neck for anyone with Lyra's eyes, considering how he had lived in such regret for six years. And silently, he cursed the prophetess for luring him through the hanging beads.

"I should've let them rape you," he growled.

He read the shock in her features, shock and fear and all kinds of unresolved emotions. Her chin quivered and a silent sob seemed to crawl up from her throat. He tried to find satisfaction in knowing that his statement had hurt, that he had struck back at Lyra by invoking cruelty on another woman, but somehow it only seared his conscience. With a spark of long-dead compassion, he stretched out his hand.

"Get in out of the rain."

Her cold, dripping fingers closed on his.

***

As he led her inside his cramped room, Blake was strangely repulsed by his sordid living conditions. Cockroaches swarmed into cracks as he lighted a firebrand near the door, and a fist-sized rat scurried along the baseboard. A corner was stained with urine, and even after he opened the window, the stench was still almost unbearable. The cot's yellowed sheets held trails of vermin droppings, while empty lemstel bottles littered the grimy floor.

Wretchedness. He saw it and felt it, and he could read the repugnance in the woman's face.

"It wasn't always this way," he said, and suddenly wondered why he had offered an explanation.

Already, she had shrunk a step from the scene. "Can I wash up somewhere?"

He went to the threshold and pointed down the hall. "There."

A squealing rat scampered between the woman's legs, drawing her close so that her shoulder was against his chest. She withdrew almost as quickly, but not before a strange tremor passed through Blake, evoking feelings he had not known in a long while. As she started away, his body odor and filthy clothes seemed strangely obnoxious to him.

He eased the door to and found a small wash basin under the cot. Undressing, he scrubbed with water from a jug, and then slipped on dry clothes from a rat-infested closet. He emptied the basin out the window and splashed the remainder of the fresh water against the urine-stained wall. He still bore stubble, but nevertheless he felt strangely rejuvenated, as if he almost cared again.

The woman re-entered. Blake sat on the cot, his hands on its outer frame as he stared at the floor.

"Why did you help me?" she asked.

He didn't look up. "I don't know."

His body language exuded anything but hospitality as the wind persisted in its mournful howl. Finally he heard the rustle of her jacket.

"I'm going," she said. "If I can't ever repay you, at least I can unburden you of me."

He lifted his gaze to find her pulling the jacket together at her breast. "The Leijan. What do you know about it?"

A frown squinted those haunting eyes.

"You were in the Valley of the Skull," he continued. "You want passage to Violesha Two. You know something about the Leijan."

She didn't reply.

"I see." He studied the floor again, but this time only for moments. From where his hand rested on the cot frame, he lifted an index finger in her direction. "So you killed a man for that jacket, somebody in the Science Branch. And in the Valley of the Skull no less."

The woman flinched as though rent by conscience and looked down to pass a hand across her face.

"Then it *is* true," said Blake, gaining a measure of admiration for this woman who had struck a blow at the U.S.S. "So the wench who condemned me for killing two men who would've raped her did some killing of her own."

A sob caught in the woman's throat. "I . . . I didn't have any choice."

"Do we ever? At what we do? Where we end up? Do we ever have a choice except what's made for us?" And he thought of Lyra, who had driven him halfway across the galaxy to wallow in the depths of depravity.

He went on. "N. G. Lasky. What do you know about him?"

Again she frowned.

Blake took a deep breath. "You're wondering why you'd even want to be around vermin-ridden trash like me, much less talk."

"I didn't say that."

"You thought it, and you were right." He reached for a rope-bottomed chair by the cot and slid it toward her. "Sit down. Please."

With slight hesitancy, she did so, bringing Blake straightening. "So Lasky. What is it you know about him?" he asked again.

"No more than anybody else. Just that he was a pirate and came across something to do with the Leijan."

"Where?"

"They say unexplored space, the edge of the galaxy. Nobody's supposed to know but him."

"You believe it?"

"I don't know."

"You've been in the Valley of the Skull. What do you make of it all? His story? The legend of a great power waiting to be harnessed?"

Words died on her lips, and she lowered her head. "None of it makes sense." She lifted her eyes to his. "That's why I was trying to get to Violesha Two, to try to make sense of it all."

"So why do you care?" pressed Blake.

"Because I've been on Brazeille Two. Because my father died there, keeping the government from maybe getting more power."

"You mean the Leijan? Then you don't believe what the Leijanists think. They want to worship it."

A cockroach at her boot seemed to catch her eye. "If I could just . . ." She looked up. "Violesha Two. All I want to do is get there, find the missing pieces, the answers."

"Then that's where we'll go," he said with resolve.

The woman started. "Who are you?" she said with incredulity. "How did you show up just in time to help me, and why did you? Is there something you know?"

His only response was a twitch at his cheek. Finally he motioned toward Shahnina's. "Back there. You gave up too much trying to make a deal. You gave them what they wanted before they could reciprocate."

"How else could I have done it? We crash-landed in the desert on the way to Violesha Two. The ship's still there. What else could I have promised them?"

"The Leijan."

"How can I promise them something when I don't know where it is, much less what it is?"

"The Black Market has a starship near here, out in the desert. They use it for running contraband to other colonies. Leave that jacket behind tomorrow and we'll go out, promise them something they want even more than money: power. After all, isn't that what everybody except Leijanists think it is, some great power just waiting to be taken?"

The tenor of his words must have given him away. "I don't think you're so convinced," she said with a penetrating stare.

Blake felt himself flush, resenting her psychological probing and castigating himself for letting her see inside him so easily.

"A whore's not supposed to think," he snapped with renewed bitterness.

His words cut deeply, for the woman stood and turned to the corner. "I guess I need you," she half-sobbed. "I need your help to get to Violesha Two." She faced him with hawk-like eyes. "But I don't need your hatred. I've done nothing to deserve it."

He saw Lyra's eyes in hers again, and he eased back to lie with forearm across his brow. *Liar,* he thought. *A liar and a whore, just like she was.*

And silently he cursed them both.

Chapter Nine

By sunrise they had left behind the suddenly lifeless Black Market sector and were making their way north through an affluent district with grassy plazas filled with traders. The odor of broiled meat stirred Blake's hunger, and he purchased food, juice, and a lemstel flask for himself. As they pressed on, he brazenly flaunted the drumstick of an Ohiloan guinea, even as he heard the woman's stomach growl, long and loud.

"Weren't hungry back there?" he asked through a mouthful of meat and bread.

She kept her eyes on the cobblestone road ahead. "I'll manage."

"Sure filling," he said with a belch.

Silence reigned but for the grinding of his teeth against food and the click of their boots. Blake knew she was hungry, just as he knew that, coming from the Valley of the Skull, she was unlikely to have credits. He smiled smugly, enjoying her discomfort. *Crawl for it, you wench,* he thought, *crawl lower than the lowest whore, lower even than Lyra.*

But the farther she walked without complaining, the less satisfaction he could muster. He knew how to treat slum women to evoke a desired reaction, but he had begun to see things in this woman that separated her from any he had ever known. What wench would have been so independent and ambitious as to enter a pleasure palace alone and try to get passage to a forbidden world? Or pass up a chance to kill her attackers? This was a girl of depth, and even through his bitterness, he found himself admiring her.

Slowing, he turned to her. "Here," he said curtly, shoving food and juice into her hands. "Stuff's not fit to eat, anyway." He refused to admit to either of them that he might have even a trace of sensitivity.

She seemed surprised, but she accepted the food and drink. "Thank you, again. You know, I don't even know your name. I'm Rhonda Gregory."

Blake sipped from the flask and went on. "Sharrel," he grunted. No woman had called him by his first name in a long time, not since *she* had, in the midst of all her lies. And he swore that no woman ever would again.

"Do you have a first name?"

"Not for you."

"You don't like me much, do you?"

He gave a quiet, caustic laugh. "You're a woman."

"What kind of reason is that?"

Blake halted, his mind reeling with bitter memories as he glared at her. "Okay, you've got her eyes, you whore. Is that good enough for you?"

She seemed taken aback. "Whose eyes?"

"Just lay off of me!" He readied to backhand her in the mouth.

His arm hung there long moments, suspended between conviction and doubt. Standing her ground, Rhonda nodded to his tensed hand. "I know you're stronger than me, that you could knock me down if you wanted to. But you think that's really going to make you feel better about her, whoever she was and whatever she did to you?"

Blake lowered his hand and walked away, dwelling not only on all the complexities inside him, but on the prophetess's bizarre words of a rendezvous with destiny with this woman.

Midday found them far north of the city and navigating a deep gash through barren crags thrusting against the desert sky. The sheer walls of the rising defile accentuated every sound: the strike of heel against rock, the rasp of pants legs, the heave of lungs. He glanced at her frequently as he led the way over house-sized boulders and up challenging pour-offs.

Never once did she ask for his help, even though he sensed that she would have accepted it. She was trim and obviously fit, as any archaeologist from the Valley of the Skull would have to be, and Blake wondered if it was not so much a helping hand she wanted, as a friendly one.

Either way, he was determined not to offer it.

Negotiating a bend, Blake caught the glint of sunlight against steel or plastic high on dark, volcanic boulders where the cliff sloughed. With a raised hand, he signaled for Rhonda to stop, and then drew his Banning and crept on. The change in angle negated the glare, and he sighted a guard reclined on a great, square-topped boulder, his weapon hand resting on his chest.

The night before in the palace of delights, Blake had heard talk of a ship readying to disembark from this place in the charge of a scoundrel named Sahtu. But an outsider didn't automatically gain the respect of Black Marketers; he had to earn it. This was a risky enough venture as it was, trying to enlist the aid of cutthroats who wouldn't hesitate to murder someone who didn't live up to his promises. If he could impress them from the start, he would gain a crucial psychological edge.

Fixing his gaze on the lookout, Blake slithered up between jutting boulders. Sharp rocks cut into his ribs and gnawed at his pelvic bone. Once, his Banning scraped a stone, petrifying him against an expected challenge. But it never came, and he pushed on, ever-higher through the massing debris.

High above the canyon floor, Blake crouched behind a large rock and studied the greasy-haired Spaniard stretched out on the sloping boulder. A knife lay unattended at his harness, while the Banning across his glistening bare torso rested in limp fingers. His swollen face was pitted, and his squat build, profusion of body hair, and virtual absence of a neck reminded Blake of the extinct gorilla of Earth.

Blake had seen his kind before, for the swarthy Spaniard exhibited the classical physical characteristics wrought by decades of lemstel and leche weed addiction. The drugs had taken such a toll on his body that Blake doubted that he could speak in more than monosyllabic terms, Blake's own fate in not-so-many more years.

Noting the closed eyes and steady rise and fall of the barrel chest, Blake crept nearer with readied Banning. He caught a whiff of the man's pungent odor and watched him stir at a buzzing insect, and then Blake was upon him.

"Wake up," he ordered.

With a startled cry, the Spaniard awoke to a Banning at his temple.

"Easy now," said Blake, reaching for the man's firearm.

As the Banning slid through the Spaniard's fingers, the beetle-browed eyes narrowed, making the already low forehead appear even more anthropoid. Blake took the weapon and nodded to the scabbard. "The blade. Hilt first."

The man grunted and eased the knife out with a grate of metal against metal. Withdrawing, Blake slipped both weapons inside his belt and motioned with the Banning to the canyon bottom. "Let's go."

The Spaniard grunted and cursed, but he did not resist.

At the base of the boulders they met Rhonda, whose face seemed to hold both admiration and confusion. Blake couldn't help but wonder if she saw in him the same contradictions that he realized himself: selfish yet caring, cowardly in his threat against her, yet cool in face of danger.

"I didn't murder this one," he said bitterly.

The sudden hurt in her face was no surprise, but somehow Blake found no satisfaction as he prodded the Spaniard up-canyon.

Within a thousand meters the rocky defile opened onto a boulder-strewn basin cradled by towering crags. A hundred meters away, powdery dust swirled through rock ruins from which unkempt men loaded crates onto pack animals. Past the ruins a great starship stretched out like a fallen bird of prey, its silver-and-black form camouflaged by a tarp sprinkled with soil.

Blake knew this place; he had once helped unload starship booty here and carry it by pack animal to the city. He also knew that two strangers prodding the lookout along at Banning point would quickly cause a stir, and he was right. Within a few steps a shout rang out, and a dozen men took up arms. Rhonda was close to him now, and he reached back and drew her nearer. Then he drove the muzzle into the Spaniard's back and threw a vice-like arm around the short neck.

"I'd sooner kill him than not!" said Blake. "It's Sahtu I've come to see. Tell him I bring him a gift, a gorilla sleeping on a rock!"

An energy bolt exploded to kick up dust at the Spaniard's feet. "No shoot!" the Spaniard screamed in a guttural. "It Lorenzo!"

"Sleep on watch and you deserve to die!" answered a slender man with European features and scraggly, dust-caked whiskers. As the European squeezed off a second near-miss with a long-barreled Banning, Blake caught something familiar about the shooter's weak chin and slick, black hair.

Panic led the Spaniard to try to break free, regardless of the muzzle, but Blake didn't want to kill him and invite the mob's wrath. So he did the only thing he could. He clubbed the Spaniard with his weapon and watched him drop.

"I could've killed him but I didn't!" he yelled, lowering the Banning. "It's Sahtu I want to see."

"You'll talk to *me* or come crawling at my feet," the European demanded. He came nearer, and with him came armed cutthroats.

"What's goin' on out here?" A shirtless man with a thick accent ran from a doorway that framed a barely clad woman. "Fellini! I'm talkin' to you!"

The European glanced over his shoulder. "Showed up causing trouble, Sahtu."

Blake seized the moment. "I bring you a gift, Sahtu!" He pointed with his Banning to the now-stirring form at his feet. "Do you always let your lookouts sleep on watch, or is that just reserved for this one?"

Sahtu's Asiatic eyes took in the scene. He was of Vietnamese stock, perhaps, a skinny and stringy-haired man with face frozen in a fierce grimace, courtesy of a jagged scar stretching from mouth to eye. He withdrew a gleaming scimitar from a scabbard in his hand, and, with a nod, ordered the force forward with him. What he didn't see was the scowl with which Fellini met the seizure of his leadership.

Blake felt Rhonda's hands sudden on his upper arm and he flinched, more so than at the upraised Bannings. Sahtu stopped before them, his eyes roaming her.

He grinned. "Lorenzo you can kill. I'll take her as my gift."

"This whore?" said Blake, glancing at Rhonda. "She's got it bad, every disease in the slums." He pried her hands free and shoved her toward him. "Take her. I don't care what you catch."

The Asian recoiled as Rhonda fell at his feet. "Get her away from me!"

Fellini alone laughed raucously, and Sahtu whirled angrily. "Enough!" growled the Asian. He turned to eye Rhonda as she came to her feet and shrank a few paces to the side, and then again he confronted Blake. "Some kinda gall comin' in like this."

Blake motioned to Lorenzo. "Wasn't so hard. If a whore and I can walk up on a sleeping fool, think what the U.S.S. could do."

Lorenzo grunted and struggled to his knees.

"Oh yeah," added Blake, slowly withdrawing knife and Banning from his belt, "he lost these back along the way." He tossed the weapons to Sahtu's feet. "I think you'll find our coming here worth your while. We've got a deal we're willing to cut you in on, for the right price."

Lorenzo gained his feet, shakily, and touched the blood above his ear. "Lorenzo say kill him," he grunted.

The flat side of Sahtu's scimitar clanged against Lorenzo's skull. "Nobody asked you, you stinkin'. . ." He added a choice epithet, and then turned to Blake. "You've got one minute to talk me out of slittin' your throat."

Blake smiled and nodded to the ruins. "Here you are, wasting your time with petty contraband, when you could have power beyond your wildest dreams."

Fellini's features lighted in recognition as he came up alongside Sahtu. "I know him. Blake Sharrel. They thought he was hot stuff at the Academy, had him rated higher than anybody else ever there." He laughed smugly. "The trash turned coward and went AWOL his first starship assignment."

Out of the corner of his eye, Blake saw Rhonda react with surprise.

Sahtu twisted the blade to let it glint in the sunlight. "Then we can't trust him," he said with a scowl. "Once a U.S.S. guard, always a U.S.S. guard. Ain't that right, Fellini?"

The European didn't respond, but Blake had plenty to say as he slung a hand toward him. "You take trash like him that washed out of the Academy and make him your lieutenant. Don't you think it'd be smart to enlist somebody with ability for a change?"

The long-barreled Banning at Fellini's hip rose again, but Sahtu's hand stayed the weapon. "*I* give the orders," he snarled, and then to Blake, "You're not makin' many friends, and that minute's just about up."

"I didn't come here to make friends. I came here to find the Leijan and its power."

"There's no such thing," said Fellini.

"It's real!" An almost maniacal voice came from the rear of the mob. "The Leijan's waiting to be worshipped!"

Beyond Sahtu, a hand stretched to the sky, and Blake looked to see a wild-eyed man with disheveled white hair and a loose-fitting robe of Rhythian spider silk that fell from one shoulder to dust-powdered sandals. Blake thought him the most emaciated person he had ever seen, with a build so skeletal that his ribs seemed ready to burst through skin. Most startling were his eyes, orbs so sunken that they appeared dark and sinister. Only in N. G. Lasky and Lyra had he ever seen the same look of possession.

"Somebody shut him up!" shouted Sahtu.

"Hashienah knows!" the man continued to cry to the heavens. "The Leijan is real!"

Sahtu kicked Lorenzo in the leg. "Get over there and break his neck if you have to."

As Lorenzo grunted and stormed toward him on short, powerful legs, Hashienah launched into a chant, but then the sudden threat of his Banning stopped the Spaniard in his tracks.

"Call him off, Sir Sahtu!" said Hashienah. "Call him off or I'll send him to the Leijan's nether world!"

Blake laughed quietly, drawing Sahtu's attention, and nodded to Hashienah. "Looks like I'm not the only one who believes in the Leijan. But I'm the only one that can get us there, me and the whore."

The Asian exhaled strongly and nodded to the ruins door.

***

In a musty, dungeon-like chamber, Blake and Rhonda sat on furs reeking with cheap perfume and faced Sahtu and Lorenzo. A band of sunlight from a high, narrow window found the Asian's fierce scowl.

"I don't like *nobody* rubbin' my men's noses in the dirt," he snapped, "unless I'm the one doin' it."

Blake glanced at Lorenzo and laughed quietly. "Some people's noses need cleaning, like guards that sleep."

Sahtu studied Lorenzo's discomfort. The only response from the Spaniard was a grunt, and when Sahtu turned again to Blake, his scarred countenance held less belligerence.

"You got a style I can appreciate, Sharrel," he said, nodding. "Lorenzo's the best I got. Used to be a guard in a penal mine, till his woman died and he fried his brain in lemstel. Still got ears, though. Even when he's dreamin' 'bout some palace wench, he can usually hear a rat crawlin' fifty meters away. And there you walked right up on him. That's somethin', ain't it, Lorenzo?"

The Spaniard again only grunted, but he glared at Blake with blood-lust.

"If you appreciate me so, why not give me back my Banning?" suggested Blake, noting that it had rested inside Lorenzo's belt ever since he had yielded it.

Sahtu grinned. "I said appreciate you, not trust you." He withdrew a pouch of leche weed from his pocket and rolled a cigarette. Lighting it, he took a deep drag and his demeanor turned sinister. "So why should I think the Leijan's anything but a lie?"

"Look at Hashienah, your own man. The U.S.S. executes anybody they even suspect of practicing Leijanism, but it's still going strong."

"A bunch of fools believin' somethin' don't make it so. A few years ago, Hashienah was a social worker with a house full of brats, then he took up Leijan worship and turned buffoon."

"Whatever the Leijan is, it's real," said Rhonda. It was the first time she had spoken since Blake had thrown her to the Asian like a pimp's barter. "I spent eight years digging in the Valley of the Skull. For thirty-three years before that, my father dug there. Now, it's over with, and all we've got to show for it is a puzzle with pieces that don't fit. The Leijan cult on Violesha Two has the answers. Whoever finds them finds the Leijan and its power."

Sahtu took a deep drag and surveyed her with a raised eyebrow. "So you're not a whore."

"She was by the time *I* got hold of her," said Blake, realizing he had to take the offensive. "Found her turning tricks with anybody and everybody, trying to get somebody to take her to Violesha Two. Spread so much disease, they even threw her out of a couple of dives."

He couldn't resist a glance at Rhonda, whose eyes showed anger and hurt as she edged away.

Lorenzo grunted and motioned to her. "Give her to Lorenzo. Maybe he love her like first woman."

Sahtu sent smoke spiraling toward the window. "Filth like you got enough disease already." Then he addressed Blake. "So that's what you came here for? The forbidden world? I ain't riskin' my neck takin' you nowhere. Not for a silly legend I ain't."

Blake took Rhonda's arm. "Let's get out of here," he said, pulling her up and turning to the door. "Let this fool go back to his petty contraband. We're going to Violesha Two and getting the Leijan. Right where N. G. Lasky told me to go."

He was aware that Rhonda spun to him, but it was Sahtu's reaction for which he waited.

"Lasky?" repeated the Asian.

A rustling from behind meant that Sahtu had jumped to his feet, but Blake never paused as he ushered Rhonda out into the sunlight.

"Wait!" called the Asian. "What do you know about Lasky?"

Only now did Blake stop and turn, finding Sahtu framed in the shadowy door. "Everything that matters."

"You knew him? How could you know him? They slit his throat ten years ago."

"He's dead, all right, but not even ten *days* ago. That job on spaceport? He and I did it. They chased us through the desert, killed him, but not before he told me everything he knew."

"You're lyin.' You want my ship and you're lyin'."

"Okay, I'm lying," said Blake, escorting Rhonda on beyond Hashienah, who led a pack animal alongside waist-high ruins defining an ancient courtyard.

"He know Lasky?" asked Lorenzo, who had followed after Sahtu.

"Lasky!" The word exploded insanely from Hashienah's lips as he whirled and dropped the reins. Seizing a rock from the crumbling foundation, he hurled it at Lorenzo. "You blaspheme the Leijan by speaking of the one who defiled it!"

Sahtu dodged as the rock kicked up dust at his feet. Pulling his Banning, he exploded a bolt against the ruins. "Next one's for you!"

Hashienah recoiled from the sudden lightning and scowled menacingly, but he held his tongue and started after the loose animal.

"Leijanist crazy," commented Lorenzo.

Blake had halted with Rhonda to witness the exchange, and now the two parties stood facing one another.

"The Leijan. Can you promise it?" demanded Sahtu, his hand still fierce on the Banning.

"In all its power," said Blake. "Enough to conquer the galaxy."

"You both better be sure," said the Asian, fingering the weapon. "Just a girl, my sister was, lookin' after me once our whore-of-a-mother ran off. Just a girl, and a U.S.S guard rapes her and cuts her throat, leaves me on my own, a half-grown boy lookin' to kill anybody that does me wrong." He nodded to Rhonda. "Lorenzo can't wait to have the wench, and I can't wait to slit one more throat."

Blake only smiled.

Chapter Ten

In the roofless section of the ruins assigned them at nightfall, Blake sat resting his forearms on upraised knees, his head slumped toward a flask in his hand. He was drunk, very drunk, but he still couldn't drown the memory of Lyra raving as wild-eyed as Hashienah. Across from him, as far as the small room allowed, Rhonda sat in silence, and though he often glanced at her in the moonlight and saw Lyra's eyes, she wouldn't return his gaze.

He dwelled also on Lasky, not so much on what the old man had told him, as on what he hadn't. What good was knowing where the Leijan was, when he had no idea what it was, much less how to claim its power?

Power, he thought, sipping from the flask. If he could just find the answers on Violesha Two, maybe he could have it. He could destroy the U.S.S., the swine who had oppressed billions over the centuries, the animals who had taken Lyra away from him forever.

His unvoiced cries brought him mumbling, finally drawing Rhonda's attention.

"Do you have to drink so much?" she asked.

Blake raised his head just enough to distinguish her, hazy across the stone floor. "What do you care?" he asked with slurred words. He sipped from the flask again.

"My life depends on you seeing this through. You're the one that promised him power."

Blake laughed quietly and stared at the flask. "If we find it, there'll be enough for all of us. If we don't, then all he can do is kill us. Either way, I win." He drank again.

"How could you value your life so little?"

"Easy, ever since . . ."

"Since her," completed Rhonda, rising and approaching him. "That's why you hate me, isn't it. Because of what some other woman did to you, somebody I never knew or had any connection with." She stopped before him.

Blake's glazed eyes narrowed. "One whore's like another."

Rhonda slapped him so hard that he reeled. "Don't ever call me that again!"

"You—" He seized her forearm and twisted it as he tried to rise, only to fall back in his drunken stupor. Rhonda pulled free and withdrew a step.

"You ought to see yourself right now," she snapped, "sitting there drowning in your own bitterness. Don't you have a shred of will or caring left? Or would you just rather wallow in your own self-pity, acting like the world owes you a favor? Did you ever stop and think that maybe it's you that owes the world something, like your best?"

"My best wouldn't be very good," said Blake, lowering his head to his flask.

"In one way I owe you so much," Rhonda went on, "and yet I've never hated anybody so much in my life. What you did out there, telling how dirty I was and throwing me to that filthy man. I was never so hurt and humiliated, and I'll always hate you for it."

"Yeah?" said Blake, looking up at her. "Then go on hating me. I don't care. But maybe *you* better do some thinking, like what woulda happened if I hadn't fed Sahtu all those lies. You see that trashy woman with him? That's where you'd be right now if I hadn't done what I did."

Rhonda turned away, a hand on her brow. She stood that way for a long while, bathed in the light of the two moons trailing across the sky, before finally facing him again.

"I owe you an apology. I was embarrassed and hurt, and it kept me from seeing things with your perception. I see now part of the reason you excelled like you did at the Academy."

"That was a long time ago."

"Then it's true what Fellini said? About you graduating and going AWOL your first starship mission?"

"No," he said, staring at the flask. "I deserted."

"It was because of her, wasn't it?"

Blake didn't answer.

"What did she do to you? How could any woman hurt you enough to bring you to your knees that way?"

"Mind your own business," he slurred.

"Then tell me something that *is* my business. Lasky. Did you really know him?"

"I knew him."

"Will you tell me what you know?"

Blake again grew silent.

"Don't I have a right to know? Won't Sahtu kill me the same as you, or do worse, if we don't deliver on your promise?"

Blake brought a hand up and found his tired eyes. He was quiet for a long while, deep in reflection. Finally the words began to come, slowly and muffled by his palm.

"I was with him all those days and didn't even know who he was till the end." He dragged the flask across the floor with a grating sound. "We were in the desert. He had a bad gut wound. Both of us knew he was dying. He told me about studying navigation, getting mixed up with pirates. They roamed space, preying on freighters. One day they stumbled on a big shipment of ore on a freighter out of the Alosian mines. They took it, blew up the ship. First thing they knew, a fleet of U.S.S. fighters was after them.

"They ran through the outer colonies but couldn't shake them. The chase went on for weeks, right into unexplored space, the galaxy's edge. The pirates' fuel cells got so drained they couldn't've made it back even if they'd had a chance. They could've stopped and given up, but it was better to die out there than in the penal mines.

"They just had a few hours' lead on the fighters and the fuel cells were about gone. They turned into a cloud of space dust to look for a habitable world. They broke onto a solar system and pulled into orbit around a planet. It was dead and black, then they came across an orbiting derelict.

"Nobody'd ever been out that far before, at least nobody thought so. But there it was, a ship, big and as black as space dust. They didn't stop to worry how it got there. They were too busy trying to stay alive. They rendezvoused and went on board, Lasky and the captain, to see if it was operational, look for fuel cells. It was pressurized, oxygen-nitrogen. It looked like a derelict freighter, but there was no propulsion system, no on-board computers, nothing. Just a maze of dark corridors converging on a central chamber that somehow seemed bigger than the whole ship. It was cold, and so dark they couldn't see the end even with their illuminators. Everywhere else there was artificial gravity, but right there off a ledge it just ended. Lasky found some kind of markings on a plaque, looked like silver, so he was pirate enough to take it.

"Then they saw it spinning in the dark, some kind of crazy sphere with three spikes sticking out, just floating there, the cold coming right out of it. Lasky swore he could hear groans and screams inside it, and could feel something awful crawl all over him.

"They started running. He talked like the penal mines didn't even sound so bad anymore. They boarded their ship, pushed the fuel cells to the limit, and about the time they burst out of that dust cloud and made a few parsecs, the fighters ran them down. They should've been thinking about how to save their necks, but Lasky and the captain were so shaken by what they'd seen, they took time to scan the plaque's markings into the computer. There were images, equations, Greek words, something about the Leijan inside that derelict. There was a sketch of the galaxy, and under it something like *let it go, worship it, it's all yours.*

"The two of them shot out of there in a life pod just before the fighters blew up the ship, but still they got caught. Lasky was just a kid without a record, so they let him off with a couple of years, but the captain got sent to the penal mines for life.

"Lasky got paroled and lost himself in the slums, but he couldn't forget, like there was something calling him back. It must've done the same thing to the captain, made him want to go back too, but not as bad as he wanted to live. He finally opened up to the U.S.S. and offered to tell them where it was if they'd free him. You know the U.S.S. If they think something's stronger out there, no matter how unscientific, they'll do everything they can to get it before anybody else does.

"They bled his memory, but they didn't realize he never paid attention to coordinates. That was Lasky's job. Not only that, but the fighter records just showed a general route for the chase, and that pirate captain had given such a wide time frame for finding the derelict, it could've been in any one of a million solar systems. The U.S.S. decided to track down the only person that knew: Lasky.

"When Lasky got wise to it, he knew they'd never let him stay free if he cooperated. So he hid out and they made him a wanted man, hunted him like an animal. Every step of the way, the Leijan kept calling him. That's what he said, calling. But it would take a starship and a crew to go back, a couple of things that only lots of money would buy. So when he heard about a million-credit shipment at spaceport, he talked me into robbing it with him. It cost him his life, the minute he told me this story."

***

The twin moons had crawled another handbreadth across the sky, yet in the corner of the ruins where she had retreated, Rhonda still kept up a stunned silence, trying to process Lasky's account. The cold, the dark, the Greek inscriptions implying that a great power lay waiting to be loosed . . . The parallels with the holy of holies boggled her mind.

Could Lasky have really stumbled on the place where the Leijan, whatever in Heaven's name it was, actually lay? Even more disturbing, could it be coincidence that the one person in all the colonies to burst in upon the back room at Shahnina's had been the very man who had heard Lasky's deathbed confession? No, it would've been an impossible coincidence. Either Sharrel had found out about the incidents in the Valley of the Skull and had sought her out, or he was lying about Lasky.

Or . . .

She felt a chill creep down her spine. A third possibility was too un-scientific, too frightening to ponder. Could the Leijan that had haunted Lasky have drawn them together? In the name of all that was holy, could it have?

She had stood for a long while, and suddenly became conscious of the ache in her feet. With that awareness came reflection on the star-key at her heel, and on what its age, as revealed in her glimpse of the moni-tor, might mean.

"The derelict," she said, approaching Blake's shadowy form, "did he say how long it took to reach it?"

"They probably ran a zigzag course, trying to lose the fighters." His voice was hoarse now, the words much slower. He sipped from the flask, and his head sagged lower. "From here, it'd take eight, maybe nine weeks."

"Then he told you," pressed Rhonda. "He told you the coordinates."

"No."

But Rhonda, images of the monitor readout vivid in her mind, men-tally was racing through interstellar space, star-key in hand.

Chapter Eleven

The hundred-meter starship they boarded at dawn was an older one taken in piracy, but it possessed a hyperspace propulsion system for extended interstellar flight. Blake stayed strapped in while the craft thundered toward escape velocity, but when it eased into the silent vacuum of space, he went alone to the round portholes in the mid-ship observation deck. He had a throbbing headache, courtesy of the previous night's lemstel, and it grew worse as he recalled Rhonda's hand hard against his cheek and her blunt analysis of him.

Just who did the wench think she was? he asked himself, pressing his face against a porthole to see Ohilo suspended in the blackness. What did she know about all the things he'd been through? He'd saved her from being raped; didn't she owe him something besides all her high and mighty judgment that didn't have a shred of truth?

But if her insights were wrong, why did it bother him the way it did? He was intelligent; the years of lemstel and leche weed had yet to dull his senses. Had she seen things in him in two days' time that he had been too full of self-pity to see for the past six years?

He reached for his flask. Maybe in a little while he would be drunk enough again not to care.

He brought it to his lips, the liquid a flame in his throat. A rough hand on his shoulder suddenly whirled him about, spilling lemstel to his shirt. Fellini was in his face, reaching for his collar, clutching it.

"I told you to talk to *me* back there," snarled the European.

Blake looked down at the hands at his lapel, and then focused on Fellini's beady eyes. "Get them off of me, *now*," he challenged. "Or maybe you'd like a little more of that hand-to-hand, like the time they dragged you off that mat whimpering and bleeding."

Fellini tightened his grip. "I know where you been the last several years. They say you're just trash that stays stinking-drunk all the time."

"Keep those hands on me and you'll find out."

There ensued a tense moment in which the European must have seen something sinister in Blake's eyes, for he relaxed his grip and his lips parted in a sneer. "I intend to take control of this ship one of these days, Sharrel. It'd be in your best interests to stay in my good graces."

Blake smiled caustically. "You're a loser, Fellini. You have been ever since I had you crawling at my feet on the training field. Even with a respected father pulling strings, you never could cut it at Academy. You couldn't measure up to his expectations, and he couldn't stand the embarrassment. I guess it was a good thing he killed himself when he did, because I can't imagine what he'd think of you now. Good graces? No, thanks. I prefer to stay in the good graces of somebody that's got half a chance of winning."

"You think you do?" retorted Fellini. "All that time you thought you were hot stuff at the Academy you were the dumbest fool around. That wench you were always with, Lyra or something? The one that made lieutenant and went crazy? You think she cared about a coward like you that ended up running like a sissy his first starship mission? Take a guess whose tent she crawled in during that survival exercise on Trinal Four, who—"

Blake seized him by the throat and slammed his head into the porthole. "You're lying!" he said, grinding Fellini's face against the glass and smearing it with blood.

"Stop it!" a feminine voice shouted above Fellini's choking gasps. But Blake only renewed his attack, wrenching cheek and mouth against porthole.

"You've got to stop it!" The voice was at his ear now, and then lithe arms tugged at his grip and he spun to find Rhonda.

"Get out of here!" he yelled, sweeping her aside.

It was all Fellini needed to escape Blake's clutches, and he slid away to double over and gasp for breath. He came up brandishing a Banning, and in that split second Blake wondered if he would see the lightning explode from the muzzle before it struck him, if he would hear the crack of the bolt in the millisecond before he died.

Fellini's wild-eyed visage held blind rage, but something stayed his weapon hand. "You'd be dead now!" he said, quaking and bleeding from the mouth and nose. "You'd be dead if you hadn't promised us the Leijan!"

Wheezing and spitting blood, Fellini staggered out.

The moment the European disappeared around the corner, Blake turned and drew back his arm, threatening to backhand Rhonda in the face. "You could've got me killed, you wh-!" He didn't complete the word, just lowered his hand and turned away.

"Why do you have to be so violent all the time?" she demanded. "Don't you have a shred of compassion?"

He spun on his heel. "You think he does? You think anybody on this ship does? The only reason we're alive right now, or that you're not in Lorenzo's quarters, is that we promised them the Leijan. It's greed these men know, not some silly thing you call compassion. It's force they respect, the kind that puts fear in their eyes. Can't you see that?"

Rhonda only brought fingers to her temple.

"You don't even know what it was about!" Blake continued. "You come in here and automatically assume it's me that's in the wrong. No matter what somebody else says or does, who's trying to rape you, it's me that's in the wrong."

Her chin quivered. "That's not true," she said through a half-sob.

"It is and you know it." He turned and started away.

"Don't go," she pleaded, and he felt her hands on his upper arm. "Please let me try to explain what's inside me, Blake."

He stopped and wheeled, her hands riding the contours of his body to rest on his chest. But his bitter glare found only her eyes as he spoke with utter coldness. "Don't ever call me that again."

And then he was gone.

***

Alone with her thoughts, Rhonda responded early to the meal summons and made her way to the empty dining deck. She found the heat shields retracted, revealing a concave porthole pushing against the starry expanse along the outside wall and ceiling. It was as if she were suspended in space, at one with the black veil encrusted with colorful points of light. She crossed to the porthole and pressed a hand to its curvature. She stared out and her mind reeled with the mysteries inside her and before her.

What was her place in all this vastness? Her purpose among the stellar bodies reaching to infinity? Scientists could describe the laws governing the universe, but what about the why? Was it chance that electromagnetic forces held together the very electrons, protons, and neutrons that formed her body, and hers alone? Or that made up the most immense stellar objects? What held all these in their places, defined their boundaries, determined their fates?

Then ancient writings and her mother's voice filled her mind, solacing and reassuring: *You and me, the stars, the being of light made it all for himself.*

"Sure pretty, isn't it?"

Rhonda turned to see Fellini at her shoulder. She was surprised to find him well-groomed and clean-shaven; only a puffed lip and lacerated nose evidenced the fight. She was even more surprised to see that except for his weak, sloping jaw, he was not unattractive.

"Please don't be offended," he continued in a voice she found annoyingly nasal, "but it's almost as pretty as you are, Miss . . ."

Rhonda wasn't immune to flattery, and not since the university had a man paid her a compliment. Blake certainly had afforded her no such pleasantries. But such a hackneyed line grated on her intelligence, and she only half-smiled. "Rhonda Gregory."

To Rhonda's embarrassment, Fellini took her reluctant hand and kissed it. "Angelo Fellini," he said. "I'd like to apologize. We greeted you pretty rudely in the basin. The U.S.S. keeps us jumpy." He touched his swollen lip. "Also sorry you walked in on that scene I had with Sharrel. Last thing we need's a bunch of fighting among ourselves, but he was bound and determined to start something. I knew him a long time ago at the Academy, and I've heard about him in the slums. He's always been a troublemaker, trying to bully his way past everybody. If he's not doing that, he's drunk or chasing prostitutes. Pardon me for putting it that way, but it's true. I've never known him to give a woman any kind of respect. I could see how it hurt when he threw you at Sahtu."

Rhonda was taken aback at his insight, which seemed to corroborate everything she had seen in Blake and knew to be true about herself. Still, she couldn't forget Blake's assertion that only greed and force motivated these men.

"Say," Fellini continued after a moment, "we've all got a long space-flight ahead. Be pretty boring for awhile. What say we visit a little, drink some brandy?"

The raucous laughter of arriving crewmen saved her answering. Blake was among them, and although Rhonda exchanged glances with him, he scornfully took a seat with his back to her at the long, oval table.

Rhonda seized the opportunity to withdraw from Fellini and approach him. "We need to talk."

He pulled out a flask and slumped in his seat.

"I need to explain some things," she said, "why I reacted like I did."

He brought the flask to his lips and drank deeply.

"Do you mind if I sit with you?" she pressed.

Only then did he turn to stare at her coldly. "I thought you'd want to sit with somebody with *compassion*. Like Fellini over there. Looks like you've already managed to get in his good graces."

He turned to his flask, and all she could do was hang her head and walk away.

Several crewmen already had seized trays and shoved their way toward a wall unit and its chemically manufactured food when Sahtu burst in. "All of you!" he shouted in his pronounced accent. "Shut up and sit down. Now."

Amid grumbling, the sweaty bodies pushed and fought for chairs, which grated across deck until all were seated. Rhonda counted twelve of them: misfits with hard eyes, lice-infested whiskers, vulgar tattoos, fingers that quivered from lemstel addiction. On Sahtu's left, Lorenzo slumped over the table animal-like; on the Asian's right, a slovenly woman giggled drunkenly. Hashienah sat at the opposite end, his pale features and wild, white hair starkly contrasting the black of space. Chance, or perhaps Fellini's conniving, left Rhonda no place to sit except at his side, directly across from Blake.

Sahtu fingered the hilt of the scimitar inside a red sash at his hip and picked at his decaying yellow teeth. "You scum listenin' to me?"

Squinting, he let his gaze wander the table and fixed on the lone person who preferred to stare into a lemstel flask. Rhonda watched as every head turned to Blake, but this man on whom she had placed so many hopes responded only by taking another sip.

She had seen such moodiness in him before, but now it shrouded her with a sense of impending doom. Confrontation brewed, and with Blake the focal point, she knew it could threaten not only the mission but their lives.

Sahtu, the grimace frozen deeper in his scarred face, poked Lorenzo in the shoulder and nodded to Blake. The Spaniard seemed to understand, for he scooted back his chair and ambled toward him.

Blake sipped again and lowered the flask. He had to be aware that the short, thick-chested brute loomed over him, but he nevertheless kept eyes on the lemstel.

"I suggest," Blake said quietly, "you get this pig away from me."

Lorenzo's upper lip curled like an animal baring its teeth.

"This ship's mine," growled Sahtu, glaring at Blake. "When I talk, you look at me."

"Or what?" responded Blake, and this time he did look, straight into his eyes. "You need me and you know it."

"People have been known," interjected Fellini, "to go against their best interests in fits of passion."

In light of the truth of Blake's words, Sahtu seemed glad for the chance to save face. He whirled on the European and cursed viciously.

"*I* do the talkin' here." The Asian unsheathed his scimitar and clanged it on the table, where the light danced in its blood-stained blade as he addressed the crew. "I'll slit the throat of anybody that does me wrong." His eyes wandered to Rhonda. "A dirty strumpet, I'll throw to Lorenzo first, then I'll cut her throat. We ain't on just another contraband run. It's power we're after, the Leijan, and nobody better get in my way."

Hashienah slammed his hands to the table and leaped up. "The Leijan's not something to give you power! It's holy, something to fall down and worship!" His outburst seized even Blake's attention, and it was he on whom Hashienah's wild eyes settled. "Blasphemer! Desecrater! You'll crawl forever in hell!"

Rhonda watched as Blake lowered his gaze to the lemstel and closed his eyes. *"Hell,"* she read on his whispering lips. *"Forever. For the last six years."*

For the first time, she truly felt for this lost and hurt man.

Hashienah continued to rave until, at a nod from Sahtu, Lorenzo stepped over and backhanded him in the face. Though Hashienah had unnerved Rhonda, she gasped at the vicious blow that sent him slumping to the deck.

Rough laughter erupted around the table. Sahtu grinned. "Just an example that there ain't a one of you we can't do without. The fewer there are, the bigger the share."

Rhonda glanced about. While an audible wave of greed swept up and down the table, Fellini sat quietly, studying the Asian with cold, calculating eyes.

After long seconds, Hashienah dragged himself up. He bore an ugly welt under his eye, and blood from his nose dripped to his protruding ribs. Slinking from the deck, he hesitated at Rhonda's shoulder and flung a bony hand toward Blake.

"It's you that did this!" he screamed. "It's your lies that's filled them with blasphemy against the Leijan!"

"Get him outa here," snarled Sahtu.

Lorenzo stomped his foot and feinted, evoking a start from Hashienah. Amid coarse laughter and the giggle of Sahtu's woman, the Leijan worshipper crept away.

"Still ain't makin' friends, are you, Sharrel," commented Sahtu with a sneer. "Heard you and Fellini left the mid-observation deck about same time. Looks like somebody cleaned the porthole with somebody's face.

That what happened to you, Fellini? Or was the wench more'n you could handle?"

In the general snickering that followed, Rhonda looked at Blake and realized just how grave his situation was. But for the power he had promised, any of four men—Lorenzo, Fellini, Hashienah, and Sahtu—would have thought nothing of slitting his throat. What could possibly stay their hands and safeguard her if the promise couldn't be fulfilled? And what if the Leijan did prove an energy ready for the tapping? Could she risk sharing it with such as these?

Her thoughts were interrupted by Fellini's address to Sahtu. "The woman. What quarters will she have?"

Sahtu grinned. "We ain't got a pleasure palace on board. *I* don't want her filthy disease. Throw her in the bunk quarters with ever'body else."

Rhonda started to protest, but Fellini spoke sooner. "Let her quarter with me."

Blake, seemingly beyond caring, lifted his head to the Asian. "It's a small crew, a big ship. Unless you're letting Fellini run things, why don't you ask her?"

Fellini's thigh suddenly brushed Rhonda's so casually it could have been an accident. "I'd like my own," she said, edging away.

As Sahtu grunted his consent, Rhonda realized that, in Blake's own coarse way, he had performed a discerning, noble gesture to protect her. Or had he done it simply out of hatred for Fellini?

Chapter Twelve

His flask empty, Blake staggered drunkenly into the shadowy cargo bay in search of lemstel. Wooden planks splintered before a short length of metal as he pried open crate after crate, finding strong-smelling food tablets, adhesive, Banning chargers, clothes with hairless newborn rats, and finally bottles of lemstel that fizzled to his handling.

He popped a cork to wild spewing and drank as foam dribbled down his chin. He felt its fire warm him inside, but somehow it wouldn't dull his mind as he had hoped and take away the images of Lyra and Fellini and Rhonda.

Rhonda. Why was he suddenly dwelling on her, when he had barely known her three days? What foolishness about the two of them standing together in common destiny had the self-described prophetess put in his mind?

He slumped to the floor, feeling the engines' vibration that jostled the uncrated bottles. Maybe he just wasn't drunk enough yet. Maybe he just needed a little longer to drown the pictures, throw his thoughts to the uncaring stars.

Filling his flask and tucking an unopened bottle under his arm, he rose from the stacked crates to turn toward the shaft of light defining the doorway.

The images came lightning-fast: movement, a silhouette, a blurred shadow like a cave bat swooping toward him. Then for an instant there were no images at all, only oblivion.

He groaned and shook his head; he was awake but he was asleep, and tiny, silvery flecks flew before his eyes. In a dreamy world, he thought he could hear the hooves of an animal in flight. He fought to pull himself from his nightmare, and with sheer will he found himself crumpled beside the crates, one arm pinned beneath him. As he came to his elbow, he found his clothes drenched in lemstel and slivers of glass marking the deck.

Stinking drunk and passed out, he thought. But the blood on his fingers as he touched his aching temple . . . Had he struck a crate when he had fallen?

Then he found it amid the broken glass: a gap-edged dagger the length of his boot. He seized it and looked at the doorway, flooded with sudden memory of the silhouette. He dragged himself up with the aid of a crate and staggered toward the shaft of light, only to reach it and lean groggily against the jamb and see empty corridor. The world swam, pulsating from black to light to black again. Somebody had tried to kill him. Somebody had thrown a dagger and it had struck hilt-first, or else he already would be dead. Then the assailant had fled like an animal, the coward.

Fighting the off-balance world that seemed to drift farther into night, Blake began to chase the specks of light that danced down the passage.

***

Alone in her starboard quarters, Rhonda stood by the oval porthole and faced the brilliant points of light set against a great, red-hued nebula of primordial gas. Such must the cosmos have been in the beginning, she thought, when all was a shapeless void awaiting sculpting by the Creator.

The Creator. For too long she had neglected Him, immersed as she had been in the secular ideology of the U.S.S. academic system. Even after finding for herself the faith of her mother, she had committed an unthinkable act, the killing of a human being. She had purged the galaxy of an evil man, all right, and her God was forgiving. But could she ever forgive herself?

She didn't think so, and in her self-doubt, she questioned whether God were with her, or whether all the grief, fear, and hopeless complexities of her quest were a divine judgment.

Her nerves frayed, she shuddered at a commotion in the corridor. She knew there were many evil men on board who would stop at nothing to satisfy their desire, and she suddenly called silently for Blake, the man she thought she hated. She edged behind the sleeping couch, whose jets were designed to suspend a person on a cushion of air, and stared at the secured yellow door. It alone separated her from the unknown, but the sounds she heard now were not of attempted entry, but groans, faint and deep.

She frowned and approached the entrance, her breaths measured. She pressed a hand to the door and inclined an ear. "Who's there?"

Still she heard only moaning, and it dawned on her that she had heard a similar sound once before, the instant she had struck Langdon. She slapped the button controlling the lock and the door slid back, revealing the outstretched legs of a man writhing on the floor.

"Blake!" She rushed out, checking left and right to find empty corridor before kneeling to him. "What's wrong?"

He turned his head, and she gasped at the sight of blood at his hairline.

"What've they done to you?" she exclaimed.

He brought a forearm to his brow, smearing blood as he shaded his eyes against the overhead lights. "Dizzy," he said groggily. "Feel dizzy."

"I've got to get you inside."

He tried to clear his senses with a shake of his head that slung blood on her blouse. "Came up from behind . . . turned and ran." With Rhonda's aid, he struggled up to lean against the door jamb and find the gash at his temple. "Head hurts."

Rhonda's arm was about his waist and her free hand on his upper arm. "Come on," she urged, again checking the passage.

A couple of minutes more and they were behind her locked door, with Blake lightheaded on the couch's cushion of air, and Rhonda dabbing at the wound above his closed eyes. As blood blotted the cloth, she saw the lines of tension in his forehead fade, his facial muscles relax, his limbs grow less rigid. He was *responding* to her, yielding to the caress of a woman, accepting her help and caring.

Even after the wound coagulated, she sat on the couch and passed fingers gently across his hair, finding surprising solace for her own loneliness and fear. His eyes suddenly opened, reflecting awareness and finding her hand. Self-conscious, she discreetly lowered it.

"How do you feel?" she asked.

Groaning, he brought fingers to his temple. "Like on a three-day drunk, like always. I can't make it all out, the cargo bay . . . Something to do with the cargo bay."

He laid a forearm across his waist and brushed the dagger in his belt. Coming to his elbow, he pulled it free.

"This. Its hilt, the bloody spot. Somebody threw it, hit me in the head. Came that close to killing me."

"Who was it?"

He sheathed the dagger and lay back, a caustic laugh in his throat. "Can't imagine why anybody'd think *I* was worth killing."

"You've done your best to make all the enemies on board you can. Can't you see? Now you've made it where somebody wants to get rid of you more than he wants the Leijan. But this?" She nodded to the dagger.

"Banning's too loud. Too many on board still want the Leijan."

"You think it was Fellini?"

"He's too smart to pass up the Leijan. Sahtu's too greedy. But Lorenzo or Hashienah . . ."

Rhonda turned and passed quaking fingers across her eyes. "I'm scared," she said with a tremble in her voice. "They'll try again. I know they will. They'd do anything to me, anything they want, if you're not here."

"I figured you couldn't just be worried about *me,*" Blake said bitterly.

She faced him. "That's not what I meant, not how I meant it to sound."

"Wasn't it? Why *should* you care about me?"

"You saved me in that back room. You've risked your life for me ever since I met you."

"I didn't help you out of compassion. I helped you because some wench filled my head with the crazy notion my destiny was tied in with yours."

Rhonda went silent, and Blake laughed cynically. "The only destiny I have," he added, "is to die stone drunk."

"Who told you about me, us?"

"Just some old hag who called herself a prophetess. I slapped her away, but she kept on, saying I had something to do, a destiny. I saw you in Shahnina's, watched the bartender lead you through the beads. Then that wench was next to me, going on again about my destiny, implying you had something to do with it. I got up, followed you to the closed door. I swore I wouldn't go in, have anything to do with you. Then you began talking about the Leijan, and something made me go in."

Rhonda looked to the porthole, where the mysteries of the galaxy swept by like a black crypt pierced only here and there by pinpoints of light and understanding. In Heaven's name, was there really something out there drawing them across space, pulling them toward a mutual destiny with it?

She turned to him, the awe of the unknown filling her. "I don't understand. You were with Lasky when he died, heard his story, just you. Then me, digging way across the colonies in the Valley of the Skull, finding—" She caught herself and stared deep into his eyes. "Have we been brought together? Has something or someone brought us together?"

"No!" said Blake, sitting up. "I don't want a destiny. I just want to die!"

Rhonda stretched out her fingers, and he turned at her touch. "You must have loved her a lot," she whispered, "for her to be able to hurt you so."

"What difference is it to you?" But he didn't sweep away her hand.

"Aren't we in this together? Will you tell me about her?"

"Leave me alone," he said unconvincingly.

"Please. I want to know."

He sat up to stare down at his trembling hands. "You're with somebody you care about, somebody you think cares about you. You open up and share your innermost self, knowing you'll be together the rest of your lives. What else could you think? Over and over, she's told you that there couldn't be anybody else, that she'll be with you always, no matter what.

"Your whole life, you've needed somebody, then she comes along and every day's worth waking up to, because you know there's somebody in all this craziness that you're special to, just like she is to you. She looks up to you, because the studies come easy for you and don't for her, and you feel good knowing you're able to help keep her from washing out. She tries to pressure you into marriage for months, but you tell her, 'Hey, there's no hurry, you're headed for a training exercise on

Trinal Four and I'm buried in my studies. We'll be graduating soon and we'll do it then.'

"Then you start noticing little changes, like she's suddenly losing interest in you, like she's not even the same woman anymore. You start wondering what's really inside her, who she really wishes she was with, and you start hating cadets you don't even know.

"But you hang on, because you gave yourself completely and can't take it back, even when she starts complaining about how possessive you are. You know what that means, don't you? You're possessive only if, deep inside, she wants to be with somebody else but knows she'd feel guilty doing it.

"Then she finally tells you she's not ready for marriage yet, that it'd be a good idea for both of you to see others, that she wants to see others. And you just turn and walk away, knowing you'll never go back, knowing you can't go back, not if you've got to share her with somebody else.

"You go for months, taking pills to get you through the night. You go to the doctor, tell him something's wrong with your heart, your blood pressure, but it's just because of her. You're dying, a little at a time, because your insides are ripped out. You know you can't keep it bottled up anymore, that you've got to talk about it with your best friend, but you can't, because *she's* your best friend.

"But there's more to it than that. You're both at the Academy and you hear rumors. She's been with a cadet suspected of being a Leijan worshipper, and you start thinking back, putting all the little things together. You're convinced the sudden change in her had to be for a reason, that all those months she was supposed to care about you so much, she must've been seeing that cadet and getting mixed up in a Leijan cult.

"You bury yourself in your studies, because it's all you've got left, and somehow you make it through to graduation, both of you. They assign her to a star base on Rhythia, and after the first few weeks of your commission, they order you to the same colony to investigate reports of a Leijan cult. So you land there, and one night you and some more officers burst in on a shadowy room and find two dozen kneeling people chanting before a Leijan symbol lighted by candles. You catch most of them right off, but a handful scatter.

"You track them with hellhounds outside the city, and when you're alone, you come around a ridge and meet her face-to-face, the one person in the galaxy who knew you for what you really are, and rejected you for it.

"You call her by name, and all the old wounds open up. But her eyes are wild, and she spits on you and calls you the vilest names imaginable before she runs away.

"You stand there shivering. You thought you knew her better than anybody else in the world, but you can't begin to understand why she's in a Leijan cult, why she's so disturbed. There's nothing else to believe except she's sick, that she needs help. The Leijanists open up with their Bannings, and when the U.S.S. marksmen behind you return fire, you run back, yelling for them to stop, telling them those people include women, that they're just mentally ill and need understanding, not killing.

"But the commanding officer shoves you aside, calls you a yellow coward for running. They force you up the ridge, and you stand there helpless and watch them unleash the hounds with those terrible fangs on the people running across the clearing. You call her name over and over, and just before the hellhounds run her down she looks back at you, calling you names that stay with you the rest of your life.

"You desert before you make it back to star base and fall back to the slums, nothing but hate in you. You hate the U.S.S. for murdering people who were sick. You hate her, for leading you on all that time just to kick you in the stomach. And you hate yourself, because you're so bitter toward a woman that deep inside you know just needed help.

"You take it out on yourself and every woman that comes along, on anything that's got a shred of connection with the U.S.S. You swear you'll bring the U.S.S. to its knees, that if you don't live to do anything else, you'll live to do that.

"Bitterness is the only life you've got left, and you just don't care about anything anymore, except vengeance and lemstel and anything else that'll drown the memories."

Emotion clouded Rhonda's eyes. He had opened up to her, and she finally understood that this lonely, embittered man's only fault was that he had loved a woman too much. *If only somebody could ever love me that way,* she thought.

"What was her name?"

"It doesn't matter." But he told her anyway. "Lyra."

Rhonda swallowed hard. "I'm so sorry, Blake, for all you went through, for not understanding before."

He looked up. "I told you not to ever call me that," he said unconvincingly.

For long seconds they stared at one another, Rhonda seeing him stripped of his rough exterior and as he really was, a person as lost and in need of someone as she. Suddenly, it was as if their different worlds made contact, creating an intimacy that saw her hand steal up to the back of his neck, that brought his face drawing near hers. Their lips were close, her eyes closing, but then he drew back as if his lost love had again whispered a three-word lie.

"Get away from me," he snapped, turning to the porthole.

"Blake, I—"

"I don't need your sympathy, and you don't need anything from a murderer."

"I don't blame you for feeling that way. I wasn't fair to you."

"Then why'd you say it? You're a woman; you don't need a reason."

She stifled a sob and he faced her again, obviously reading her troubled features even as she hung her head.

"What's *that* all about?" he demanded. When she didn't reply, he seized her upper arm. "I asked you what you're crying about!"

She looked up at his sudden roughness, yet she felt neither anger nor fear. "You put on this front," she said through emotion. "You try to make everybody believe you don't care about anybody else, try to make yourself believe it. But I know now that nobody who once gave himself so completely to somebody could be as insensitive and uncaring as you make out like. That's why I know I can tell you what I've kept bottled up in me, why I know you can understand."

Brushing at her eyes, she told him of her parents and her faith, of her animosity toward the U.S.S., of the way her father had died and how she had killed Archaeology Secretary Langdon to keep the Leijan out of their hands.

"You didn't know I hated them as much as you do, did you," she said when she had finished. "But even with all the hate, I keep telling myself I didn't have any right to do what I did, to take a life that nobody but God has the right to."

Blake exhaled in disgust. "Get kicked in the gut a few times and see if you believe there's a God."

Rhonda went on. "I try to tell myself it was self-defense, that I didn't have any choice, but I'm not even sure that's really true. I hate myself for it, and then when I see you doing something violent, no matter how justified, it's me I see, and I throw all that hate I've got for myself on you."

Rhonda's hope for a caring, understanding response died in his bitterness. "So what was it about the Leijan the two of you couldn't let the U.S.S. find out?"

She tried to hide her hurt, but still it surged. "How to unleash it."

Blake straightened. "So how do you?"

She only turned and stared at the distant red nebula.

Chapter Thirteen

Nights can be long in interstellar space, as long as a person wants them to be. Stretched out on a cushion of air, Blake wanted this one to be very long, because of the sudden hope he felt in the presence of the woman at rest on the nearby bunk. He slept for hours, and when he finally awoke with a hangover and a throbbing knot at his hairline, he turned to her and found her bosom still rising and falling in peaceful sleep.

She wasn't beautiful in the same sense Lyra had been, but her finely chiseled features held an intelligence and maturity that rendered Lyra childlike by comparison. He had never been able to communicate with Lyra on his own level, and unintentionally had dominated, but Rhonda was his intellectual equal and incapable of subordinating herself to anyone she thought wrong. Strangely, he realized it was Rhonda and not Lyra who held the attributes he now deemed most important in a woman, and he suddenly wondered why he had ever found Lyra so captivating.

The blood pounded in his head and he sat up. No. He wouldn't let himself be attracted to this new woman fate had brought into his life. His first love had been a lie, and it would be his last. He would love only her and hate only her until he died alone and bitter.

Reaching for his flask, he fled her quarters.

Trained for flight, Blake noticed the blip on the unattended detection monitor as soon as he entered the control deck in the ship's nose, where one hundred eighty-degree portholes opened to the stars and formed a backdrop for crewmen: Sahtu at starboard, sharpening his scimitar; Lorenzo, as usual, at his side; Fellini staring through the porthole; and the helmsman asleep at his post.

"A far-ranging comet?" asked Blake.

Lorenzo looked up and grunted. Sahtu continued grating blade against whetstone. The helmsman's head nodded in oblivion. And Fellini turned to scowl.

"Nobody gave slum filth like you permission to be up here," the European snapped.

Sahtu glanced up just long enough to see who had entered. "Slum filth and Academy filth, just like you, huh, Fellini?"

Blake went to the detection post and studied the blip carefully, cross-referencing the information with computer data on various interstellar objects. Failing to get a match, he intuitively overlaid the blip with that which a U.S.S. starship would evoke and whirled to Sahtu.

"You're sitting around like the ignorant lemstel runner you are, and we're headed on a course to rub elbows with a U.S.S. ship!"

Sahtu's eyes went wide, his hand tightening on the scimitar. "Johannsen!" he shouted, rousing the dozing man near Blake. "Check it out."

The Swede scooted lethargically to the monitor as Blake yielded ground. He studied it and turned without alarm to the Asian.

"Blip's on a course that'll bring it close in about a minute, but it could be anything."

Blake slung a hand to the monitor. "That's a ship! Don't any of you know how to cross-reference?" He glared at Fellini. "Where were you? Out whoring when the Academy taught that? Your father would be proud, all right."

Sahtu was on his feet now, approaching the blip to study it for himself. "You sure?" he demanded of Blake.

"A star cruiser or a pirated one. It's not on an intercept course, but if we get any closer we're setting ourselves up for trouble."

Fellini was at Sahtu's shoulder now. "Johannsen! Veer starboard."

"Yes, sir." The man swiftly scooted back to the helm and reached for the controls, but claw-like fingers stayed his hand.

"You take *my* orders, nobody else's!" said Sahtu, slinging the Swede's arm from the console.

"Then you tell him to veer starboard!" shouted Fellini.

Sahtu spun to brandish the scimitar. "And I don't take orders from you!"

Lorenzo, who had followed Sahtu, grunted loudly. "Stinking trash," he said, and shoved Fellini in the chest.

Blake knew what kind of men these were; he had been one of them the last six years. So he was not surprised to see a brawl ensue, a primitive response to immediate danger with which they had no idea how to cope. Then a sudden hail came in over communications, followed by a demand for identification. Blake leaped for the helm, shoving Johannsen out of the way to lay in a course change so sharp and with such acceleration that the combatants flew across the deck.

"Get off those controls!" screamed Sahtu from where he lay.

"I'm taking this thing outa here!" yelled Blake, maximizing acceleration and glimpsing the sudden light of the unidentified ship streak the black of the larboard porthole and dive away. "There it is!"

Lorenzo was on his knees now, and Sahtu shoved him forward. "Stop him!"

Looking back just as Lorenzo leaped, Blake caught him savagely in the face with his elbow. The blow staggered the Spaniard and bloodied his nose, and he just stood there like a bighorn ram between jousts and shook his head in confusion. Meanwhile, the ship's acceleration ceased, allowing free movement on deck. As four men rose up against Blake, he came to his feet and pulled the dagger.

"Which one of you wants this back?"

Sahtu's hand stayed Lorenzo from charging. "I had you disarmed at the ruins."

"Looks like a lot of your orders go ignored."

"Who gave it to you?"

Blake nodded to Fellini, who stood with his hand at his Banning holster. "Maybe it was Fellini." Blake turned to glare at Lorenzo, and then at Sahtu. "Or the Spaniard. Maybe even some Asian pig. Whoever threw it at me in the cargo bay turned and ran like a yellow coward before I could ask."

Sahtu relaxed his grip on his scimitar. As if only now remembering their immediate plight, he turned to the detection monitor. "Johannsen. Get over here and check that ship out."

The face-off between Blake and the three crewmen continued while Johannsen did as directed. "Out of range. No sign they're after us."

Sahtu was shaking, in anger or fear. He looked at Fellini and lifted his scimitar so that the lights imbedded in the floor glinted from the blade. "You ain't dumb enough to kill somebody that can take us to the Leijan. But Lorenzo . . ." He cast penetrating eyes on the Spaniard.

Lorenzo grunted defensively. "Lorenzo no run from nobody."

The Asian turned back to cross-examine Blake. "When did it happen?"

"Several hours ago."

"What were you doin' in the cargo bay?"

"Getting drunk. Whoever did it will try again. Don't you think you better give me a Banning? Lose me, you lose everything."

Sahtu studied him a long while. Once or twice his eyes shifted to Fellini and Lorenzo, only to return to Blake. The anxious silence finally ended with the Asian turning to Fellini. "Give him yours."

"But—"

Sahtu brought the blade sweeping up against Fellini's heart.

"*I* give the orders, remember? Give it to him."

Flushed and trembling with rage, Fellini detached the holstered weapon from his belt and handed it over.

"Thanks," Blake said sarcastically, and looked down to attach it to his own belt.

Light glinted in his eyes as something flashed toward him. Suddenly the point of Sahtu's scimitar was at his throat.

The Asian sneered. "I'd hate to kill you when I got reason not to. Don't expect me to take it so good next time you touch those controls." Withdrawing, he turned away. "Somethin' else, Johannsen."

The helmsman's eyes widened; Blake saw that he was hardly more than a kid. "Yes, sir?"

Sahtu was before the Swede now, an arm's length away. "Fellini ordered a course change and you jumped at it. Nobody obeys orders I don't give."

And with savage efficiency, he came up with the blade and slashed the man's throat.

Blake had seen men die before, by his own hand and by others. But now, watching the kid writhe in a bloody pool as Sahtu's sister must have done, he somehow was sickened for the first time in a long while.

And strangely, Rhonda's face filled his mind.

***

Without a sun rising and setting or a moon to display phases, interstellar space held no such thing as time, only a chronology of events. In the larboard barracks cramped with bunk beds and crew, Blake drifted off to sleep many times with the Banning across his chest and his eyes on the triangle of stars filling the porthole. Repeatedly he read the menacing glare in Hashienah's wild countenance, especially as the two stretched out on bottom bunks only an aisle apart. Again and again, Blake slipped into the Catholian Ray stall with Banning in hand to let the rainbow of light cleanse his skin and clothes and melt his stubble. He walked the corridors under the watchful scowls of Fellini and Lorenzo, and ate numerous meals as Sahtu's violent outbursts persisted.

Blake also noted the increasing attention Fellini paid Rhonda; the European invariably managed an adjoining seat in the dining deck and made small-talk throughout the meal. To an extent she reciprocated, but whether out of politeness or interest, Blake wasn't sure.

One thing was certain, though. It troubled him, because somehow it conjured up images of a woman he had loved, crawling inside that foul-breathed washout's tent on a dark, distant world.

***

Secretary of Archaeology Langdon abruptly thought of his older daughter, trapped in a world beyond medical intervention, as he watched a wizened man make his way to the head of an elliptical table about which he and a dozen other Science Cabinet members sat. Perhaps Langdon's memories were stirred because of the elderly man's awkward gait, so reminiscent of that early stage when his daughter's dying motor neurons had first manifested themselves, even as she had planned a wedding that would never be. Now, at only twenty-six, with her amyotrophic lateral sclerosis progressing rapidly, she lived every day at the whim of thought-controlled wheelchairs and voice synthesizers.

The wizened chairman stopped against the backdrop of a concave window that framed rows of starships, silvery in the Kansas sun. When he turned squinting eyes to the table, his features were troubled, his arthritic fingers trembling at a temple as ashen as his face.

"N. G. Lasky is dead," he said with quaking voice. "All our years of searching, and one kill-happy fool ends it." At a muffled roar, he glanced toward the window; in the distance, a starship rose amid red and orange fire. "The greatest technology the galaxy's ever known, and we can't control a single finger on a trigger."

A man with a hawkish face slammed his fist to the table. "Then it's lost. The Leijan's lost forever."

The wizened man faced him. "What if it's not? What if Lasky told somebody and they find it? There's never been a power to rival us. We've ruled with an iron hand that's kept peace for ten centuries. We've crushed people's spirits so they don't dare rise up against us. There's the Black Market, but they're too satisfied with petty thievery to be a threat. But what if a visionary comes into power?"

He took a moment to steady himself. "Somebody was with Lasky, a man named Blake Sharrel. A retina scan caught him when they robbed a spaceport on Ohilo. They tracked the two of them through the desert. A fool shot Lasky, all right, but the autopsy showed he stayed lucid for hours before he died. You know the power impending death has on people. Psychologists tell me a deathbed confession was possible, and nobody was with him but Sharrel."

"So who is this thief?" asked the hawk-faced man.

The wizened chairman shuddered. "With what he might know, as dangerous a man as there's ever been. The highest-ranked cadet ever to come out of the Academy. A deserter during a Leijan uprising on Rhythia six years ago. A cult sympathizer." His voice dropped to a hoarse whisper. "That's why we have so much to fear. Lasky was just a pirate. He didn't have the vision to go back for the Leijan or do anything if he had it. But Sharrel . . . We've got to find him, stop him, if there's even the slimmest chance he knows where it is."

He rasped an aged-blotted hand across his brow. "But there's more to it." He nodded to Langdon. "You've all probably heard the whispers. The last forty-one years, the digs in the Valley of the Skull were in the charge of Gerald Gregory. Eight years ago, his daughter Rhonda Gregory joined him. They seemed loyal enough, but we failed to reckon with the greed that comes with knowledge.

"In his inspection, Archaeology Secretary Langdon came across incontrovertible evidence that the Gregorys found the holy of holies. They attacked him and left him for dead, then plotted to steal the shuttle and escape. Rhonda Gregory did so, but not before her father blew up the site and whatever evidence that led them to treason."

He motioned again, this time inducing Langdon to turn to a burly man with vengeful eyes and a pilot's wings on his uniform: Pierce.

"That's not all," the wizened chairman went on. "We have Captain Pierce's statement that the daughter was headed for Violesha Two when they crash-landed on Ohilo. We believe now she intended to rendezvous there with Sharrel all along. After that, an unidentified ship was sighted along a course from Ohilo to Violesha and took evasive action when hailed."

"So what's the big worry? They'll never make it through the Web," observed the hawk-faced man. "Anyway, we don't even know if there's anybody alive on Violesha Two."

The wizened man shrugged. "There's a lot we never know, even when we pretend we do. But Rhonda Gregory knows something important enough to commit treason and go to a forbidden world. But it's strange. The Leijan can't be there. The planet was carefully selected all those centuries ago, and that pirate captain, Lasky's commander, said the Leijan was in orbit around a planet far distant at the galaxy's edge. That's why we've got to let their craft through to Violesha Two."

Langdon heard a murmur sweep the room. "But they destroyed the most priceless archaeological find in history," he argued.

Up and down the table, he found the same incredulity in face after face.

"That wench stole my ship, kept me at Banning point for days," added Pierce with a sneer. "She left me to die in the desert. It took me three days to stagger into Ohilo's capital, notify my wing commander. I've got just what she deserves." He slapped his holster.

The wizened chairman breathed sharply. "You men are thinking with your emotions, not your minds. Can't you see? If we're to get the Leijan, we've got to let them accomplish whatever they've set out to do on Violesha Two, then hope they'll head into deep space for the Leijan itself."

Pierce cursed under his breath. "With all due respect," he said with thinly veiled contempt, "you people are scientists, not military men. You think they're gonna lead you to the Leijan if they've got a fleet of starships on their tail?"

"Not a fleet, one craft," said the wizened man. He pointed to an associate with a ring of reddish-gray hair. "Under utmost secrecy, the two of us have spent the last eight years developing a two-man ship with full interstellar capability. Not only can it cruise faster than a starship, but it has exceptional stealth properties. With that vessel, you could chase a starship from here to Andromeda and never show yourself."

Langdon's eyebrows rose.

"What I propose," continued the wizened man, "is that we let their ship, assuming it really is the two of them, through to Violesha Two, and stay poised for pursuit in the stealth craft just outside the solar system."

"Chasin' 'em's one thing," contended a still-skeptical Pierce. "Catchin' up's somethin' else. Two men can't go up against a whole pirate crew."

"No need to," explained the chairman. "Their purpose would be to relay their bearing to a full fleet following at a discreet distance."

A hook-nosed cabinet member, who thus far had kept silent, stirred restlessly. "I'm a scientist, not a metaphysicist. I've never believed in the Leijan, and I still don't. Frankly, I'm astounded the rest of you are so scared of something that couldn't possibly exist in the cosmos as we know it. The only power there is, is governed by the laws of physics. I've never understood why the U.S.S. has been so concerned with Leijan cults and the Valley of the Skull and all that metaphysical bunk. Let them have it. We can't be hurt by fairy tales."

"But what if it *is* real?" spoke up Langdon, who for months now had neglected his stricken daughter, but not his extramarital dalliances, in a consuming quest for understanding. "There's things in the Valley of the Skull that go against everything that scientific principle demands. Have you ever calculated the odds that the Great War was averted at the very moment that, all those light years away, the Valley of the Skull became void of inhabitants? Or that simultaneously, Leijan cults sprang up on Earth with the identical serpent sign I saw for myself in the Valley?

"And what about the Earth-like artifacts and Greek writing and human bone fragments? *Something* was going on in that Valley for eons, and whatever it was, it was tied in with Earth. It's like there were people banished there, in some way I have no idea how to explain when it pre-dated interstellar flight. And when they got there, the whole Valley was just a furnace, with volcanic fires pouring up out of twin sinks. Yet they lived there somehow, right in the middle of it, and worshipped some bizarre power in the holy of holies. I'm a scientist, all right, but I'm also smart enough to know there's only one place that man's ever thought of in those terms, and that place is—"

"*Scientists.*" The hook-nosed man interrupted sarcastically and then broke into laughter. "You're not scientists. You're dreamers telling each other fairy tales. Please, let's restore a little sanity to all this."

The wizened chairman rapped the table. "Even fairy tales sometimes have a basis in fact. I do know one thing: No matter how much we learn, we're still like little children walking along the seashore, playing tag with the waves while the whole ocean's still out there. I admit I don't know what the Leijan is, or even *if* it is. But I say we can't afford to just sit here, when the means may be at hand to find out for the first time. I'm calling for a vote."

Only the hook-nosed man cast a dissenting ballot, and he rose enraged. "All of you are fools," he said, storming out.

Langdon watched him leave, and then passed fingers along the scar in his skull. "You'll need a scientist for the mission. You've got one."

"Yeah," added Pierce, finding his Banning grip, "and an awful anxious pilot."

Chapter Fourteen

As the pirate ship neared the Web, Blake slept only fitfully, awaking repeatedly with a pounding head and racing heart. After a swig of lemstel and a few deep breaths, the problems would pass, but the weakness and jittery spells of his waking hours seemed immune even to drunken stupors. The episodes came in waves, broken by periods of calm, but Blake was beyond analyzing the signs. Alone and searching for bitterness through a cloud of lemstel, he spent his waking hours smoking leche weed or drooping over a flask.

This day found him doing just that, sprawled in the officers' quarters corridor with forearms on upraised knees. He was only vaguely aware when someone exited the cabin at his shoulder and went aft, and not until he heard a knock did he look to see Fellini at Rhonda's door. He heard her muffled voice, Fellini's indistinct response, and, after a pause, the door sliding open. He watched with strange emotions as the European entered, carrying something in his hand.

The door closed behind him, and Blake lifted the flask loosely by the neck and drank deeply. *The filth. Both of them, just like Lyra.* Lemstel dribbled down his bristly chin. *Let him have her.*

But even in his stupor, he couldn't help but remember the spark she would have ignited in him in her cabin if he had not doused it with bitterness. Dragging himself up, he staggered down the corridor to stop at her closed door as he had that night at Shahnina's.

***

Rhonda was asleep when a knock sounded, and as she approached the door and asked who was there, she had a raging headache and was not yet alert. Interpreting the subdued reply as Blake's, she opened to find Fellini.

"Evening, Miss Gregory," he said, holding forth a flask and two wine glasses that tinkled against one another. He brushed inside without invitation and the door automatically slid shut. "Here's that brandy I promised you a long time ago."

Rhonda made certain the door remained unlocked. "I didn't ask you in, but I would like to ask you to leave."

He glanced at the brandy and smiled. "Stuff's pretty rare. You'll be glad you didn't pass it up. A girl like you's pretty rare too. Come on, let's have a drink. The Web's going to be on us before we know it. No telling what to expect. Can't we be friends while we can? I was hoping we already were."

"A friend," she said, "doesn't come in a woman's cabin uninvited."

Fellini placed the glasses on a small table and popped the brandy cork. "This stuff'll soothe even the most doubting heart."

"Really, I'm not feeling well."

"You know," he said, pouring the brandy, "there's twelve, fourteen people on this ship we don't even need." He extended her a filled glass, only to see her shake her head. He shrugged and sipped from it himself. "All you want to do is get to the Leijan. Have you ever stopped to ask yourself, why share it with so many people who wouldn't know what to do with it if they had it?" He drank again. "I just wanted to let you know it doesn't have to be that way."

"What are you saying?"

"The ship's big, but it doesn't take a big crew to run it. I've been planning on taking over for quite a while. This just might be the time to do it. We don't need all the scum aboard this thing. We don't even need Sharrel. You do know everything he does about the Leijan, don't you?" He stared at her as if judging her reaction. "With what I know about the ship's automated systems and you knowing where the Leijan is, we could have it all for ourselves."

"I see. So you want to murder everybody."

He poured himself another glass of brandy. "Your words, not mine."

"And me? You planning to kill me too, once we get the Leijan? Why share it with *anybody* if you don't have to?" She watched his swarthy features go red. "This is what it's been about all along, isn't it? All the compliments, going out of your way to sit with me, you've just been playing me so you can have the Leijan all for yourself. Well, you can just go to—"

Fellini flung the contents of the glass in her face and lunged for her. "Sharrel's right, you are a whore," he growled, seizing her arm, "but I'll bet not a diseased one."

"Let me go!" she yelled, struggling fiercely.

***

Outside the sealed door of Rhonda's quarters, Blake heard the piercing cry, and he drew his Banning even as he slapped the button on the wall. The door slid open with a *shoosh* and then he was inside, white-hot with rage and leveling the weapon on a wheeling Fellini.

"What the—"

"I think you heard her," slurred Blake.

Fellini smiled nervously and eased his grip on Rhonda, allowing her to pull free. "Come on, Sharrel," he said, holding out a palm in supplication. "I was just having a little fun. You know how it is in deep space."

Blake nodded to the weapon in his hand. "How's your Banning look from that end?"

Fellini flushed. "You—"

116

Blake lunged, driving the muzzle between Fellini's eyes. "You want it back? I'll give it to you bolt at a time!"

Rhonda had withdrawn, and Blake hesitated with his finger still on the trigger and sought out her brandy-drenched features. He was determined to kill the filth, splatter his brains against the wall, but strangely he wanted Rhonda's approval. He wanted it, but as he studied her over Fellini's shoulder, she only shook her head and mouthed a silent word that carried the same meaning.

With a sharp breath of disgust, Blake lowered the weapon and buried a fist in Fellini's abdomen to double him over with a loud *whoof.*

"I should've killed you!" he said as Fellini sank to a knee, clutching his midriff and gasping for air. "Get out of here!"

His own lungs strangely heaving, Blake watched as Fellini crawled to the door. The world began to swim, and before the European was fully into the corridor, Blake staggered and groped for support. What he found was Rhonda, her arm about him, sustaining. Then his light-headedness vanished as quickly as it had come, and he found himself looking into her eyes from centimeters away. He could feel the warmth of her body, sense the delights of her curves, and all the pent-up feelings of six years suddenly burst free and he crushed her to him, his mouth fierce against hers.

He could taste the brandy on her lips even as she refused to yield, groaning the displeasure she couldn't vocalize. He felt her arms slip inside his, and then push against his chest as she wrenched her face to the side.

"Blake, no," she pleaded.

But Blake, his inhibitions lost in the intoxicant, only dug his fingers into her shoulders and fought to find her mouth again.

"Stop it!" she said.

Her arm jerked free, and suddenly he felt a stinging blow in his face.

Jolted as if by electrical charge, Blake relaxed his grip and just stood there, his cheek continuing to burn as he stared at her. Her eyes flashed with anger as she withdrew a few steps, and then she pressed a hand to her face and turned to lower her head. Suddenly short of breath, Blake reeled drunkenly and backed away until his hand found the closed door. Leaning into it, he slid down to become a heap at its base.

He shook his head, trying to clear his senses. Maybe all he needed was a swig of lemstel, he thought, or a few drags of leche. He reached in his pocket for the bag of weed and rolled a smoke with trembling fingers. He found his motor skills strangely dulled as he fumbled with a techno-lighter. He finally ignited it, only to witness it sparkle and fizzle but fail to sustain a flame. He tried it a second time, a third and a fourth, with similar results.

Oxygen, he thought, something clicking in his memory, *can't burn without oxygen.*

He started in sudden, fearful realization. *The ship had manufactured oxygen only in spurts for days, and now a deadly gas was being pumped in its stead.* He lifted his head to Rhonda, only to see her sink to her knees.

"Feel dizzy," she said weakly. "Can't catch my breath."

"Life support out," he muttered.

Rhonda raised her head and stretched a hand toward him. "Blake," she wheezed.

Blake felt a part of himself drifting away. He laughed a choking, fatalistic laugh, hearing it as if from a distance. "I die, I win."

Rhonda slumped to the floor. "Help me," she whispered, laying her head on her extended arm.

He turned to see dying before him the person he had loathed just because of her womanhood, the one whom fate or an inexplicable alien force had brought into his life. She had touched all his half-dead feelings and made him think about living again, only to kick him in the stomach as Lyra had. Now, at the end, his bitterness redoubled, yet strangely, the sense of caring wouldn't go away. He cared about her, no matter that she too had spurned him.

"Hang on!" he said, fighting for air and struggling to his feet.

He searched for the release button and found it, and then he was through the door and staggering up the corridor. He passed Fellini, writhing on the floor, and reached the spiral upper deck ladder. At its base slumped Hashienah, wheezing and choking on his vomit. Every click of Blake's boots against rungs was a clash of will against body, but finally he gained the upper level to seek out the gauges and computer read-outs of the life-support system. He didn't need confirmation but he gained it: The system produced deadly gases, not oxygen, and pumped the mixture through the air ducts. Fighting the haze of lemstel and poison gas, he called on his Academy training and feverishly slowed the deadly flow by manual override. But oxygen. In the name of all the laws of physics, why couldn't he stimulate the production of oxygen?

He called up a troubleshooter graph on the monitor and pinpointed a gaping hole in a vital valve of the primary support system. Desperately he tried the backup, only to find that the graph showed it integrally sound but stymied by damage to the controls.

Sabotage, he thought, *but not total.* For in the core oxygen-producing mechanism, behind a panel in the larboard hull, lay the means of activating the system manually, *but only from outside the ship.*

His every fiber screaming for air, he reeled around the corner for the starboard air lock. He struggled against dream-like disorientation to reach the access hatch and spin the wheel, and then crawled inside to seal it and scramble with aching lungs for the external periphery module. The EPM was a small craft designed for effecting outside repairs, and the transparent bubble composing its upper three-quarters warped his reflection in its sphericity.

He popped open its hatch and clambered in to reseal it and fight for breath. Surprisingly, his lungs found oxygen trapped inside. He sprawled in the seat, careful not to activate the flow of poison gas through the lifeline connecting module and ship. By remote control, he neutralized the air lock's artificial gravity and initiated decompression. Normally it required sixty seconds, time too precious to waste. As the module drifted from its base, he strapped himself in, waited anxious seconds, and blew the airlock's outer hatch.

Instantly, the starry expanse sucked him into its depths, the sudden acceleration popping his neck, and then he was adrift in a black void with myriad points of light. In seconds the module hit the end of its hundred-meter lifeline and rebounded toward the ship. The harness squeezed his ribs, and he slapped a hand to the rocket controls just in time to brake and avoid crashing into the hull.

Suddenly in control of his fate, he activated the spotlights and studied the hull. Simulator-trained, he had never been adrift outside a starship in interstellar space; it seemed suspended in a vast, black sphere jeweled with many-hued stars, nebulas, galactic clusters. Without a nearby frame of reference, there was not even the sensation of motion, only stillness, as eternal as the dark and silence.

As his subconscious took in such details, he used small bursts from rockets to take the EPM closer to the ship and skim along the hull to larboard. The spotlights crawled along the charred heat shields as he searched for, and found, a panel delineated by cracks. Suddenly, as he directed the EPM robotic arms to the panel's locking mechanism, his breaths began to come in short spurts as if he had just sprinted a desperate race.

Time running out, he told himself. *Gotta do it, gotta get it open. Dizzy, can't see. Why won't you open? Come on, it's just you and me.*

There. Spilled your guts open to all the galaxy. Can't breathe. Gotta have air! Where's the controls? Everything going black. Is that them? Turn. Turn the valve. Latch on to it and take it to the grave with you!

With a great wrenching of the robotic controls, Blake felt the valve give. In death throes he flailed wildly, brushing against a switch and reeling to a sudden burst of rocket fire that carried him away from the ship. There, floating alone in a tiny, spinning bubble in interstellar space, he felt a sudden alienation from his body, as though his inner self were drifting away and soon would be apart.

The tranquility was strangely transcendent; all he wanted to do was close his eyes and yield to it, to sleep and never awaken. But when he shut them against the blurry stars, he suddenly saw Rhonda, and somehow she seemed to cry out the words of his flophouse dream, something about who could go, who *would* go.

No! he screamed silently. *I don't want a destiny. I just want to die!*

But like one looking on a scene from the outside, he saw his trembling fingers straining to reach the switch that controlled the lifeline's air flow.

Chapter Fifteen

Her head resting on her arm, Rhonda stirred and became aware of fresh air caressing her cheek. Rolling to her back and raising a knee, she moaned and opened her eyes to the grilled ventilator shaft high on the wall. It hummed gently, and she listened for long seconds before memory flooded her. She had been dying, and he had been with her.

She sat up groggily and looked to the door. "Blake!"

Only the soothing vibration of the ventilator broke the stillness.

She came to her feet, her head swimming. She clutched the air bunk for support, his name on her lips again. She was alone, and fear enveloped her, for she didn't know what had happened.

She staggered into the corridor, where she found Fellini stirring on the floor.

"What's happened?" she asked. "Have you seen Blake?"

Fellini only squirmed and groaned, and Rhonda reeled past him toward the prow. At the upper deck ladder she found Hashienah slumped in his vomit and trying to rise with the aid of a rung.

"Blake? Has he been this way?"

Hashienah only sneered, and Rhonda hurried from the sickening odor of gastric juices and lurched through the mid-ship hatch. A gathering of men with impeded motor skills drew her to the portside observation deck, where she found Sahtu and Lorenzo. The Asian sat by a porthole cursing indiscriminately, while Lorenzo stalked about, grunting and flailing his short, powerful arms like a scared gorilla looking to vent its emotions. Unprovoked, he turned on a groggy man who sat with lowered head and sank his teeth into his shoulder, growling as he did. His victim yelled and fell away, and Lorenzo resumed his pacing.

"Just like an animal," someone said drunkenly from behind Rhonda. She turned to see that Fellini had followed.

In contempt, Rhonda turned her back on him and withdrew to catch Sahtu's eyes. "Where's Blake?" she pressed. "Tell me!"

Lorenzo snorted like an enraged bull, and Sahtu cuffed him on the side of the head as he came near. "Shut up and be still," snapped the Asian. Then a pale, huffing man at the entrance drew his attention.

"Couple in the bunk deck, can't wake 'em up," the crewman reported groggily.

"Drunk?"

The man shook his head.

"Don't you see what's happened?" spoke up Fellini, gaining Sahtu's scrutiny and Lorenzo's glare. "We all passed out, the life-support system. It went out or somebody sabotaged it."

Lorenzo grunted. "Then how come everybody not dead?"

Fellini nodded to Rhonda. "Maybe she knows. You think the two of 'em will share the Leijan if they can help it? Sharrel knows starships. He could've cut off the air, thinking he'd kill everybody but him and his whore."

"He's lying!" charged Rhonda. "All of us were together. Blake went down the same time I did. Fellini hit the floor too, but it was a fist that put *him* there."

Fellini went red and Sahtu laughed. "Hers?" suggested the Asian.

"He sabotaged it!" said Fellini.

The Spaniard grunted. "Lorenzo find him. Lorenzo break his neck."

Sahtu came to his feet, brandishing his scimitar. "You do and you won't have a neck to break. I'll cut it ear to ear." He turned to include Fellini in his warning. "Nobody touches Sharrel. Nobody but me."

"Bet him already dead," grunted Lorenzo.

Rhonda shuddered. "Have you seen him?" she demanded, sensing a threat perhaps already carried out. She faced Sahtu. "Make him tell us. Make him tell what he knows!"

Fellini sneered. "Maybe the Spaniard did come along and find Sharrel out cold. Maybe he did break his stinking neck."

Sahtu went crimson and leaped toward the European. "He's alive and takin' me to the Leijan!"

"Hope Sharrel rot in hell," said Lorenzo.

"Blasphemers! All of you will rot in hell!" said a maniacal voice.

Rhonda spun, catching the odor of vomit, and saw Hashienah stumble on-deck.

"Desecrate the holy place and the Leijan will call down fire!" he ranted.

Sahtu brushed past Rhonda and brandished his scimitar before the Leijanist. "I'll cut your tongue out!" Then he turned again, the veins at his temples bulging red. "Fellini, get up there and check out the life-support system. The rest of you spread out and find Sharrel."

"You don't have far to look."

Rhonda whirled to the entrance, her heart hammering.

"Where devil you been?" asked Lorenzo.

"Saving all your necks."

Blake. Across her lips it swept silently, powerfully, the name he had yielded to her so grudgingly. But Rhonda's elation degenerated just as swiftly into depression as he met her with a piercing glare.

"Maybe," he added bitterly, "I should've been more selective."

Lowering her head, she turned away, guilty that he had opened a door to his soul only to have her slam it in his face.

She looked up as Sahtu slapped the flat side of his scimitar against Fellini's shoulder. "Check that upper deck like I told you," ordered the Asian.

"No use. I just came from there," said Blake.

Sahtu's eyes narrowed. "Fellini says you sabotaged it."

"It was sabotaged all right, but pretty amateurishly. They took out the main system, but just the computer and manual controls on the backup."

Fellini turned to Sahtu. "How would he know all that unless he did it?"

"Because while you were groveling on the floor," said Blake, "I was on the way to the upper deck, fighting to my last breath. Good thing it was me too, because none of you fools would've had any idea what to do. I took the module out, got the backup system going by tearing into the hull. You'd all be dead now if I hadn't."

Rhonda turned at his revelation, remembering how in her quarters he had stoically accepted impending death and even longed for it. *He cares,* she thought. *He wanted to die and I reached out to him, asked him to help me, and he did. He did it for me.*

Blake turned to Sahtu. "If you're looking for a saboteur, take a look around you. The Spaniard there doesn't have sense enough, but if he did, he'd probably be too stupid to realize he was killing himself too. Now Fellini there probably had the know-how. It was an amateurish job, like I said. But like most of the crew, he's too greedy to give up the Leijan.

"But just ask yourself who might have a reason for us not getting there, even if it cost him his life."

Fellini was the first to turn and stare at Hashienah, and the action prompted a similar glare from Sahtu. With all eyes on him, Hashienah backed away in alarm.

"He lies!" he asserted. "I want to get there worse than any of you. I gave up my children, everything I had, for the rites. I want to kneel at the feet of the Leijan and worship it."

"You keep talking like it's a person instead of a power," said Fellini.

"The only person he's gonna fall down in front of," growled Sahtu, his fingers twitching on the scimitar hilt, "is me and this blade, if I ever find out he tried to kill us."

"Lose the backup system," said Blake, "and you won't have to worry about revenge. You'll be dead. You need to post guards on it, units of three. If by chance you put the saboteur up there, it'd be too easy for him to overpower a single companion."

"I'll go," said Fellini, turning to Sahtu. "But I'll need a Banning."

A sarcastic smile crept over Sahtu's lips. He turned to the three crewmen who stood nearest the portholes and gestured to the entrance. "Now," he ordered.

Anger darkened Fellini's face as he watched the men start away on unsteady legs. His reaction elicited a grin from Sahtu before the Asian again addressed Blake.

"The backup. Is it gonna get us through?"

"This ship probably hasn't been serviced since it was pirated. It might last ten years and it might stop pumping in ten minutes."

Sahtu stepped nearer. "Answer me. Will it make it through the Web, on to Violesha Two?"

Blake laughed, with a bitterness only Rhonda understood. "You don't have any more guarantees out here than anywhere else, Sahtu. The only sure bet is that we're all gonna die, today, tomorrow, the next day. Yeah, odds are the system'll get us to the Web, just as the odds are that they'll blow us out of the galaxy soon as we try to break through. You even given any thought how to get us inside that solar system?"

Sahtu rasped his thumb along the edge of the blade and glanced at Fellini. "Ever' U.S.S. guard I ever saw was nothin' but a stinkin' coward, but I guess you two already knew that, didn't you? Once we meet 'em head on, they'll turn and run, and what the missiles don't get, my scimitar will."

Rhonda read the disgust in Blake's face, but it was Fellini who spoke first.

"Cracks. We've got to look for a seam in the Web and sneak through. Trying to fight our way past is crazy."

Sahtu snickered. "Fightin's always crazy for a coward, ain't it."

Blake turned away with a wag of his head. He started for the door, but stopped and pivoted to Sahtu. "I didn't save this filthy ship to have it blown up from incompetence."

Rhonda saw the scimitar flinch in Sahtu's hand, and Blake must have as well, for he had more to say. "Go ahead and use that thing, if that's what you want, if you've given up getting the Leijan. You can go ahead and kill me now or just hold off a few hours and let those U.S.S. ships take care of all of us. It's the same difference."

"You got a better plan?" demanded Sahtu.

"At least I've got one. That's more than any of you do." He stepped nearer Sahtu, as if to ensure that the Asian understood him completely. "We've got two things going for us. First, the element of surprise. It's been a long time since somebody tried to break through the Web, and the guarding ships are probably complacent by now. They won't react as fast as they should. We've also got the advantage of a U.S.S. ship ourselves. For a while we won't set off any alarms. Maybe we can get closer that way, come in under a ruse, ask for help. If we're close to the Web by then, maybe we can burst through, outdistance them."

Lines etched Sahtu's face, and he turned to study the stars through the portholes. Rhonda realized the thought of accepting Blake's plan grated on Sahtu's bloodthirsty pride, but she also knew the Asian's greed. So she wasn't surprised to see Sahtu turn again, a grimace on his scarred visage.

"We've got a U.S.S. ship," said the pirate. "We've got surprise. Next thing we'll get's the Leijan." He sheathed his weapon and strode from the deck.

One by one the crew dispersed, until there were only Rhonda at a porthole and Blake at the entrance. She looked at him, remembering how she had pushed him away in her quarters. Why had she done it? Because he had been drunk and boorish? Because she believed herself too good for a lemstel addict ruled by hate and selfishness? But she understood him now; she understood and still she had forced him away.

She approached within a mere pace of him. She didn't know what to say, didn't know if he now hated her for herself, rather than because she was a woman.

"You've done so much for me," she said with a tremor.

Blake only stared at her, and she grew so uncomfortable that she lowered her gaze.

"Back in my quarters," she whispered, "you were ready to die, wanted to die." She forced herself to lift her eyes. "I asked you to help me and you did. Deep inside, you care, don't you? About living, about others, about me."

She could still taste the lemstel from his lips, still see the flushed imprint of her hand on his cheek.

"Anything I did," he said bitterly, "I did for me, to get the Leijan."

Turning his back on her, he walked away to leave her standing alone in a suddenly misty world.

Chapter Sixteen

Like meteoroids pulled toward impending doom in a planet's atmosphere, everyone seemed drawn to the control deck in the ship's final approach to the Web. Blake understood; they had been struck by their own mortality and faced either the end of their lives or a frontier forbidden for centuries. Either way, mystery awaited, and only in the company of others was there a measure of security.

For once, noted Blake, Sahtu had manned the essential posts. True to character, the Asian laid his own fingers on the weapons and communications panels, with Lorenzo at his shoulder. Fellini he ordered to the helm with a wave of his scimitar and a warning against insubordination. Surprisingly, Blake found himself directed to the navigation and detection screen; in this life-or-death situation, Sahtu seemed eager to defer to his proven abilities.

Though Blake never glanced behind him, he knew that Rhonda had crowded in with the bodies reeking with sweat and lemstel to stare at the black void ahead. He caught himself dwelling on the events in her cabin, and his anger surged anew. He hated her for it. He loathed her, and even worse, he loathed himself for caring enough to throw aside his bitterness and save her. But she would never hear him say he cared.

By detection screen, Blake saw the Web before anyone else as a tightly woven network of red, blue, and green blips encompassing a red giant star and planetary system. From his earliest Academy days, he had studied the Web, for many cadets eventually served a hitch in this convoy that comprised a full third of the U.S.S. fleet. Deployed geometrically to maintain missile range with any craft that might approach or depart, the fighters were physical manifestations of a U.S.S. obsession to quash Leijanism.

The U.S.S. had the greatest scientists civilization had known, thought Blake, the greatest military might. Yet they feared the Leijan and its worshippers as nothing else. Did they know something he didn't? Did the Leijan really hold the power to crush this mightiest of empires? Or was it something incredibly evil, to be feared by individuals and governments alike?

Remembering the icy grip at his throat in the desert, he wondered if there were some things better left alone.

He dared a quick look at Sahtu and nodded to the communications panel. "They're on-screen. Get that distress call out."

His words must have seemed too much a command, for Sahtu only lifted his gaze to the sweeping portholes and the flaring red star in the sea of black.

"You hear me? We've got to send it *now*."

The Asian grumbled, but his fingers nevertheless engaged the universal distress signal. When Blake glanced up again, he saw Fellini's anxious hands seize the helm.

"He hits those controls before we're ready and we're dead!" warned Blake.

Sahtu clanged his scimitar against console, and the startled European relaxed his grip.

Every second now seemed protracted, every action of Blake's confederates magnified: Sahtu's eyes shifting between porthole and weapons panel, Fellini's fingers twitching before helm, Lorenzo's chest rising and falling. Then Sahtu cupped his hand to a receiver in his ear.

"They got it. Now the trash demands we tell 'em who we are."

"Keep 'em sweating," said Blake. "By now they've scanned us, know it's a U.S.S. ship. For all they know, our main communication's out. Keep easing on in."

Anxious seconds passed as the Violeshan sun grew until Blake could distinguish its sphere. With peripheral vision, he caught Rhonda edging close, and somehow he longed for her touch, even though he could never have it. Then Sahtu spun, wild-eyed and cursing.

"They're orderin' us to answer or back off. I'll shoot the filth out of the sky."

"No!" said Blake. "We've got to push 'em to the limit. They won't fire yet. They don't figure on trouble." He glanced back to sweep Rhonda aside. "Strap in."

He didn't see her withdraw, but his thoughts stayed with her, even as Sahtu shouted.

"They're sayin' back off and tell 'em who we are or they'll shoot!"

Blake searched a screen at his elbow for enemy missiles. "Keep pushing 'em. We could evade from here."

"Gotta shoot the trash!" screamed Sahtu. "Gotta blow 'em sky-high!"

"Push it on in!" said Blake.

"Gotta shoot, I tell you!"

"Push it on in!"

"They're givin' us ten seconds. Ten seconds and they fire!"

"Keep pushing!"

Six, counted Blake, *five, four, three, two.* In his screen he suddenly saw an entire sector of fighters split ever-so-casually directly ahead. "Full throttle now!" he told Fellini.

Fellini lunged for the controls, but hesitated with eyes on Sahtu.

"Do it!" screamed the Asian.

Fellini slammed hand against throttle and shoved it to the limit, and with sudden thunder the ship accelerated frightfully, snapping Blake's head back. The force of many G's constricted him in his seat, dizzied him, contorted his face, but he could cast eyes on the forward porthole and see the Violeshan sun ballooning crimson against the blackness. He looked to the screen to find the breach in the Web widening, even as the ship came abreast and exploded through. *They'll fire,* he thought. *They're gonna shoot.* But when he searched again for missiles, he found only undisturbed void.

"We're through!" he announced. Then sudden light bathed the deck and he looked to the larboard porthole to see lightning streak the dark.

"What are you doing?" he exclaimed, watching by screen as one of their own missiles surged harmlessly into space. When he looked up, he found Sahtu grinning sadistically.

"Just wanted to greet the scum," snapped the Asian.

"They'll come after us!" warned Blake. But as he studied the screens and waited, something incredible happened. Nothing. Without a single missile fired or even a hint of pursuit, the fighters had yielded the one forbidden solar system in the galaxy to an unidentified ship.

"We did it!" yelled Fellini.

"The Leijan!" screamed Sahtu, leaping to his feet to thrust scimitar above his head. "There ain't nothin' to stand in our way, nothin' to keep us from gettin' it."

A half-dozen vulgar voices rose up in exaltation, but Blake just sat staring mutely at his screens. He had attended the Academy and served on a starship; he knew as well as anyone the desperate measures enacted for centuries to isolate Violesha Two. He had expected the Web to react slowly, but never could he have imagined the ease with which they had sliced through. It was as if the U.S.S. had let them in. But how could that be, when the government feared Leijanism so obsessively?

A hand slapped his shoulder and Sahtu's boisterous voice rang out. "You promised me power, Sharrel, and by the devil in hell it's gonna be ours."

Blake unbuckled his harness and stood to face him. "They had the technology and firepower to blow us out of the galaxy, but they didn't even try."

Sahtu only grinned to reveal leche-stained teeth. He gestured to the red orb adrift in the emptiness ahead. "Think what's out there, what we're about to get. So the U.S.S. has a bunch of idiots. What do we care? We made it. We done somethin' nobody else ever had guts to."

"There was a reason nobody did. They weren't *let* through."

Sahtu held his scimitar aloft again. "Power, Sharrel." He turned and brandished the weapon before his crew. "Power enough for all of us. Enough to conquer the galaxy!"

As the deck erupted in mad revelry, Blake turned and found Rhonda's pensive face flooded by the light of a swelling crimson sun, and he wondered what forces were at work to have brought them this far.

***

They orbited a world forbidden for centuries and stared at its mysteries.

It hung before Rhonda in the black void, the sun bathing it in vermilion. Indigo clouds swept like strokes from an artist's brush across a terrain without seas, and swirled hurricane-like above deserts broken by crags. Earlier, they had passed from night to day, the sun exploding from the planet's rim magnificent and huge, and in the entire hemisphere shrouded by dark, she had seen no lights to suggest cities.

She glanced around and found Blake beside her at the starboard porthole. Behind them, lemstel flowed freely, so that the two were relatively alone and Rhonda was free to speak frankly in a hushed tone.

"They stranded a million cultists down there, from all walks of life. They could've taken a world and done anything they wanted to with it. But there weren't any lights."

Blake exhaled impatiently as he studied the planet. "I've got bigger worries."

Rhonda waited, knowing he had more to say.

"Something's behind this," he went on, "the way the U.S.S. let us through like it did. Either somebody on board's conspiring with the government to get us to lead them to the Leijan, or the U.S.S. is doing it on their own. Maybe they figured out who pulled that robbery with Lasky. Maybe they've been tracking me every step. You too."

"Do you know what you're saying?" she asked incredulously.

"Exactly."

"Then that means they'll follow us, kill us as soon as we find it."

"Just like Sahtu will, the moment he figures out it's not down there." He backhanded the porthole and pivoted to her. "Okay, you're here, so what is it you know? What did you come here for?"

Trembling, Rhonda glanced around to find lemstel and leche weed still passed freely, verifying that the crew had forgotten them in boisterous celebration. "Do you believe in a Supreme Being, a devil?"

He nodded to the larboard porthole and the stars that stretched to infinity. "The first astronomers thought the stars were windows to Heaven. We've gone to the stars. You see a God out there?"

"Then you don't believe in a hell either."

The sudden twitch at Blake's eye spoke volumes, and Rhonda wondered if he could deny what he had crawled through for so long.

She pressed a hand to the porthole and stared at the forbidden world. "Lasky. Did you believe him? The story about the plaque, what it said?"

"He was dying. He didn't have any reason to lie."

She nodded to the marketers. "They all think it's some kind of power they can get, but I don't think it is. I don't think it's something *anybody* can get for himself."

"Then what is it?" he demanded. "You were in the Valley of the Skull. You came all this way. You know something."

She ran trembling fingers along the porthole and a quiver entered her voice. "The ancient Jews, early Christians, did you ever study them?"

"No."

"Then you don't know about their concept of Lucifer or Satan."

"Superstition."

Rhonda stared at the planet below. "They called him anointed, perfect. They said he walked in the deity's *shekinah*, radiant glory, and became 'the shining one,' Lucifer. They said he wasn't satisfied being a subordinate, that he rebelled and was banished with his cohorts.

"They think he ended up not only prince of Earth, but prince of the powers of the air, implying that when we went to the stars, he'd be there too. They believed if a man died unrepentant he'd go to Gehenna, a first century trash dump where they burned the executed. They used it as a metaphor for a place where the unrepentant dead would go on living bodily in perpetual fire. And Gehenna, in English, means hell."

Blake turned away with a wag of his head, but then whirled upon her. "I don't want nonsense, I want answers!" he said in a barely contained whisper. "Are you going to give them to me or do I have to knock the—" His eyes dropped, and he suddenly seemed subdued by the words he had almost uttered.

Hurt by the first threat in a long while, Rhonda tried to bury it in anger of her own. "I can't give you answers. I can only tell you what I think. And I think Gehenna and hell were names for a real place, and that place was the Valley of the Skull."

Blake started. "Are you crazy?"

"Sharrel."

Rhonda turned to see Sahtu staggering drunkenly toward them, a bottle in his hand. He guzzled from it and lemstel dribbled down his chin.

"We've done our part," he slurred. "We got you and your whore to Violesha Two." He clumsily unsheathed his scimitar to let it glint in the deck lights. "Now's time you put up or—"

"You passing that thing around?" Blake interrupted with a nod to the bottle. Accepting it from the willing Asian, he drank long and hard, and then wiped mouth with sleeve and surveyed the revelers. "It's been a long trip. Everybody's been under a lot of stress. Why don't we stay in orbit a while, let everybody celebrate some more."

The scimitar flashed up, and Rhonda gasped as it came to rest at Blake's throat. "No," said Sahtu, his countenance suddenly fierce. He pressed the point just deep enough to indent the skin at the jugular vein. "We came here for the Leijan, and you're tellin' me right now where to set down, or I'm stickin' this thing through your filthy neck."

"You push that thing any farther," said Blake, "and you won't have to worry about the Leijan, 'cause I'll take its secret with me."

Sahtu tightened his grip on the hilt. "All this time you been sayin' just get you to Violesha Two and the Leijan's mine," he snarled. "We're here now. Ten seconds and you're dead. Count 'em off. Five left!"

A thousand one. Rhonda saw the reflection of the lights in the curved blade and knew that Blake could never draw his Banning in time. *A thousand two.* She wondered if he would still be conscious when the blade thrust into his neck, if he'd still be alive when he sank to the floor. *A thousand three.* Tell him a lie, any lie! *A thousand four.* Blake's lips parted, words forming in his throat only to be choked by the blade. *A thousand—*

She whirled to the planet in desperate search, and a startling feature struck her almost simultaneously. "There!" she said, stretching out an arm.

Spinning back to the gleaming scimitar, Rhonda found Sahtu turning his scarred countenance to the planet and relaxing his grip. As the blade withdrew, Blake looked as well, and Rhonda joined them in focusing on one particular blight on the planet's surface. Although she had known only mystery and violence for weeks now, she shrank from what she saw. The shadow patterns in the red-tinged plain suggested the imprint of a huge, human skull in the planet's crust.

"Canyons and badlands," suggested Sahtu, suddenly sobered.

"No," Blake said with awe. "A city. It's a city."

But Rhonda had already realized it. A great city stared up from below, its skull-like features perfectly delineated in the hemisphere's late-evening shadows. In all the known galaxy, only Brazeille Two held a similar feature, and its skull valley had not been stumbled upon until centuries after the cultists had been stranded here. Yet, independently, these people had built a near-perfect replica.

How could that be? In Heaven's name, how could that possibly be?

Chapter Seventeen

Rhonda stood with Blake and a crew of interstellar pirates on a world hidden for centuries and stared past a silhouetted spire at the distorted sun sinking into a cloud of deepest indigo. There were eleven of them, and at their backs lay the starship and their sole link with the galaxy as it had been known for generations. Ahead, concealed by crags and ridgebacks, lay the great unknown of the city. A stiff wind howled from the shadowy, ogre-like formations and tugged at Rhonda's collar, and suddenly it carried a horrid stench.

"Do you smell it?" she asked, edging near Blake.

"Something dead."

"It's coming from . . ." The words seemed to hang in Fellini's throat, and he turned to Sahtu. "The city, it's coming from the city."

Sahtu's woman gasped.

"Nothing stand in Lorenzo's way," said the Spaniard. "He get Leijan no matter what."

Sahtu spun angrily to Blake. "You're the one had me land away from the city. What do you know about this place, that stink?"

"I had you land here because we don't know if there's hostiles there or not. Probably just a dead animal between here and the walls."

"It's rotting flesh, human flesh," said Fellini. "I've smelled it before. I know what it is."

"Don't be a fool, Fellini," snapped Blake. "Bodies on a battlefield don't smell any different than anything else dead."

Lorenzo grunted, nodding toward Fellini. "He yellow U.S.S. filth, not want to go in."

Sahtu's eyes became slits as he scowled at Blake. "We got more than one piece of U.S.S. filth stinkin' up this place, but one that'll be dead as that smell if he don't come through. I want to know what it is we're lookin' for in that city, how we'll know when we find it."

Blake laughed quietly. "How do you describe power? What nuclear energy looks like? Electromagnetic forces? Lasky *couldn't* describe it to me. All he could do was tell me where it is."

"Then tell me," growled Sahtu, his hand moving to his sheathed scimitar.

Blake's own hand found the grip of his Banning. "I'm not as big a fool as you give me credit for. What do you suppose would happen if I did?"

"You'd be dead the next minute," interjected Fellini, "and anybody else that turned his back."

Sahtu glared at the European. "Just be sure you don't turn yours," he snarled, his fingers playing on the blade's hilt.

Blake shook his head, a laugh of disgust in his throat. "You've been flashing that thing around this whole expedition, Sahtu. You've had it at my neck twice, and I've watched you slit the throat of the one crewman you really needed. Aren't you a little behind times? Wouldn't being an eighteenth-century pirate suit you better? Somebody like you doesn't need the Leijan. You can't even think in those terms. You can't think past the most primitive level, your sister's murder, the need to get revenge. Just what would you do with the Leijan if you ever got it?"

The jagged scar creasing Sahtu's face turned scarlet. "I'd kill anybody and everybody that didn't do like I said. I'd pick out a planet and be its king. No, I'd go from planet to planet, wielding the Leijan like this scimitar, bloodying it left and right. I'd rule the whole galaxy and crush anybody that got in my way."

Blake looked down at the swirling dust and nodded, and then lifted his head to the European. "You, Fellini. Surely you've got loftier ideas than that."

The man smiled smugly. "I'd claim the U.S.S. star fleet for my own, command it like the starship captain I ought to be."

"Of course," Blake said sarcastically. "You've got your father's expectations to live up to. But what happens when you run into the galactic king?"

Fellini fixed eyes on the Asian. "There can just be one king."

"Lorenzo lost woman he loved," interjected the Spaniard. "Soon he take *all* women, find another one to love. Then he drink all lemstel he want, smoke all leche weed." He stiffened, the great muscles in his arms tensing, and with eyes narrowing below his protruding brow, he glared at Sahtu. "And he no take orders from nobody no more."

Sahtu shifted uncomfortably.

"Blasphemers!" exclaimed Hashienah, his emaciated form a silhouette off to the side. "Give me the power and I'll kill all of you right now. Every one of you that blasphemes the Leijan. Everybody that wants to do anything but fall down and worship it!"

Sahtu unsheathed his scimitar. "Tomorrow you can fall down and worship the king of the galaxy, or you can start by doin' it right now."

"I suggest," said Blake, "we don't draw any more attention to ourselves than we already have. We don't have any idea what we're facing behind those walls. They may already be watching us."

Rhonda turned with the rest of them to the spires that stood like ghostly sentinels against the rapidly darkening sky. With his scimitar, Sahtu gestured to the hatch ladder.

"Inside," he ordered. "Tomorrow belongs to us. The Leijan belongs to us."

Rhonda watched the marketers file up the ladder and through the hatch. On the heels of the last, she clutched a rung, only to be stopped by Blake's hand. She looked to see him momentarily cast eyes up to the hatch and shake his head almost imperceptibly. She understood, and as the last crewman disappeared, she edged with Blake back in under the ladder.

"We've played our hand to the hilt," he whispered. Then he seized her shoulders in sudden demand. "You've got to tell me what you expect to find in that city."

"Please don't be so rough with me."

He withdrew his hands, but the grimness stayed in his face. "Do you hear me? I've got to know what's over those walls, what you're looking for. Both our lives depend on you squaring with me."

What could she tell him? That she had come all these light years on a hunch, a woman's intuition? That she had no idea what might lie inside those walls? That this whole mad expedition was just to search for missing pieces in an eons-old mystery?

He gripped her shoulders again and shook her. "Tell me," he demanded quietly. "He's going to kill us. Don't you understand?"

His actions startled her, but she went ahead and offered an answer. "I'm looking for a clue, anything to verify what I think the Leijan is, that might tell me where to find it."

"I already *know* where to find it. I just don't know how to harness it so I can overthrow the U.S.S. and send them to the grave along with every last whore like y—"

Astonished, she swept aside the inner hurt at his unfinished word. "He told you! Lasky told you where it was! Why didn't you tell me?"

"What've you ever told me? I just listened to every last one of them say what they'd do if they ever got it, but you've never even told me that much."

Suddenly she was overwhelmed by mysteries yet to be unlocked. "If it's what I think it is, there's nothing any of us can do, except what's got to be done."

"Sharrel! Whore!"

Rhonda stiffened at Sahtu's cry and turned to see his boots clang down the ladder. The boots found a lower perch, and then the upper rungs framed the Asian's shadowy face. Now he brandished a Banning, not a scimitar.

"You've got a short memory, Sharrel," he growled. "You know what happens to any filth that don't follow my orders. I got a reason not to kill you for now. Before long, I don't plan on havin' that reason." He spat at their feet. "Lorenzo might be dumb enough to let you go wanderin' off without us, but I ain't Lorenzo. Now get up here."

Rhonda, the bearer of the grotto's secret, climbed up toward the hatch with Blake, the keeper of Lasky's knowledge.

***

Reeking with leche weed and lemstel, Blake lay in his lower bunk in the cramped barracks as the first true night in a long while brought deep sleep to the crewmen about him. But Blake's mind was too fitful, despite the drugs. As the eerie light of triple moons crawled across the floor, he thought of Lyra and again had trouble conjuring up the old bitterness. He dredged up the one memory that before had sent such hatred through him, that of Fellini bragging of sharing his tent, and more, with her. Was it true? Did it even matter anymore?

Even when he tried to convince himself it did, the bitterness still wouldn't come, for it was swallowed by memories of Lyra's terrified screams as the hellhounds tore at her. What was the matter with him? He wanted to be bitter; he wanted to hate her and every other woman to his last breath.

So why did he suddenly look at her not as the woman who had led him on in such a lie, but as the programmed cult victim she had been? Could it be that, those last few months together, he had been so self-centered that he had ignored the signs of a troubled person crying for help? Was he just as responsible as the U.S.S. for the events leading up to the hellhounds' attack? For six years, he had taken satisfaction in hating the world, firm in his conviction that he was an innocent victim, but now he wondered.

He wondered too about how his bitterness toward Lyra had given way to more noble considerations of Rhonda. He had never admitted it to himself before, but now he realized it was she, not Lyra, who dominated his thoughts.

His fingers resting across the Banning on his chest, he closed his eyes and smelled again the freshness of Rhonda's hair, saw the smoothness of her tanned cheeks, felt the firmness of her rounded charms as he had crushed her to him, only to taste the sting of her hand.

He opened his eyes in new-found bitterness and saw a moonlit blade sweeping toward him.

"Burn in eternal fire!"

He heard the mad cry only in retrospect, for raw instinct ruled him. He fended off the blade with his forearm but still felt the prick of steel in his chest. A brooding silhouette exploded into his vision as he rolled to his shoulder and seized a bony wrist. He struggled for the weapon and heard a maniacal voice scream *Blasphemer*!" and then he closed a second hand on the wrist and wrenched the blade free. It clanged to the floor and Blake fell beside it, the sudden shift loosing his assailant.

"Hashienah!" Blake glimpsed the figure lunging into the corridor as pandemonium erupted from the bunks. He scrambled to his feet, only now remembering to seize his Banning from the blankets. Then he was after the man, fixing on him all the pent-up hatred of six years.

The coward. It had been him from the start! The one who'd tried to murder him in the cargo bay, the zealot who would've sacrificed himself to prevent some sort of blasphemy. What madness was it that possessed cultists and demanded their very lives?

Blake didn't know, but he was certain of one thing. He would kill the Leijanist!

Ahead, Hashienah darted into the mid-ship passage that led to the outer hull. By the time Blake reached the passage, the emaciated man had surged past a sleepy-eyed guard, who now came to his feet and issued a challenge. But Hashienah already was whirling the locking wheel, throwing the hatch open to flood the corridor in moonlight. Poised against the night and the mysteries of the ages, he spun to the confused guard and the onrushing Blake.

"Burn!" he shouted. "Every last blasphemer, burn!"

Without extending the ladder, he turned and leaped into the shadows.

Blake brushed past the guard to stop in the hatch and stare into the night. Hashienah had sprawled to the ground, and now was on his feet, limping toward the spires silhouetted by sinking moons. A fierce oath on his lips, Blake knelt in the moonlight to bring the Banning up with both hands and find the bare back in the sights. He had him, the filth.

But suddenly there seemed another in his sights, a woman whose flowing hair trailed in the wind as she fled wild-eyed across a clearing, a pack of snarling hellhounds almost upon her.

Lyra. She'd been the same as Hashienah. Tortured and driven, seized by madness that had deserved only his understanding, not his hatred.

Lowering the Banning to watch Hashienah disappear into the shadows, Blake couldn't help but wish that Rhonda were there to witness his sudden empathy and compassion.

Chapter Eighteen

The sun, wispy in azure clouds, rose between ridgebacks to throw Rhonda's elongated silhouette and those of ten others upon the hewn blocks of a four-meter rock wall guarding a city of mystery. Right and left, as far as she could see, the shadow patterns of daybreak delineated the cracks of age. But it was the bizarre etching, ever-repeated along the crumbling rim, that seized her attention.

"What the devil it mean?" grunted Lorenzo, his voice subdued by more than just the necessity of remaining discreet.

Sahtu glared at Blake and the crewman who had guarded the hatch during Hashienah's escape. "Snakes crawlin' on their bellies like you two. If that filth gets the Leijan before me, I'll . . ."

Rhonda didn't hear, for she was suddenly back at the holy of holies.

"Quite a decoration," said Fellini.

She exhaled impatiently. "We're on the Leijan colony. Don't you know the sign of the Leijan?"

"Then it's gotta be here," Sahtu exclaimed under his breath.

"So's that awful stench," added Fellini with a nervous glance around.

Sahtu stepped closer to the partial breach before them. "You cowards stand here holdin' your noses. I'm goin' in."

"If I were you," spoke up Blake, "I'd think about it before I went bounding over that thing. Whoever built it was looking for trouble."

Rhonda had stepped forward to inspect the blocks with an archaeologist's touch. "Unless," she thought aloud, "they never intended it for a fortification."

"What else would it be?" pressed Fellini.

Rhonda didn't reply, for Sahtu tapped Blake with the flat of his scimitar and nodded to the breach. "Let's go. Now."

Lorenzo was first up the talus to become framed in the V at top. "Nobody there," he grunted, and disappeared beyond.

"Get back here!" ordered Sahtu, scrambling after him in distrust.

Caught up in the excitement and in the particular anticipation she alone held, Rhonda followed, the rubble sloughing under her boots. She gained the breach to taste the stench and face an ancient city amid ashen flats and irregular gullies. Parthenon-like structures rose in ruins, some from foundations resembling low-set Mayan pyramids. Their columns, painted ochre by lichen, stood cracked and jagged, while the encircling steps fronted an eroded thoroughfare extending from the wall to disappear in the haze ahead. In places its cobblestone surface lay plain, but elsewhere it held the same catacomb-like dust that swirled through the pillars.

But what made Rhonda gasp with *déjà vu* was that she immediately equated the scene with the Valley of the Skull, as if the design of the structures, their placement, the landscaping, even the pattern of erosion, had been carefully planned to coincide with specific topographic features in the Valley. Even the wall served as a reminder of the barrier cliffs.

Blake suddenly was at her shoulder, his voice a whisper. "He'll kill us. Be ready." Then he was past, dropping over to join Sahtu and Lorenzo in the city.

Before she could even process his warning, a bristly face brushed her cheek and she heard additional discreet words. "You and me can share it. Just get me there first."

The putrid breath told her it was Fellini. She shrank from his touch and descended inside.

Sahtu and Lorenzo, their boots kicking up little dust clouds, had wandered toward a left-side edifice, but as Rhonda started in their wake to take in an archaeologist's dream, Blake seized her arm.

"Stay close," he said, unsnapping his holster. "We might have more than Sahtu to worry about here."

She glanced at the ruins ahead. "If there's anybody alive to keep up the cult's sacraments, we've got reason to be careful. They practiced human sacrifice."

They waited for the stragglers, and then followed Sahtu and Lorenzo up the edifice's lower steps, where the Asian rummaged through the debris of a toppled column. Lorenzo, meanwhile, had gained the upper level to run like a grunting animal in and out the double line of pillars.

"He's calling too much attention," whispered Blake, catching Sahtu's eye. "We don't know who's here, how dangerous it is."

The Asian motioned to Lorenzo with his scimitar. "Get down here!" he quietly commanded.

Lorenzo, still scurrying about between broken columns in frantic search, slung a fist in reply. "Die, wicked-eyes!" he yelled. "Lorenzo find Leijan, he no take orders no more!"

Sahtu went livid with rage and slapped a hand to his Banning, only to have Blake stay his arm.

"Think about it," said Blake, nodding to the weapon. "That thing'll attract more attention than he ever could."

The fact that Lorenzo had disobeyed without tasting Sahtu's scimitar had not gone unnoticed, and while the Asian's glare was still fixed on Blake, Rhonda watched two men scramble up to join the Spaniard in search. Sahtu wheeled to them and his rage redoubled.

"Down here now!" he half-shouted, only to see another order ignored.

Fellini snickered. "You think they're gonna listen to you anymore when the Leijan's here somewhere? You think they—"

A sudden thud from above precipitated a scream that died in mid-utterance, and Rhonda saw a crewman tumbling down the steps, heels flying. He came to rest, head-down, at Sahtu's feet, blood oozing from a neck bearing a brightly feathered arrow. Shock reigned for a split second, and then Blake clutched Rhonda's arm and half-dragged her down toward the thoroughfare, reaching for his Banning as he did.

Over her shoulder, Rhonda saw another whirring arrow chip a column at Lorenzo's skull, forcing the Spaniard into retreat with the others. Simultaneously, Blake pulled her to the ground and, pivoting on a knee, found only empty ruins down the sight of his Banning. But Sahtu was firing wildly, prompting the men beside him to do likewise, the bolts exploding against columns and sending rock flying like shrapnel.

Blake spun to the terrified faces. "There's nothing there. Don't drain your Bannings!"

Sahtu was the last to cease, but he continued to clutch his scimitar and Banning as he spewed profanity. "Can't let 'em pin us down!" He leveled another quick burst that found only sky and ruins.

"For the sake of all that's holy, give me a Banning!" implored Fellini, cowering at the bottom step.

"Can't pin us down!" repeated Sahtu.

Fellini buried his face in debris and threw an arm over his head. "Do something. Somebody do something!"

Blake cursed. "Is that the gallantry that brought her into your tent that night on Trinal Four? You want your Banning back? Come take it, you—"

The rest of Blake's challenge was lost on Rhonda, for as she sought his eyes she realized he must have spoken of Lyra. Here, thousands of light years from anything that should have reminded him of her, it was still she he thought of in a crisis, and Rhonda didn't know why it should bother her the way it did.

They lay there anxious minutes, vainly searching the encircling ruins for a glimpse of their attackers. But the only movement was a haze of dust that crawled along the flats and a whirlwind that rose out of a snaking gully.

Blake finally stood, but kept a finger on his Banning trigger. "They've backed off, but you can bet they're still out there."

"Gotta get outa here, back to the ship!" pleaded Fellini, only now raising his head.

"Stinking coward," grunted Lorenzo.

Rising, Sahtu snickered cruelly. "The Leijan ain't for cowards, is it, Lorenzo. Maybe I *better* send that filth back."

"Just a Banning," Fellini whined. "All I want's a Banning!"

Sahtu merely turned to study the columns. "I ain't lettin' no puny Stone Age weapons keep *me* from the Leijan. We can stop a whole army with what we got."

Blake exhaled sharply. "Not if you go draining your Banning shooting at something you can't even see."

Sahtu turned his fierce scowl upon him. "Then I'll kill what I can see. Now where is it?"

"You're barely in the city. Is this where you'd keep something that valuable?" He looked down the hazy thoroughfare and nodded. "We've got to go further."

Sahtu cursed under his breath, but he nevertheless struck out down the avenue with his woman, and an unarmed Fellini and four pirates with upraised Bannings went with them.

"What about him?" asked Rhonda.

Blake turned as she pointed to the wounded man on the bloody steps.

Sahtu glanced back and grinned. "One less to share it with," he said without losing stride.

Images of Langdon and the grotto bombarded Rhonda's conscience. "We can't just leave him there."

"No," said Blake. "We can't."

Rhonda never had been so surprised, but she didn't hesitate as Blake motioned her up the edifice while he scanned for hostiles with ready Banning. When she reached the prostrate form and knelt, Blake was there too, hovering over her, his weapon continuing to guard. She slid her fingers down the bloody neck to the carotid artery, and then shook her head and stood. The moment she found Blake's eyes, she was amazed to read the same compassion of which his actions already had spoken.

Under sustained threat, the nine crept on beside a winding gulch with an impassable bed that at least would offer quick cover from another volley of arrows. As Blake reconnoitered the bordering ruins, she stayed close to his side. An ensuing exchange, a mere murmur in the howling wind, was most eloquent in what she didn't say, that she had discovered a startling facet of his personality and yearned to know even more.

He seemed to lag purposely, and she fell back with him. Maintaining his reconnaissance, he whispered almost angrily. "Okay, you're here, so what good's it done? The city, the way it looked from orbit, these ruins, is this what you came here for?"

His sudden gruffness seemed so foreign to his earlier demeanor. "I don't know. I just know that . . ." She shook her head. "Before, I've been here before."

He clutched her shoulder just long enough to glare at her. "Will you give me a straight answer just for once? If whoever's out there doesn't kill us, Sahtu will."

"I don't have any answers yet. All I know is I've been in a place like this before. It's almost like this one was designed from the other even though they couldn't've had contact, because the other one's the Valley of the Skull."

He gave her a quick, hard stare before again surveying the ruins.

"I think," she went on, "that whatever it was that the inhabitants of the Valley worshipped was real, and that somehow, across all these light years, it led those banished cultists to build this city as a shrine to it."

"You know what you're saying?" he asked, checking their flank.

"Well enough to know that an archaeologist has no business saying it, that whatever the Leijan is, it's got the power to override every law of physics and exert influence and control we can't even begin to understand."

Blake seemed to shudder. "Is that so hard to believe? Didn't it bring the two people together who knew so much, or so little, about it? If it wasn't for it, I'd still be in some dive drowning every last memory of her."

Rhonda's jaw trembled. "Why do you have to talk about her all the time?"

"I don't."

"You talk about her and think about her, even here, all these light years from where she was. We have arrows coming down out of thin air to kill a man at our feet, and still you talk about her."

"What do *you* care?"

She turned away and the decadent city blurred. "Hasn't it been long enough?" She looked back at him, emotion hanging in her throat. "Can't you ever forget about her? Don't you know it bothers me to hear you talk about her all the time?"

"I didn't know you felt that way, Rhonda."

It was the first time he had ever called her by name, and it suddenly unleashed her pent-up desire to have him pull her close and tell her everything would be all right. But at the same time, it raised pangs of guilt, for she remembered the time he had tried to do so.

"When I look at you now," she said, "I see somebody different, somebody I'd . . ." She looked down for an instant. "I wish you wouldn't keep letting her crush all the good things in you, because I see you the way you used to be, the way you still are, inside. I see you for the person I'd like to have as a friend."

The confusion that masked his face stayed suspended in Rhonda's mind as they pushed on under a sun wheeling toward zenith through building clouds. The stench worsened, and eerie shadows that played in the adjacent ruins led anxious eyes to see things that weren't there, or were they? Frayed nerves and fear of the unknown brought Banning fire toppling pillars more than once, yet when the rock ceased to fly and the dust settled, only debris remained.

In late morning, through a near-impenetrable haze of dust that choked her throat, Rhonda thought she could discern a widening of the avenue ahead. Such, she knew, would coincide with a broad alkali flat with a Matterhorn-like pinnacle that guarded a pair of cavernous sink-holes in the Valley of the Skull. They had always been mysteries to her father and to generations of scientists before him; geologic evidence suggested that they had been the source of the volcanic fires that had seared the Valley for eons. But *everything* had been a mystery in the Valley, as it was here.

She grew queasy and realized they must be nearing the stench's source. With each step the pungency intensified, carried by a wind that seemed to howl wraith-like through hazy ruins that rimmed a plaza ahead.

"Listen to it," said Fellini. "It almost sounds alive, like it's—"

The howl grew more distinct, stopping everyone in mid-stride. As Rhonda listened, she realized she heard more than wind, and she inclined an ear to distinguish it. It was almost like moaning, wails, cries of agony in the dust-blown flat ahead. Then an abrupt cross-wind shifted the thick haze for an instant, and six Bannings shot up to fix on five outlines shimmering indistinct in the plaza.

Sahtu's woman screamed. Rhonda shrank close to Blake. The face of every crewman went pale.

"What in devil?" muttered Lorenzo.

"I see it!" said Fellini. "Let's get out of here!"

"What do you see?" demanded Blake.

"Shoot it. Somebody shoot it!"

Fellini's hysteria was contagious, and it swept through Rhonda with a flurry that threatened to panic everyone.

"Listen to it!" ranted Fellini. "We've got to get out of here. We've got to go!"

Blake stepped over and backhanded him in the mouth. "Shut up! You hear me? All of you!"

Blake rubbed his knuckles as he withdrew, but the blow quieted Fellini, who shot a quick glance of surprise at him before slinking away to tend the blood on his lip.

"Now, all I see," said Blake with authority, "is a bunch of hazy outlines, and all I smell is rotten meat, and all I hear is, what? The wind? You're not afraid of the wind, are you, Lorenzo?"

The Spaniard grunted.

"And if it's not the wind," continued Blake, "then it's more like somebody being tortured. Don't tell me you never tortured anybody, Sahtu?"

The Asian sneered.

"Either way," Blake went on, "it's only arrows we've got to worry about. It's not like we're up against something that's not flesh and blood."

The moment he said it, Rhonda remembered all the scattered pieces of a cosmic puzzle and wondered.

The uncanny moans and wail of the wind died in the deep-throated roll of thunder. Rhonda turned her face to the dark clouds for a moment, and the stinging rain reminded her of the inflexible laws of physics.

Blake had more to say. "So what are we going to do?"

Scattered drops pitted the dust at Sahtu's boots as he slung his sword hand toward the plaza. "There ain't nothin' up there that this can't slit the throat of."

"But those cries, that stench," argued Fellini.

"Lorenzo hear wind, smell rain, and yellow coward," grunted the Spaniard.

Sahtu turned his fierce scowl on Blake. "You're takin' us in," he ordered with a sweep of his scimitar.

Damp powder clinging to her boots, Rhonda followed Blake into the shrouded plaza that stretched toward a dark, mitre-shaped mass, a small peak maybe. As the wind gusted, she caught fleeting glimpses of five forms deployed with almost geometric precision. Each of the five seemed to spring vertically from foundations that flared on either side: almost upside-down T's. Whatever the nature of the stench and moans, they issued from their very midst.

A few steps farther and the rain began to settle the dust, revealing the scene a detail at a time. Blake, in the lead, must have pieced it all together before the others, for he suddenly hesitated. Then Rhonda gave a little cry and instinctively drew close, needing an arm that Blake didn't offer. Sahtu fought for air like a man kicked in the stomach. Lorenzo shrank to grunt like a terrified animal and shoved the crewman nearest him. Fellini muttered a scared oath that became the retching of a nauseated man.

In the clearing ahead were the ashen bodies of five men, all but one stilled and in an advanced stage of decomposition. But it was the position of the bodies that was startling, for the five had been crucified upside-down on upturned crosses of wood that marked the points of a pentagram outlined by a stone foundation.

And the man who still squirmed to cries of agony, rivulets of blood and rain streaking his tortured body and face, was Hashienah.

Chapter Nineteen

Fear chilled Rhonda to the marrow as a gloom settled over the plaza. She shuddered with the distinct sensation that something evil lurked nearby, but a quick scan across the deep-cut gully to her right, and over the shoulders of the crewmen behind, found only ruins and twisting thoroughfare.

Detail gave birth to detail as her unwilling legs carried her forward a step behind Blake. Except for Hashienah, the victims appeared aged. Iron spikes at their feet, and in the extremes of their outstretched arms, held the five framed against a great upthrust of volcanic rock that lay beyond widely separated shadows that suggested abysses. The dead watched with frozen grimaces as vultures tore at shreds of flesh with sharp, red talons.

But their agony was over, while Hashienah's continued. Rhonda had particular insight into his torture, for her archaeological study of Earth's Roman Empire, coupled with her religious training, had left her with a macabre fascination for Roman execution. Now, in all its graphic horror, she actually witnessed a bastardized form of crucifixion. The force of Hashienah's weight against the slender spike through his ankles had produced a visible tear in ligament and cartilage, bringing blood streaming down his legs. The upside-down position had pulled knees and hips out of socket, leaving the bones protruding awkwardly. The strain on his chest was most apparent, the exposed rib cage showing his severe laboring for every breath. Spikes in each bloody wrist extended his arms along the crossbeam so unnaturally that his shoulders had dislocated. He was semi-conscious at best, his fingers twitching and his head rolling slightly as vomit trickled from his mouth.

But those were scientific observations, cold and unemotional, while the true horror of crucifixion could be understood only on a personal level. Hashienah's wrenched face spoke volumes: cheek muscles distorting, the mouth drawing to one side, the tongue swelling between lips cracked and bleeding, the eyes bulging in anguish, disbelief, and fear.

Again, Rhonda was awed by the power the Leijan had to possess. The walled ruins were a shrine, and what purpose could there be for these victims of reverse crucifixion at the points of a pentagram, long an unholy symbol, except as sacrifices?

"He just wanted to worship the thing. You know what they'll do to *us*?" exclaimed Fellini. "We've got to get out of here!"

"Somebody do something," said Rhonda. "Get him down. Please."

"It's too late," Blake said quietly.

"We can't just let him suffer."

"Leave him where he is," snapped Sahtu, regaining his bloodthirsty vindictiveness. "Traitor had it coming."

"Nobody's got that coming, not even him," said Blake, and he lifted his Banning mercifully toward the crucified man who three times had tried to murder him.

Rhonda couldn't believe that the person who uttered those words was the same man she had watched kill her helpless assailants in the back room of that Ohiloan dive. She fixed eyes on his weapon and watched it rise against the backdrop of the foundation, and as the rain-slick barrel leveled against Hashienah's breast, she saw it quake in fingers suddenly frozen.

Blake's gasping curse, and the sudden oaths of withdrawing pirates, called her attention to Hashienah. An involuntary cry died in her throat, for Hashienah's breast suddenly crawled with inflamed welts that popped out in relief, the ridges altering the streams of watery blood.

But they were more than welts, for they formed letters, and the letters words, and they were essentially the words Lasky had found in a derelict ship at galaxy's edge: *Free me, kneel, it's yours.*

But that wasn't all. There was an annotation in Greek that set Rhonda reeling with memories of her mother. Then she flinched to the crack of Blake's Banning, and Hashienah's suffering suddenly was over, welts giving way to charred flesh.

The report stirred a half-dozen men out of shock, and Sahtu brandished his scimitar before Blake. "What was it? Tell me what it was!"

"You can read as well as me," said Blake, lowering his weapon and turning away.

Sahtu seized his arm and slung him around. "I said tell me!"

The Asian's scimitar suddenly was at Blake's heart, but Blake maintained his composure. "Who am I to understand what we saw? I'm as shook up as you, but I know coordinates when I see them."

"You're lyin'!"

"Let's just get out of here!" said Fellini.

"Lorenzo saw, no read," grunted the Spaniard.

"Well I read plenty," said Blake, staring into Sahtu's eyes. "I just saw what the mind can do when you're the kind of zealot Hashienah was. Are you that much of an idiot that you can't see for yourself that he found out where the Leijan was and they killed him for it? They crucified him, and still he found a way to tell us, and it's nowhere on this planet."

Sahtu turned crimson, the veins in his neck bulging. "You told me it was here. I'll kill you!"

A short, powerful arm swept up from behind and a bony fist slammed into Sahtu's jaw, separating him from his weapon and knocking him hard to the bloody base of the cross. He looked up dazed and surprised to see Lorenzo towering above, Banning in hand.

"He know coordinates, get us Leijan," said the Spaniard, nodding to Blake. "Wicked-eyed devil know nothing."

Enraged and humiliated, Sahtu went livid but held his tongue in face of the muzzle. "If you think he saw coordinates, make him tell 'em. If he's got 'em all to himself, make him tell 'em."

Rhonda realized that Sahtu knew the dim-witted Spaniard well, but she didn't reckon on Blake's anticipation. When Lorenzo turned to direct his weapon on him, the Spaniard found Blake's Banning already leveled on his chest.

"Easy, Lorenzo," Blake said calmly. "From the looks of things, we need all the men we've got to get out of this."

"You tell Lorenzo coordinates," he demanded.

"What do you think would happen if I did? If everybody here knew them? It wouldn't just be me that'd catch a knife in the back, so would you. Look at Fellini over there. He's already drooling over it. You think he wants to share the Leijan with you, Lorenzo?"

"Lorenzo kill Fellini first," said the Spaniard.

Fellini withdrew a step, casting nervous eyes for cover that wasn't there. "Don't let him do it, Lorenzo. Don't let him turn you against me. You know I'm with you."

The Spaniard faced him, his eyes slits beneath the protruding brow. "Lorenzo no want coward trash on his side. Maybe he kill you all."

Fellini slung a hand toward Blake. "It's Sharrel that can't be trusted. Don't you see? There was writing on Hashienah's chest, maybe even numbers, but we can't trust the filth. Look how he's led us on."

"Then maybe *all* of you better kill me," said Blake, "if you came this far just to decide you don't want the Leijan after all."

Lorenzo turned back to him in confusion.

"Leave him alone!" shouted a crewman. "I don't care who else you kill, but don't touch Sharrel. He was standin' closest. It said somethin' about the Leijan being ours, but that other stuff might've been coordinates. We can always kill him later."

Lorenzo grunted. "He take Lorenzo to Leijan, else—"

A sudden *whoosh* presaged a thump and a scream that died in a single expulsion of air, and Sahtu's woman slumped to the dust at Fellini's feet, a feathered shaft in her back. For a moment it froze everyone. Then an arrow came out of the sky to embed in the beam at Blake's head, and all of them dropped to the cover of crumbling foundations half a meter high.

"They're everywhere!" said Sahtu.

Prone in the dirt, Rhonda slid her face up along the rock and looked past Hashienah's body. An army of skeletal and ashen men were pouring down from the columned ruins. Naked but for G-strings, they bore the scars of self-mutilation along rib cages as protruding as their eyes were hollow. As the scores in the forefront came screaming like banshees, they nocked arrows to bows and unleashed an incredible hail of missiles into the sky.

She had only moments to take in the scene, for Blake gave a cry of warning and fell upon her, shielding. Instantly came the staccato of arrows peppering the ground about her, and a sudden groan told her that somebody had been hit. Then Blake was on his elbow, his weapon hand resting on the foundation as he squeezed off bolt after bolt into the attacking horde.

Rhonda watched them fall in masses, to Blake's Banning and others, but still they came, cutting the sky with repeated volleys of arrows: human and feathered tides that wouldn't slow. The hostiles seemed impervious to fear and to the moans of the fallen, trampling them to press the attack and keep up the fusillade. Iron-tipped shafts fell like grapeshot, striking the crucifixion beams, imbedding in Hashienah's corpse, glancing from the rocks that were at Rhonda's eyes.

"There's too many of 'em!" yelled Sahtu.

Blake concentrated his fire on the leaders. "Turn. You've got to turn!"

But it was a stampede that seemed immune to discouragement, and Rhonda remembered the voice of her mother: *Don't be afraid of the terror of the night, or the arrow that flies by day. A thousand might fall at your side, ten thousand on your right, but it won't come anywhere near you.*

A crewman took an arrow in the side, setting him flopping. Fellini, cowering beside him, came up insane with fear to wrench the Banning from his hand and fire wildly. Yet, even with five weapons still hurling blue bolts of energy, the screaming hostiles stormed ever closer to draw stone hatchets and knives. A volley of Banning fire would fell the entire front line, but twice as many would swarm across the downed bodies to take up the fight.

"My Banning's drained!" shouted a crewman, throwing it aside to seize that of the wounded man at his shoulder.

A handful of weapons against a horde of thousands. Rhonda couldn't help but think how ironic it was that even with the most lethal handguns ever developed, they were no match for savages bearing Stone Age weapons. By sheer dint of numbers, the hostiles were overwhelming them, and when Lorenzo grunted that his Banning also had failed, Blake whirled to her.

"When I fall, take the Banning. Don't let them take you alive!"

"Here they come!" said Sahtu. "We gotta get outa here!"

He scrambled over the mortared rocks to fall clumsily at his woman's arrow-riddled body. His men went with him, those with weapons firing a quick salvo from their knees. Then they were up, hugging the ground, volleying, zigzagging at right angles to the swarming mass and making for the shielding ruins on the thoroughfare. Rhonda knew that the marketers were open targets, but she also saw that within seconds even the crumbling rocks wouldn't stay the warriors and their weapons.

"Let's go!" said Blake, seizing her arm to clamber across the wall. Then a crewman caught an arrow to sprawl to the ground, and Blake dragged Rhonda with him as he retreated toward the deep-cut gully. Thunder boomed simultaneous with the crack of his Banning and they were at its bank, stumbling and sliding down through the mud.

"Stay down!" Blake urged, flattening himself against the sloughing ridge to rest his Banning hand at its rim.

Rhonda looked back and no longer saw an indistinct legion, but hatchet-wielding individuals almost upon them. Blake fired, turned, and fired again. Their bloodcurdling cries were in Rhonda's ears, every detail of their hideous faces with sunken orbs and pointed cheekbones before her eyes. She could taste the hanging dust, feel with her cheek the quake of a thousand legs scourging the plaza.

She slid on down to gully's bottom and huddled with her face against Blake's boot as reflections of energy bolts played along the opposite bank. They were going to die. The thought exploded into her mind like thunder shaking the ground at her hip, and with it came another thought. They were going to die and she'd never told him that she *loved him*. She loved him, this coarse, bitter man who already had saved her life twice, who only minutes ago had shielded her with his own body, who even now fought for her against impossible odds.

His name was on her lips, and she looked up to stretch out a hand to his shoulder, wanting to share death if not life, and a pair of bestial eyes in a cadaver-like face burst into her vision. Out of the backdrop of swirling clouds, an ashen arm and hatchet suddenly swept down, and before she could scream, an energy bolt toppled him headlong to the gully bottom beside her.

Now she screamed, choked by the smell of burnt flesh, and it presaged a second gruesome face at Blake's shoulder, and then a third. One hostile dropped to an energy bolt at the gully's brink, and when the lifeless arm draped over the rim, the fingers loosed a flint knife that splattered the mud. But the other man fell unmarked on Blake with hatchet, the two of them tumbling down beside her, their arms in death locks. Rhonda fell away, seizing the knife as she did, and then a Banning cracked at point-blank range and Blake rolled the body from him in time to fire at the frenzied mass of warriors pouring from above.

At the last instant his eyes caught hers and his Banning began to swing in her direction, and then he crumpled under the sheer force of numbers. She saw a hatchet glance off his skull, and as she said his name, she grasped the knife in both hands and plunged the point toward her breast.

But as she did, the hand of a savage warrior stayed it.

Chapter Twenty

Oblivion. Blackness. A faraway pounding that strained to break the bonds of unconsciousness. The intonations of many voices in a strange tongue and the euphoria of gliding effortlessly.

In his half-awake world, Blake strangely relived the moment when he had stood below Hashienah's cross and watched the rain carry blood to the ground. The scene called to mind another crucifixion victim, one who once had held the worship of millions. Blake had always dismissed the story as unscientific and immaterial to life as he knew it, but now he appreciated as never before exactly what that man must have endured if he had truly given himself, as some had claimed, as the ultimate sacrifice for every individual.

Then the rain seemed to blot everything out, opening the way for his senses to return little by little. He found his legs outstretched to a little dust cloud rushing through a mist as his boot heels cut trails to the force of bony arms hooked under his shoulders. It was a minute more before he realized that two persons dragged him backward through a throng of dancing Leijanists, who chanted and brandished weapons against the sky. He had heard such chants only once before, when he had burst in on that shadowy Rhythian room, and only his stupor kept the hairs from rising at his nape.

His vision clouded by blood, he turned his head in compensation to look through the stirring horde and glimpse the rise and fall of a stone hammer. The break through the leaping, near-naked bodies closed, and then reopened, and Blake saw a half-dozen Leijanists spread-eagling a wounded crewman against a lowered cross as another hammered a spike through his wrist. Heaped nearby were the decomposed bodies that earlier had marked the crosses, while slowly rising up beyond, to the groan of a rope and the grunts of tugging warriors, was a second beam bearing a crucified marketer. He appeared unconscious, but as the beam reached vertical to slam into place upside-down and bring full force to bear on his spiked feet, a cry of anguish broke from his lips. Another pirate, with a splintered arrow in his shoulder, kicked and screamed as Leijanists dragged him toward a third cross. Meanwhile, the crucified body of Sahtu's woman already stood sentinel beside Hashienah's corpse.

Five crosses, five victims. Did that mean he had to wait his turn? He and Rhonda?

Fear jolted him and he called her name, the word dying in a throaty rasp. What had they done to her? They could only nail *him* up for the vultures, agony that could go on for days, all right, but that was all. They could do as much, and more, to Rhonda, the animals. She had depended on him to take care of her, to see her through this whole impossible venture, and he had let her down. He loved her and he had let her down.

He loved her. The revelation astounded him and unleashed a barrage of memories of a time when he had believed himself never again capable of such feelings. She had reached through all the scars and rekindled his caring and sensitivity, made him want to live again. She had restored meaning to his life, given it flavor so that the morrow had again held hope and promise, until now.

He couldn't lose her. Not at the very moment that he realized how much he needed her.

Surging with adrenalin, he dug a foot into the ground to wrench an arm free. As the remaining guard sank with his weight, Blake twisted around to catch himself on a knee and drive a vicious fist into the lowered face. The man fell away, and Blake wheeled and went down under a volley of blows and wicked kicks. When the Leijanists backed away, he could only groan and writhe in the dirt, but this time they tied his hands at his back before picking him up, and he had no choice but to be docile.

Dazed with pain, he was only half-aware as they dragged him past the pentagram foundation and the three upright crosses. But when he dropped roughly to wallow at their feet, he turned his head and found the great rock brooding nearby and a dark abyss gaping at his shoulder. He instinctively shrank, for sheer walls thirty meters wide defined blackness without end. From its depths surged an updraft, cold and musty.

Something nudged his hip, and he raised his head to see a scarred beam against his back and many pale arms withdrawing from it. Crudely rounded and parallel to his body, the timber stretched eighteen meters past his boots and a similar distance beyond his head. He first thought it an instrument with which to force him over the edge, but they quickly dragged him up and slammed him back against it. He kicked and squirmed, but there were too many hands holding him fast, and he knew that he hadn't been spared crucifixion even for a little while.

His senses seemed magnified as he awaited the agonizing thrust of nail into tissue. He felt the rain and sweat dripping from the man hovering above and smelled the foul breath. He grew sensitive to the splinters at his tied hands, tasted blood and salt on his lips, heard the chants degenerate to a chorus of near-growls. Then something cut into his legs just above the ankles, constricting circulation. A hand slid in under his back and the same sharp tightness struck the bends of his elbows, pinning him against the beam. Only then did he realize he was being bound, not nailed, but was his fate any less inevitable?

They backed away, leaving him to face the falling rain, and then they gathered along the timber to drag it until there was nothing at his shoulder but open space and dark. The sky suddenly fell away, like the sun setting in rapid-speed film, and in its wake came the great rock's mitred summit, its talus core, its thick base. Then a rock bastion passed before his eyes, fading swiftly to shadowy twilight and utter blackness. Then came twilight again, and semi-brightness through which a crucified crewman sank to give way to clouds and falling rain. Groggy, Blake finally realized that he revolved with the beam in open space as Leijanists at either end wheeled it across the sinkhole.

His head swam as many grating rotations brought him to a standstill midway across. He was face-down, his leather bonds creaking as they gashed his skin and stretched to the pull of his weight. He moaned from the excruciating stress on his shoulders; his arms seemed ready to pop from their sockets. With extreme effort, he craned far enough to catch the drip of rain and glimpse the multitude of legs dancing on the rim to the resumed chant, but then he could only let his head dangle toward the night. The leather continued to groan, gradually yielding to his weight, and even in his torture, he thought how much Sahtu would have appreciated it: suspended face-first by weak thongs over a bottomless pit, with nothing to do but wait and dwell on the moment they would snap.

But was it execution, or sacrifice to some ungodly thing he didn't even know what was?

Time became elongated; he measured every breath, and each throb of his pulse registered in his swollen arms and legs. The clouds broke, and the refracted light of day grudgingly gave way to twilight. As shadows blanketed his chest and thighs, his own echoing groans seemed to grow louder, and he glanced at the rim and realized that it was because the chanters had become silent and crept away.

A sudden, sharp creak of leather petrified him in morbid anticipation. Thongs popped at his arms, and he cried out and felt the chasm sucking him down head-first. His cry bounced back hollowly as bonds knifed into his boot tops. The cords stretched and groaned ominously but held, dangling him upside down to swing pendulum-like over a terrifying pit.

His hands still tied behind, he could only fight the unyielding bonds and look up at the beam swaying across a night sky gemmed with stars. He thought of Rhonda and his undemanding love for her, and then of Lyra and an immature, self-serving kind of love. He considered the dying old man whose story had hurled him onto a trail of mystery, and the inexplicable power that had brought Rhonda and him together only to have it end here.

But the most vivid image that exploded into his mind was that of a cross streaming with blood. At first he thought it one of the five sentineling the plaza. But as he mentally scanned the vertical beam, he saw that this cross stood upright, though it too held a crucifixion victim. Blake even seemed able to hear the moans. But this scourged man strangely was marked by two distinguishing features: the first, a gaping wound in his rib cage, the second, a peculiar wreath of interwoven thorns bloodying his skull.

The image vanished, replaced by a woman's face bearing the puffiness of a lemstel addict. Her lips were moving silently, but he distinguished the unspoken syllables and pieced them together: *"Great things are destined for you."*

Leather popped at his heels and a foot came flying from its bonds, again setting him swinging to and fro to a rhythmic screech.

"It's a lie!" His bitter shout echoed. "It's a lie!"

With each arc through the stiff updraft, the heel fixed at the beam slipped inside its bonds, yet he still squirmed violently in the fight to free his hands. To his primal yell, the thongs stretched at his wrist but wouldn't break, and as he sucked in air for a last desperate try, he lifted his eyes to the cord giving at his heel.

He started, pricked with *déjà vu.* Beyond the pitching beam, star fields began to eddy, individual spikes of light and nebular clusters gravitating inward to swirl against a black cloak. He had seen this before; he had been here before. Even after glancing away to kick vainly with his free leg toward the beam, the jeweled sky still whirled. It welded suns, clusters, spiral arms into an almost human-like appendage. It was a hand, brilliant yet wispy, and as it came hurtling out of infinity, Blake knew he was no longer alone.

Hope welled in him, a sudden burst of strength snapping the thongs at his wrist. Then he was stretching a numbed hand to the sky, seeking the mysterious presence that seemed so distant, yet so near. He had to have it, had to let it shelter him under its wing, as though it were the culmination of every breath he had ever taken, every heartbeat that had pumped life into his arteries. The hand came nearer, the extended index finger yearning for his own from so close that he could feel its warmth.

Suddenly demands from a voice not his own reverberated through the cavern, something about who could go, who *would* go.

The cord at his heel snapped, sending him plummeting.

"Me!" he shouted, the beam surging skyward. "Send me!"

A hand as warm and pliable as his own closed on his fingers, its brilliant aura cradling him with the gentleness of a feathery caress. All at once he possessed such discernment, of what really mattered and what didn't, that he grieved for the life he had wasted to selfishness and bitterness. How could he have lived that way? Survived a single moment without the hope that this being exuded? He was alive now, for the first time ever, and he overflowed with fulfillment and peace beyond his wildest dreams. He felt a oneness and harmony with all that had ever existed or was yet to come, and all he wanted to do was bask forever in the radiance of this being that hovered over him like a hen over her chicks.

In later reflection, he would remember the succeeding events only as a blur, external details failing to register on senses deluged by euphoria. As quickly as it had come, the brilliance receded, and he found his extended arms clutching the splintery beam overhead, the stars again fixed in the sky and his dangling legs buffeted by a howling, gale-force updraft.

Even as he hooked a leg over to secure his hold, he stretched a quaking hand to the stars that sparkled so suddenly far away.

"Come back!" he called, thirsting for just another instant in its presence. But the only response was the trailing of a blazing meteor across the sky.

He was alone, straddling the beam, his mind spinning with the mysteries of the cosmos, yet accepting. He realized that a few minutes ago he would have dismissed it as a freakishly powerful updraft coupled with the delusions of a dying man. But that was before he had known the being for himself, experienced a love that must have transcended the sum total of all that existed in the galaxy, understood that only through it could he ever be complete.

He belonged to the being. He was his, and it could never be any other way.

Chapter Twenty-One

By the light of a trio of fist-shaped moons rising through columned ruins, Blake crept along a beam bridging a second dark and forbidding sinkhole and heard again the moans that had drawn him here. The threat of Leijanists held his tongue, but it could not quell his anticipation. Even so, he prepared for the worst, that the form hugging the timber's underside would not be her. And though he realized he knew nothing of such matters, he found himself praying with the simplicity of a child.

An updraft chilled his face, and splinters gnawed at his hands and knees, and then he was close enough to distinguish the leather strips overlaying the girder. The creaking bonds had yet to stretch much, suggesting that the victim wasn't in imminent danger. Still, he couldn't bring himself to call her name and face the truth so soon.

"I'm going to help you," he whispered simply, for the memory of the being of light was so strong that he intended to rescue whoever it was.

The only reply was a moan of delirium, and then he was kneeling at the thongs supporting the upper body. "Can you hear me? Are you able to talk?"

A slight stirring shifted the bonds just enough to reveal dangerously frayed leather. "Don't move," he whispered.

Realizing that alone he had no hope of turning the beam even the half-revolution necessary, he sprang to the far set of equally worn thongs. Straddling the timber to feel the victim against his calf, he slipped over the edge and crooked an arm over the top. Clinging upside-down, he didn't even check the shadowy face in his feverish race against time, though the curves that brushed him told him it was a woman. He hooked a leg under her and up over the girder, pinning her against wood with his own body, and then he frantically set to work on the stubborn knot at the ankles. He worked blindly, his own thigh obscuring the moonlight. In desperate frustration he finally wrenched it in two, feeling the burden of her weight, and reached for the bonds at her arms. Only then did he come face-to-face and see the eyes open, and for a moment, even suspended over a sacrificial pit in a city of crazed zealots, he brimmed with happiness.

Rhonda was alive.

"I'm getting you out of here," he exclaimed quietly.

The eyes closed and he jerked the cords until they broke. He caught her on his shoulder, and with an arm about her back, he worked their bodies to the girder's top. Snapping the bonds at her wrists, he pulled her limp form close and let his stinging eyes wet her hair. He lifted his gaze to the stars, and a silent cry played on his lips.

It was you. Whoever you are, you kept me alive, kept her alive.

He carried her through ruins bathed by moonlight, his boots padding in the dust as their eerie triple shadows trailed alongside. She hardly stirred, and he felt her chilled shoulders and was afraid for her, knowing that she might have lapsed into shock. The ordeal had wrenched him of strength, and he staggered along under her burden, his temple and shoulders throbbing with pain. But the psychological trial had been worse, and he worried that her womanhood had netted her even greater trauma.

He traveled the winding streets toward the rising stars with almost careless indifference, making no attempt to hug the shadows; exhaustion overrode all but the instinct to place one foot after the other. Yet he struggled on at peace, strangely secure that the being of light guided his steps. Indeed, an hour from the pit, he caught the moonlit skyline of a toothy ridge far ahead and realized that, as if by design, he had chosen a more direct plaza-to-wall course than their route of the previous day, although this one bore ninety degrees from it.

The moons rose higher, casting ogre-like shadows through the bordering ruins. Once, he skirted a decadent wall with faded murals that told a story of banishment to this world, of the rise of warring factions endlessly seeking control of the City of the Skull. The murals spoke also of unholy rites climaxing at pentagram or pit, the sacrifices drawn first from enemies, and then from the aged. In the columns above, Blake thought he glimpsed movement, but when a gritty wind whipped his face, he realized it was only a dust devil stirring debris.

Midnight found the moons playing tag near zenith, the one rising last overtaking the others. For the rest of the night they hurtled side-by-side across the stars, and by the time they sank golden into the ruins behind him, Blake breached the outer wall and gained a low line of hills. Even so, he didn't feel safe until a half-hour later when he stumbled across a pool of starlight in an eroded maze of spires. It was water, captured in a rock basin, and at its brink he collapsed to taste its bitterness with a cupped hand and pour a little between Rhonda's swollen lips.

Satisfied that he had thwarted any life-threatening dehydration, he laid her head against his shoulder and eased back to shield her from the cutting wind. Stroking her hair and feeling needed for the first time in a long while, he looked up at the rocky silhouettes hovering spirit-like, and beyond at the inscrutable stars flung across an eternity of time and space. The being of light was out there somewhere, looking down, but now it lived inside him as well.

***

Rhonda's throat was dry and her joints ached as she opened her eyes to a blur of brightness centimeters away. She stared for long seconds before she realized it was sunlight against the blood-caked stubble of a man snuggling close, and it stirred dreamy memories of a familiar voice, reassuring as if from afar, and of supporting arms absorbing the rising and falling of boots down dark streets.

She eased away to see his face clearly against their surroundings, and threw her hand to her mouth in disbelief.

"It's *you*."

Blake awoke with a start.

"I thought you were dead!" she said. "The hatchet, the way you fell!"

Blake checked the guarding spires even as he edged up. Relaxing, he turned to study the abrasions at her forearms and ankles. "How bad are you hurt?" Then his voice dropped to an awe-filled whisper. "Another second and I'd have killed you. I'd have killed you to keep them from . . ." He paled and stretched a concerned hand to her shoulder. "They didn't—"

She smiled through a sudden sting in her eyes. "It's okay. *I'm* okay. I've never been so good, I don't think ever."

Blake scanned their surroundings. "We're lucky, maybe more than lucky. That pit, a little longer and you'd've fallen."

"That was you!" she said, hazy memories flooding her. "You got me out of there. Carried me when I thought you were dead and I'd never get the chance to tell you I l—"

"Don't think about it," he interrupted. "That rough a time, it's better to forget."

She placed soft fingers along the dried blood at his temple. "Look what they've done to you. And your throat, you can barely talk."

He gently took her hand and lowered it. "We've got to push on, make it to the ship. I don't know how safe we are here, not in daylight." He nodded to the pocket of water. "Drink all you can. Tastes bad, but it'll keep us alive."

***

Under the eye-squinting brightness of day, it was difficult for Blake to accept anything but what his senses told him was real, such as the black lava passing under his boots, the serrated volcanic ribs in the folds of the land, the gritty wind at his back. Still, his senses had told him he had been plunging to his death in that abyss. But how could he dismiss the memory of what had ensued, when it remained so vivid that it seemed he were living it yet, feeling even now the transcendent love that had cradled him?

Blake glanced at Rhonda, forging onward at his side, and considered how close he had come to losing her. Suddenly his every fiber screamed for him to tell her that he needed and loved her, that he would always love her. Then cold, calculating logic took over, reminding how she had once pushed him away, and he realized that she could never love someone like him. He would hold his tongue in check, but he couldn't restrain the feeling inside him, for it was an unselfish love that didn't demand love in return.

But things perhaps more important than the relationship of a man and woman also concerned him, and he found a deep breath that hurt his battered ribs.

"You haven't told me," he said quietly. He nodded back toward the hidden city. "What we saw, found, if it was what you were looking for."

"I . . ." She stopped and brought a quaking hand to her face. It was as though in light of all that had happened, she had not yet considered the implications. "I'm afraid."

Stopping with her, Blake resisted the urge to put a protective hand on her arm. "They can't get us now, not out here, I hope."

"It's not them I'm scared of, at least not in the same way. They're just people like you and me. They can't do anything besides make us suffer, kill us." She shuddered. "But we're up against things we weren't meant to understand, couldn't understand."

Blake frowned, but he remembered the being of light.

"I came all this way looking for something to convince me I was wrong," she continued. "I tried to see things the way I wanted them to be, the way I prayed they'd be. But I saw all of it for the shrine it was: the sign of the Leijan, the landscaping, everything laid out like the Valley of the Skull, the reverse crucifixions on a pentagram like it was meant to blaspheme Christianity, me tied like a sacrifice over a—"

She started, reaching for his wrist to study the rawness. "They had you, just like me!"

He disengaged his hand, letting his sleeve slide down over the wound. "It's all right."

"You got out, saved me from getting killed. How? How did you do it?"

"Later. Go ahead."

She trembled again. "Even before we found Hashienah, I was afraid I knew what it was they worshipped. No, *who* it was. Then those awful welts all over him, how could that happen? You went to the Academy, studied science like me. How could that happen? The same words that Lasky told you were on that derelict, the ancient Greek?"

He breathed the furnace-like air and glanced behind them. "We've got to keep moving, get there while we're still strong enough."

They walked, silence encompassing them like a shroud. He felt the wind chill him despite the searing sun, for he had begun to understand the implications. Finally, he forced hoarse words.

"I told them it was coordinates. It kept us alive. If you know Greek, I guess you're the only one who really knows what it said."

When her reply came, his spine crawled as if with blood-sucking parasites.

"From the time I was old enough to understand my father's work in the Valley of the Skull, it was obvious he saw the similarities with hell, but wouldn't admit it even to himself. I know it sounds crazy, but I was there, studying it every day like he did for forty-one years. Don't ask me how those Earth people got there before space travel. Maybe their consciousnesses were drawn there at death. Maybe they were given new bodies. Even now, with all our scientific knowledge, what do we really know about what happens when we die?

"We kept finding etchings in Greek, a few in Hebrew, that talked about the inhabitants worshipping some kind of being. The Hebrew called him Abaddon the destroyer, and the Greek, Belial the worthless one, or Apollyon, exterminator. There were hints that he came there every solar year or so, accepting sacrifices in the holy of holies."

Blake passed a hand along his face, remembering the sensation of evil he had known in the desert. "You're telling me it was Lucifer, aren't you."

"Is there any other being in myth or history that fits the picture so well?"

"You're really serious about this. So what's it mean to us? What was that Greek on Hashienah?"

She stopped and the wind began to howl. "I wish I could remember, my mother, what she taught me, the oral traditions. It was the number *twenty* and something like *unveiling*, or *a striking disclosure.* It's something important, but I just can't put it all together, can't remember."

He tugged at her arm, and he hiked on in silent reflection for a long while. Then her touch again halted him.

"There's something else I haven't told you," she said, "something I couldn't before, because I was afraid I couldn't trust you."

She lowered her gaze. Blake suddenly remembered the sting of her hand at his face, and realized anew all the reasons she could never love him.

She looked up. "Just before my father died, he found the holy of holies. Langdon, the archaeology secretary, that's where I killed him, Blake. I killed him to keep him from finding out everything we knew. Dad, he'd found a little star-shaped artifact, an inscription that talked about an entity imprisoning the Leijan, and somebody else coming along exactly a thousand years later to let it loose with the star-key."

Blake stared at her, and continued to stare as she told again, in heart-wrenching detail, the story of her father's sacrifice, and of her loss.

This time, Blake put a caring hand on her shoulder. "I'm sorry, Rhonda," he said, his voice strangely choked.

She breathed sharply, seemingly defiant against emotions that threatened to cripple her. "Just before the U.S.S. shuttle landed, I tested the artifact, found out its age to the day."

"You believe the Leijan's supposed to be released soon, don't you."

There was only the rush of the wind in reply, and his hand was no longer merely gentle on her shoulder.

"Tell me, please."

She stared straight into his eyes. "Thirty days, thirty days more and the star-key—Blake! It'll be a thousand years old, and only you know where the Leijan is."

He turned away, slowly, and brought a trembling hand to his face. "That's what you meant, isn't it? That there was nothing we could do except what had to be done." He wheeled to her. "The artifact, where is it?"

Her eyes froze on his in a way they had never done before, and then she nodded to her boot. "The heel."

He lifted his head to find the inalienable laws of physics exhibited in heat rays dancing on the horizon.

"No," he said, shaking his head. "I can't buy all this." He studied her again. "How can you say that Lucifer, even if he did exist, has been locked away when there's still so much evil going on?"

"I didn't say his sphere of influence wasn't still around. But I think that the entity that's the personification of everything evil was taken out of the scene a thousand years ago when we were on the verge of destroying ourselves. I think we would've destroyed ourselves if it'd been any other way."

"Taken out by who?"

"If there's a devil, there's an antithesis to him."

"You really believe all this, don't you. You, a scientist."

She held her head high. "You believe what you know inside."

The memory of the being of light rekindled inside him. "So what happens when he's turned loose?"

"I should know. I do know, but I just can't remember."

He glanced at the swollen sun. "We're four weeks away from that derelict by starship. So what are we going to do? We know where it is, maybe what it is, how to let it loose, when it's supposed to happen. We're the only ones who know any of that. Is it us? Are we supposed to be the ones to let something that evil go, a power that can't be controlled?"

His chest rose before he went on. "Now I'm going to tell you something *I've* kept quiet about, the woman who called herself a prophetess, the one who told me my destiny was tied up with yours. She said you'd have a key in your hand, and that together we'd stand as servants to fulfill everything."

Rhonda started, her mouth gaping in awe. "What are we dealing with? Why you and me? It's like it's summoned us, brought us together, kept us alive. It's like it's still calling, even now."

"Something's behind it, all right, but I'm not so sure it's the Leijan."

"What do you mean?"

He lived again the transcendent love, and knew he was incapable of expressing in words what had happened. He tugged at her arm and they struggled on through volcanic rocks.

"Why won't you tell me?" she asked.

"If I knew how, I would." Then a spark of the old bitterness surfaced. "And anyway, what've you ever told me all these weeks? Up until now, you've told me just enough to suit your own purposes. So what's so different about now? How come all of a sudden you think you can finally trust me so much?"

Blake saw the hurt cloud her eyes. "Don't you know?" she asked quietly.

With every rise and fall of his boots, Blake wondered just what she had meant.

Chapter Twenty-Two

On the floor just inside the ship, Blake and Rhonda found the other survivors spent, too shaken by battle and minor wounds even to secure the hatch or post a guard. There were three of them: Sahtu, staring blankly, his fierce countenance subdued by dried blood and a swollen jaw; Fellini, trembling beside him, the shirt at his shoulder darkened by a grazing arrow; and Lorenzo, lunging back wild-eyed like a cornered animal.

"Easy, Lorenzo, it's us," said Blake.

"Thought you dead," he grunted.

Sahtu slowly turned and mumbled an epithet almost matter-of-factly.

Blake studied Fellini cowering in a fetal position. "Still displaying your gallantry, huh, Fellini?"

The European faced him to reveal an ugly gash at his cheek. "The Leijan," he muttered in a quaking voice. "You promised us the Leijan."

Blake caught sudden peripheral movement and found Lorenzo bringing a Banning up from the floor. In the instant that it took the Spaniard to level it on him, Blake cursed himself for whisking Rhonda on board so carelessly. Was his mind so dulled that he couldn't foresee that others might have escaped too?

"Kill him," droned Sahtu in a whisper.

Fellini stretched out a hand. "My Banning," he demanded unconvincingly. "Last one left."

The Spaniard's finger flexed anxiously on the trigger as he stood to scowl at the two men on the floor. "Lorenzo not take orders no more. Now on, Lorenzo give orders." He shifted his eyes to Blake. "You saw Hashienah, know coordinates."

"He didn't see *anything*," contested Fellini, hatred bringing life to his voice.

The Spaniard drove a brutal boot into Fellini's ribs. "Coward shut up. Lorenzo kill!"

From beside the groaning man, Sahtu was laughing quietly, the laugh of the near-deranged. "Here," he mumbled. "All along, he said here. Shoot the lyin'—"

"He saw coordinates!" screamed the Spaniard. "Lorenzo kill you, wicked-eyed devil, you say different."

"I saw them, all right, Lorenzo," Blake said calmly. "And I heard N. G. Lasky too. There's enough power waiting out there for you to have all the women and lemstel you want, and not ever have to take orders from any more filthy pigs like these two."

"You tell Lorenzo coordinates now."

"What good would it do you if I did? You're no navigator, Lorenzo. You wouldn't have any idea how to feed it into the navigation system and get anywhere. Who you going to get to help you? Those two vermin that've ordered you around all this time? You still want to take orders from them? If so, I'll go ahead and blurt out those coordinates. They'll have you crawling at their feet like always."

The slow-witted Spaniard mulled over his words for long seconds, shifting his eyes back and forth between the men on the floor and Blake and Rhonda at the muzzle of his Banning. Finally he grunted. "You put coordinates in computer, set ship go there."

Blake shook his head. "You need me, Lorenzo, her too. If we feed those exact coordinates in, we'll all three be dead by nightfall, and you can thank your two friends there for that."

"What you do then?"

"We'll feed in the kind of coordinates that'll force us to make course adjustments all along to ever get there. You know what that means, don't you? You've got to make sure she and I stay alive or this ship'll never get to the Leijan."

Lorenzo grunted and lowered his weapon. "We go now. Lorenzo find woman to love."

"Look at the shape you're in, that we're all in. We've got to be alert for the Web. We're safe here for the time being, provided we seal the hatch. We've got to clean up, get some food and water, doctor our wounds, rest. The Leijan's been waiting for a thousand years. What's one more day?"

Or thirty, he thought to himself.

***

Twelve hours later, the five gathered in the forward control deck as the craft rocketed up through the stratosphere. Laying in a course for the Leijan, Blake never saw Sahtu's quick hands on the weapons panel, but he felt the sudden vibration that told him a warhead had been launched.

"What are you doing!" Blake yelled.

Sahtu had regained enough of his bloodthirsty nature to grin malevolently. "I'll show 'em."

Blake ran to peer over the Asian's shoulder at the moving blip on the weapons screen and note the coordinates of its target. Cursing, he wheeled to the larboard porthole, just in time to shield his eyes against a brilliant flash and watch a mushroom cloud rise where the City of the Skull had been.

"You vindictive filth!" he said, turning on the Asian.

Sahtu laughed.

"They try kill us," muttered Lorenzo.

"What's the matter, Sharrel?" snapped Fellini, the security of the ship in flight shielding his cowardice. "Turning into a sissy again like that Academy whore always said you were?"

For an instant Blake wanted to tear Fellini apart, but he glanced at Rhonda and his demeanor changed.

"Hadn't they been through enough?" demanded Blake. "So a dozen generations back their ancestors were threat enough to be put off in that forsaken place, but what about those people? Did they ever have a chance to know right from wrong? To even have an idea what life was about, when they'd been so indoctrinated with Leijan worship their whole lives? We'd've done the same thing in their place. We were the intruders there, not the other way around."

Even Blake himself couldn't believe his compassion for such a bloodthirsty horde trying to appease some evil entity. Until this moment, empathy had seemed impossible, and as he found Rhonda's face he saw astonishment equal to his own.

As the ship neared the Web, however, Blake didn't feel at all forgiving. His spiritual experience notwithstanding, he couldn't easily dismiss his deep-rooted hatred of the U.S.S. He didn't trust the scum. They'd let them through earlier, but would they be waiting with warheads this time? What did they have up their sleeves?

He didn't know, but just before they reached the fleet, he looked again at Rhonda, strapped in behind, and wished he had told her he loved her even if she could never love him back.

Within seconds, however, Blake was glad he had spared her such a burden, for precisely at the moment that the Violeshan sun receded far enough for the detection screen to identify individual craft in the Web, the very thing happened that he half-expected: The two ships along their course drifted lazily apart. The first time hadn't been a fluke. They were letting them through, defying hundreds of years of precedent. Somehow the U.S.S. knew they were going after the Leijan, and would chase them to the end of the galaxy to get it.

"Full power, dead ahead!" he commanded.

Fellini, his hands at the controls, hesitated just long enough to glance at Sahtu, and at Lorenzo beyond with drawn weapon. "Orders from who?"

"Now!" exclaimed Blake.

"Tell me!" shouted Fellini.

Sahtu flushed crimson but held his tongue, and Lorenzo smiled gorilla-like and caught Fellini's eyes. "We go."

They shot through the gap without a single warhead speeding in their wake, and Blake spun just in time to stay Sahtu's hand on the weapons panel. "Don't waste a missile. We'll need all we got. That fleet's gonna chase us till doomsday."

But as he studied the detection screen, he was astounded to find no pursuit; indeed, the two ships merely shifted back into configuration and quickly receded out of detection range. He turned to Rhonda, and then to the anxious eyes of the marketers.

"Nothing," he said. "They're not coming after us."

He looked up to see a ribbon of stardust streaking the forward porthole. Out there somewhere, along that outermost spiral arm of the galaxy, awaited a dark planet and an orbiting derelict ship, and in it, the Leijan. But why hadn't the U.S.S. pursued? Why had they allowed them through twice, only to let them go their way?

"It doesn't make sense," he said as he activated the automatic warning system. But his concerns were lost in Lorenzo's lusting grunts for women and lemstel, and in the excited words of Sahtu and Fellini, who, with the credulous philosophy of treasure hunters, seemed to believe again that the Leijan and its power did still await them.

***

In the cramped bridge of a tiny craft hurtling silently toward unchart- ed space and its mysteries, Langdon searched the star-studded shroud ahead for the pirate ship that had fled Violesha Two. Pierce, beside him at the controls, had eased the craft into the ship's wake at solar system's edge, and now their quarry, racing onward at post-light speed, dragged with it a time-space pocket that included the two men and their craft. Although the fugitive vessel was beyond the range of Langdon's naked eye, he continued to stare and deliberate.

He remembered all the boot-licking and bribery to which he had lowered himself in climbing up through the Science Branch to the Cabinet. He fumed as he considered how he had been within moments of solving history's greatest riddle and rising to the apex, only to be thwart- ed and left for dead. No woman could treat him that way without retribu- tion, neither wife nor mistress nor teenaged daughter. He had but one soft spot for anyone in the universe born with two X chromosomes, and she, a victim of neurodegenerative disease, he was totally powerless to help.

Pierce's reflections likewise focused on Rhonda Gregory. "Hope you're right about this, that she's on board that thing." He clenched a fist. "Skyjacked." He thumped a photo dangling from the console; it was of an elderly, bedridden woman with Pierce's eyes. "Couldn't even get to Nova Scotia in time for the funeral, thanks to that wench. Could've gotten busted to airman, the way it all went down, this after twenty years of breakin' up Leijan uprisings. You don't know how much I've got hingin' on this mission. I've got a second chance and I'm makin' it good."

Langdon nodded to the instrument panel. "How we doing?"

The burly pilot studied the blip on the screen and noted the readouts. "Whatever these anti-detection shields are, they work. Not a sign they got any idea anybody's within a half-light year of 'em."

Again, Langdon studied the wispy star clouds ahead. "Just don't get us too close, compromise our stealth capabilities. There's too much at stake to lose it all through incompetence."

Pierce slammed an angry hand against console. "Any incompetence won't be on the military's part. Back at that cabinet meeting I never heard so many supposedly smart people talkin' so much idiocy. It's just me and you now. Don't feed me that line about the Valley of the Skull bein' hell. What do you think's really out there where we're headed?"

Langdon remembered his glimpse into the skull-lined holy of holies. "Whatever it is, it's powerful, maybe more so than your whole sacred military. That's why we've got to get it before they do."

"Some kinda weapon?"

Langdon only stared through the porthole.

"Who made it? Where'd it come from?"

Still no answer.

"Is it a power a man can get for himself? Or a couple of men?"

Langdon turned to stare into his eyes, and then the mysteries of the cosmos through the porthole again seized his attention.

And he wondered if the Leijan was indeed something that a scientist might harness for his own purposes, and whether it might empower a daughter otherwise doomed to a hell of her own.

Chapter Twenty-Three

With the Violeshan sun a receding speck and the next course change several hours away, Blake sought the larboard barracks to rest his bruised body. Entering, he studied the empty bunks; except for his own, only one remained claimed, by Lorenzo, too conditioned to subservience to seize officer's quarters. The empty berths reminded Blake with a twinge of guilt just how many people already had died in search of something they could never have. Was it worth it? Would whatever they found along that spiral arm make up for all that had been sacrificed?

Silently, he called on the only one who might give assurance and peace, but the being of light now seemed very far away, while the summons to the derelict grew stronger. Suddenly, such self-doubt plagued him that he turned to search out the companionship and solace of the woman he had tried so long to hate.

***

Passing the mid-ship observation deck, Rhonda found herself drawn to the glimpse of the spiral arm through the series of round portholes. She steadied a trembling hand against glass smeared with Fellini's blood and considered the secrets waiting in that faraway haze. She sank inside, feeling like a child walking along a beach, picking up a shell here and there, while the ocean of truth stretched untapped into the horizon.

Then it came as a ghost-like image in the glass, a movement behind her that had a sinister quickness about it. She spun and a vice-like hand clamped over her mouth. Her scream was muffled as a body reeking with sweat pinioned her arm and forced her against the porthole. She reached to gouge the scarred face, but a flashing scimitar stilled her hand and pricked the tenderness under her eye.

Sahtu scowled as he trembled in rage. "You're mine!" he growled. "You and everything else on this ship. I'll kill that Spaniard and anybody else that don't follow my orders. I'll take whatever I want."

Their legs became tangled, and as he lowered his weapon to leave, her boot heel caught under his foot and dislodged, spilling the star-key to the floor.

Eyeing it, Sahtu froze and nudged it with the point of his scimitar. "What is it?"

She could only shake her head.

He knelt and took it, and it lay almost tenderly in his palm as he stood to set the deck lights dancing in its gleaming points.

"Cheap slut," he snapped with a glare. "You'll turn a trick for any-thing, even a stinkin' tin talisman."

It clanged to the deck and he stalked away. She was shaken by his threat and by the sudden disclosure of the artifact, but she retained the presence of mind to remove her boot, slip it back inside, and hammer the heel in place by striking the deck. With a shudder, she faced the stars again to find the cryptic spiral arm watching from afar.

***

Blake's pulse rose the moment he came upon Rhonda at a mid-ship observation porthole, for her jaw trembled and her cheek was strangely pale.

"What's wrong?" he asked.

She looked up and lowered her hand to reveal a trickle of blood at her cheekbone.

Anger boiled inside him. "What happened?"

"Sahtu."

The old hatred came raging. "What did he do to you?"

"I'm all right."

He brushed the blood roughly with his thumb. "Will you tell me the truth just for once?" he snapped impatiently.

"Please don't yell at me. I don't need you yelling at me when everything else is so against me."

As quickly as he had flared, Blake mellowed like a scolded pet, and it amazed him. "I didn't mean it that way. It's just that I've known from the start I'd have to deal with that devil and wish I'd done it before now." He touched her blood-streaked face again, this time with tenderness. "Now will you tell me what happened?"

She dabbed at her pricked cheek. "No more than this, and his boot catching my heel and tearing it off."

Blake flinched. "Did he take—"

"He thought it was a charm. I put it back."

Blake relaxed a bit, but he eyed her boot. "There's adhesive in the cargo bay. What else did he do?"

"He just grabbed me, said I belonged to him like everything else on the ship and that he'd take it all when he kills Lorenzo."

Blake looked away to clench a fist. "The trash was too big a coward to come up and tell *me* that. He's played big-shot all this time, had them so scared they wouldn't even sit down or stand up without asking him. Now that Lorenzo's got the only Banning, he's got to crawl in front of those same people. So what's he do? He picks out the one person that's not a physical match for him and tries to prove he's still got what it takes to lord it over somebody. Well, we'll just see if he's got nerve enough to try that with me."

He wheeled to leave, but Rhonda's hand stopped him. "He's armed, that sword!"

"That'll just make it even."

"It's not worth it. Can't you ever let anything rest?"

"It's worth it to make him realize you're not meat waiting to be taken."

"Don't make me the reason," she said angrily. "Don't you remember? I'm *supposed* to be a prostitute. The real reason is that you're so filled with hate and bitterness you'll find any excuse to vent it. If you really cared about my feelings, you'd stop and think where I'd be if something happened to you. Don't you know you're all that stands in the way of those three animals doing what they want to with me?"

She turned away to stare blankly through the porthole and her voice dropped to a quaking whisper. "I thought you'd changed, that you'd really come to care about somebody besides yourself, but maybe I was wrong."

Blake wanted to reach for her, hold her close and tell her that he really did care, that he loved her and that the being of light would always guard them. But he couldn't. "I didn't mean to hurt you, not again. I guess I've done that a lot, haven't I." He noted the porthole smeared with blood beyond her. "I'm sorry it was somebody like me you ended up with. You deserved better. Okay, I'll let Sahtu get by with it for now. But this time you're wrong about my motives. Not long ago you'd've been right, but then two things came along to change all that, made me care enough to throw out the bad memories and make room for hope."

The sincerity of his words brought her turning, and never had he seen her eyes so receptive.

"There's something inside me now I can't explain," he continued. "Back in that city, they tied me over a sinkhole just like you. I didn't have a chance, neither of us did. The cord at my arms broke, and I was just dangling there, upside-down, about to die.

"Then I got a mental picture of one of those crucifixion beams, or I thought it was. But this one was right-side-up and had a man with a wound in the heart and a wreath of briars on his head. Then all of that went away and I looked up and the stars squeezed together like a hand, bright as a thousand suns. It came down to me, and I knew I wasn't alone anymore, that there was somebody hovering over me. I heard a voice asking who it could send, who would go, and right then I knew it had to be me, that it couldn't ever be anybody else. Then the cord broke and I was falling and crying out that I would do it, that whatever it was that had to be done, I would do it.

"Then it was like I was just being cradled there, that incredible light all around me and not even making me squint, love I can't even begin to describe giving me such peace that I never wanted it to leave. I wanted to be with it forever, and then it was gone, and I was back at the beam, holding on. I looked up and all the stars were back in place, but something real was still inside me, and still is, every time I reach for it."

Her eyes seemed filled with awe beyond measure. She formed words that died in her throat, and when she finally spoke, it was with the voice of someone who had glimpsed the wellsprings of the cosmos. "That's how you saved me, wasn't it?" She laid tender fingers on his arm. "Oh Blake, that's how *it* saved us."

Blake took her hand and squeezed it. "A scientist like you should be telling me it was all a hallucination."

"Is that what you think?"

He shook his head.

She smiled. "You believe what you know inside, what you have inside."

He noted how she was framed by myriad stars. "Okay. That's what happened, so what's it mean? I felt such peace, but now in all this vastness I'm just . . ." He shook his head. "Scared. That's the only word that fits."

Her palm grew sweaty against his. "The Leijan, it's got to have something to do with the Leijan."

"Yeah, what? Why me?"

She glanced at their clasped hands. "Maybe it's both of us. Maybe that's why we've been brought together, kept alive. We're the only ones, just us. There's nobody else in the universe with the means to free it."

"What are you saying? Whatever that being of light was, it was good, the embodiment of love. You think it wants us to turn loose maybe the most frightening power that's ever been?"

He felt her shudder as she disengaged her hand to turn to the spiral arm. "An *unveiling, twenty.* I know it holds the answer. It's got to. Why can't I put it all together?" Then she found his eyes again. "The U.S.S., why didn't they follow us? Is there any way Fellini or Sahtu or even Lorenzo could've made a deal with the U.S.S. to let them through?"

"Those greedy pieces of trash would sell their own souls for a shot at the Leijan. But nobody'd be fool enough to think they'd hand over that kind of power if they ever got it. Besides, I've heard their names bandied about in the Black Market for years. The U.S.S. wouldn't solicit a spy from that cutthroat group. It'd plant one of its own, somebody that was knowledgeable about the Leijan and intelligent, somebody with a historian's grasp of its importance and a scientist's ability to understand and seize it."

Sudden hurt filled her eyes and her chin began to tremble again. She started to speak and turned away.

"What did I do now?" he asked testily.

No answer.

"I asked you what I did wrong."

"If you're accusing me of something," she half-sobbed, "at least have the courtesy to say it outright."

"What are you talking about?"

Again, there was no reply.

"Talk to me!"

She turned and raised her head haughtily. "Anytime you don't get your way, you still have to yell, even after the being of light. You and I both know there's only one person on board that fits that description. I guess that would explain a lot, wouldn't it, sending a U.S.S. archaeologist to a sleazy dive to persuade the last person who ever talked to Lasky to take her to the Leijan."

Again, she looked away, and he glanced down, shaking his head and half-laughing in disbelief. "If I'm looking for candidates, I don't have to look that far. I've got an ex-U.S.S. officer standing right here. Don't be ridiculous. I never said you had anything to do with it. How could you even think that of me, after what we've been through together? How could you even believe it for a second after all I've done for you? Don't you know I love you?"

He caught himself too late and just stood there speechless, watching her turn, seeing the surprise in her face and the indefinable expression in her eyes. Then anger at his lack of self-discipline swept aside the embarrassment, and he found himself barking out words.

"Okay, I said it. I wasn't going to. I wasn't ever going to tell you, but I've said it now and you know it. I know you couldn't ever really care about somebody like me, but that doesn't make any difference. Yeah, you're the other thing that made me start caring again, and if I never get anything more out of this than that, well, you've already done more than I had any right to expect. Just don't say anything. I've said too much already. We'll just go on about our business and act like this never happened and we won't ever have to mention it again."

She stared at him until her eyes seemed to burn into his soul, yet he couldn't look away, didn't want to look away. When she finally spoke, it was with emotion as deep as the mysteries between a man and a woman.

"I started to tell you something once, Blake, but you stopped me. This time, I won't let you. When I first met you, I thought you were the crudest and most selfish and brutal person I'd ever met. I couldn't bring myself to respect you, not when it looked like it was your own fault you lived the way you did. Then I gradually began to understand, saw how you were once so caring you let it destroy you. I hated her, even though I'd never met her, because of what she'd made you, the way she got in between us every time I thought you were about to look at me for who I really was, instead of just another woman waiting to hurt you.

"You kept saying you didn't care about things anymore, that there wasn't anything left to do but die. But while you were talking, I was watching. I saw you crawl out of my cabin to save my life and yours. I saw the kind of courage and determination you had, in the control deck and in the city. I saw your compassion, the way you helped that wounded crewman and kept Hashienah from suffering even after he'd tried to kill you all those times. I was there when you stood up to a whole army by yourself to keep them from taking me. And then when I saw you fall, you know what I did? I drove a knife toward my heart, and it wasn't just to keep them from raping and torturing me."

Her cheeks glistened, and she took his hand.

"I did it," she whispered, "because I couldn't bear to go on without you. I did it because I love you, Blake."

He stood stunned for long seconds, not knowing what to say, how to respond. Then elemental need seized him, and he took her in his arms and drew near, only to hesitate, remembering.

She smiled, her eyes welling with happiness. "I won't push you away, not ever again."

He crushed her to him, his mouth seeking hers.

Chapter Twenty-Four

Supported by a cushion of air in Rhonda's cabin, Blake awoke to the freshness of her hair and warmth of her breast gently swelling and falling in peaceful sleep. To the witness of the being of light, they had plighted a troth more binding than any that an atheistic government might sanction, and now they snuggled as husband and wife, his shoulder and arm cradling the hollow of her neck. He stroked her hair, and though she didn't stir, her fingers across his bare chest responded with a caress.

Happiness welled inside him, yet, disturbingly, it was Lyra who suddenly dominated his thoughts as she hadn't in days. He nudged his face into Rhonda's hair and couldn't help but imagine it was Lyra whose head nestled against his cheek, she whose charms warmed him. Guiltily, he stretched his free arm across to hold her even closer, but the image remained. He had forgotten, until now, the feelings he had known in Lyra's arms, the giddiness of first love, the light-headedness that had swept him off his feet and carried him on a dizzying ride of emotions newly discovered. They had been schoolboy sensations that he knew no one else could ever give him, no matter how much he wished, for he had entrusted himself too completely once and the scars ran too deep.

Yet, there was no denying he loved Rhonda, in a different, more mature way. So what, if he could never know the same giddiness in her arms? He realized now that true love wasn't some irresolute feeling that ebbed and flowed with the tide of emotion, but a commitment, and his commitment to Rhonda was unmatched in his past, for it didn't demand even acceptance in return. With Lyra, the relationship had been a lie, because of her fickleness and his inner need to be first in her heart, but this was the kind of unselfish love he had known in the presence of the being of light.

With that rare insight into self, Lyra's image faded, and he lay at peace again in Rhonda's arms.

Awakening, she moaned pleasurably and stretched, but then Blake felt an abrupt shudder grip her.

"What's wrong?" he asked, withdrawing enough to see her face.

She clung to him. "Just hold me. I'm so scared. What's this all about? Why is it like something's drawing us out there, making us go?"

He ran a solacing hand down her hair. "Before the being of light, I didn't believe in destiny. I didn't want a destiny. Now though . . ." Again, he put his arm around her. "Whatever's out there, we'll face it together, and the being of light won't ever let us face it alone."

"But to what end? What is it you've got to do out there, we've both got to do?"

He passed a hand over his face. "I promised the being of light that whatever it was that had to be done, I'd do it, and I meant it. But I just don't know. Why couldn't he tell me? Why wouldn't he tell me? Here we are, three and a half, four weeks away, and that thing's supposed to be let loose in how many days now? Twenty-seven? Twenty-eight? How could we let something that horrible go? Or is there supposed to be somebody there we've got to stop? Why can't we just turn back, forget all this?"

He turned to stare angrily at the ceiling, but her touch brought him about again.

"What about us?" she asked. "Oh Blake, what about us? I've just found you. We've found each other. What's going to happen to us? Why can't we be like everybody else, just go off somewhere together and hold each other and not have to worry about the being of light and the Leijan and all these things we don't understand?"

"That's what brought us together," he reminded her. Then emotion choked him. "Whatever it is we're supposed to do, I know it's more important than the lives of two petty little people. But why did he let you become such a part of me, if he didn't mean it to be forever?"

She snuggled close again, holding him as if she would never let go. "Nobody ever said it wouldn't be forever," she whispered.

But the sob in her voice and the mist in her eyes told him that her heart said otherwise.

***

Measurable only by chronometer, the days came and went for Blake in mystery and hope. With Lorenzo unable to cope with his new-found authority, even the designated eating and sleeping periods suggesting time's passage were abandoned in favor of his lemstel sprees, food binges, and behind-sealed-door episodes of drifting off into drunken and gluttonous oblivion.

Except for Blake's periodic trips to the forward control deck to make course changes, he rarely interacted with the marketers. Sahtu he invariably found seated at the weapons panel, honing his scimitar. On the occasions when Lorenzo, flagon to lips, wandered on deck to flaunt his power, Blake saw the loathing redden the Asian's scar and degenerate into something even more sinister when the Spaniard ambled away with drawn Banning. But Blake knew something Sahtu didn't. While the Asian glared at the departing Spaniard with vindictiveness, Fellini studied them both with cold, calculating eyes that bespoke greed and a coward's desperation.

With the situation so volatile, Blake knew it was only a matter of time before it erupted into violence. He just hoped that whatever the outcome, it would lessen the odds against him, for he knew the marketers remained a force with which he would have to reckon.

Blake tried not to stay absent from the cabin and Rhonda for excessive periods, for these were days of budding love and deep worries. For long hours they stared out the porthole at the spiral arm slowly growing distinct against a velvet cloak. It held so much, yet so little. He would stroke her hair when she trembled, and she would melt into his arms to gain solace and hope. When rest beckoned and the lights dimmed, they would cling to one another on a cushion of air, sharing a love like that of the being of light, but through the porthole still shone puzzles awe-inspiring and frightening.

The ship sped on until far-flung star matter engulfed it, and they looked upon constellations never recorded, stars whose light never had been seen except as part of a milky haze ribboning the sky. The loneliness was immense, for the heavens opening up reminded Blake of his own insignificance in the galaxy. And this galaxy was but one of billions, all separated by unfathomable distances, floating in a boundless sea of nothingness impossible to comprehend.

Meteors and comet fragments pelted the hull frequently now, sometimes severely enough to rock the ship. But Blake, his mind no longer clouded by intoxicants, worried more about his occasional shortness of breath, his episodes of rapid heartbeat, his headaches upon awakening: all signs of impending failure of the backup life-support system. Without burdening Rhonda with his suspicions, he climbed to the upper deck and confirmed his fear. Slowly it was failing beyond repair.

No. He couldn't have found her love just to be cheated of it so quickly. How could everything be so against them? Didn't the being of light care anymore?

He thought about shoving aside the intensifying summons and turning back, but now they were weeks beyond any outpost. Then he considered searching nearby solar systems for a habitable planet, but what kind of life would that have been, merely to survive, haunted by what they should have done?

Then he took hold of himself and remembered a calling more important than his life or Rhonda's, and he promised again that if the being of light carried him to the derelict, he would do whatever it was he had to.

Blake didn't speak of the failing system, even to Rhonda. But every time they clung to one another, he held her just a little tighter, squeezing the most from every moment and taking in every sensory detail: the fresh scent of her skin cleansed by Catholian Ray, the tenderness of her fingers caressing his shoulders, the buoyancy of her hair as he pressed his cheek close.

The moment he made the last course adjustment marked the twenty-seventh day by chronometer from Violesha Two. He sat at the navigator's post, feeling the subtle tug of centrifugal force as the nose of the ship veered from a brilliant star cluster toward a mass of Stygian black that all but filled the forward porthole. For days Blake had been observing its approach, recognizing it as galactic dust. Like all such areas in the galaxy, this one crawled with enigma, only more so, because the derelict described by Lasky lay inside. Blake went to the porthole to see the dust cloud fully from this variant angle for the first time, and cringed in awe. For this gaping dark that readied to swallow them bore an uncanny resemblance to a great, black skull adrift in the starry expanse.

"What the devil?"

Sahtu's awe-struck voice told Blake the Asian was at his side, and then Fellini was there too, and the three just stared in stunned silence for long minutes. They started at the first microscopic grains that pelted the glass, and turned to the side portholes to watch the thickening dust darken the stars. Gradually it blotted out even the nearest, and it was as if they sped through a nether world loath to share its secrets.

Fellini's fingers dug into Blake's arm. "The instruments can't work right in these hell clouds! We could burn up in some sun, get sucked into a black hole, not even know we're in trouble till it's too late!"

Blake wrenched his arm free. "Back off. *Now*."

Fellini withdrew, only to confront Sahtu. "You've got to make him get us outa here!"

"Just Lorenzo give orders."

They turned to see the Spaniard staggering drunkenly on deck, a bottle of lemstel in hand. He reeked of leche weed, its effects reddening his face and slurring his words.

"He's trying to get you killed, Lorenzo!" charged Fellini. He slung a hand to the forward porthole. "See where he's taking us? We're blind in here!"

Lorenzo came closer, his narrowed eyes fixing on Fellini. He stopped directly in front of him, and before the European could react, a huge hand seized him by the collar and dragged him close. "No want Leijan, huh? Lorenzo no want share it with Academy coward."

He shoved Fellini against the porthole and reached for his Banning as he turned to Blake. Blake, however, had anticipated the threatening move and now chose his words carefully.

"Two days, Lorenzo, three at most." He nodded to the forward porthole. "That's what we came here for, isn't it? To get the Leijan, its power? You're the captain now. You tell us whether we're going on in, or if we're just turning and running so somebody else can come along and take it."

Lorenzo took a long hard drink, the lemstel dribbling down his chin, and when he lowered the bottle, a grin creased his broad, flat face. He nodded to the prow.

"We get Leijan, Lorenzo take all women he want. Maybe even give Sharrel one." His eyes shifted to Fellini. "Then kill cowards."

***

While Blake was away, Rhonda slept, and dreamed. She dreamed of callously crushing a man's skull and hearing his cry in hell, and of abandoning an injured, helpless pilot to die in the desert. Then she dreamed of swift and terrible judgment meted out to her for perpetrating such uncaring acts.

The scene shifted, the decades rolling back, and she relived a moment long submerged. She was a child again, sitting on her mother's knee on the veranda as a night breeze swept through the Valley of the Skull. She turned to see her mother's lips moving, but the words were strangely quiet, impossible to discern. Rhonda shifted uneasily, knowing she had to hear, and she leaned inside those comforting arms and listened.

Her mother was talking of her faith, of ancient writings in Greek. She mentioned an *unveiling* and *twenty,* and Rhonda squirmed, restating it with perplexity in her young voice. But her mother shook her head and told her no, that she had heard it wrong. Rhonda concentrated with all her being as the woman repeated it, and this time she understood.

"Revelation," said her mother. "Revelation twenty. The old serpent was about to cause everybody to blow up the world, but a being locked him up and threw him in an endless pit to keep him there a thousand years. He's always been at war with us, that old serpent has, but the writings say he won't win. But they were written a long time ago, and maybe the men who wrote them hadn't been told everything yet, and that's what scares me.

"Your daddy would probably just laugh if I ever told him this, but sometimes I have funny dreams about a bright light sweeping down out of the sky, telling me things. But it's not a dream because it happened again not twenty minutes ago, sitting here wide-awake, staring at the stars.

"The writings say that when that thousand years is up, somebody will come along and let the serpent loose. If the right ones do it, the ones the being of light chose, then the serpent will gather up all the bad people and make war on the good. He'll do that, and the being of light will rain down fire and kill the wicked. He'll throw the serpent in a lake of fire and sulfur and keep him there forever. It'll be over, Rhonda. All the evil will finally be over, and we'll be happy together always.

"But the being of light's given me a terrible vision. If anybody but the chosen ones lets the serpent go, the light can't win. If even one prophecy's not fulfilled, the chain's broken and none of them will be, not ever again. It'll show the serpent he's the strongest. It'll give him the drive he needs to destroy the light, and then it won't be the serpent that's thrown in the fiery sulfur, it'll be you and me, everything that's good, even the being of light.

"Oh Rhonda, my precious darling, what can I do to help us, to help you, to help the being of light who loves us so?"

Rhonda awoke with shortness of breath and a mind swimming with awe. For a moment her mother's voice still seemed to echo and it was difficult to separate dream from reality. But her raging headache was real enough, as was the sound of the door sliding open and Blake entering.

"Rhonda. Look outside. We've reached the dust cloud."

"Oh Blake!" she exclaimed, jumping from the bunk and rushing toward him. "I remember. I remember and I'm so scared."

"Hey, what's wrong?"

She melted into his arms and trembled uncontrollably. "Just hold me. Tell me everything's okay, that you won't let anything happen."

"You know I won't, not if I can help it. Now what's the matter?"

She withdrew just enough to look into his face. "I had a dream. It came back to me. I know what this is all about. Oh Blake, we've got to get there, let the Leijan loose."

There was a stunned look in his features, but he waited for her to say more.

"'Unveiling,'" she continued. "In Greek it's the same as 'revelation.' *Revelation twenty,* first-century writings that originated on Patmos, the Aegean Sea. That first section on Hashienah's chest, the words everybody could read, about turning it loose and kneeling and getting it all, the Leijan must've done it somehow to prod the marketers on. But the being of light knew you and I were there too, and gave us a clue nobody else could understand, so we'd know what to do, what we've got to do."

And in hushed tones no one could overhear, she told him of her conviction that only the release of the Leijan at the fated time by the destined ones could ever set in motion the events that would culminate in total harmony in the universe.

When she finished, Blake's face showed a man reeling with things he couldn't process. "You're sure. You're sure it's us that's got to release it."

"Who else could it be? Sahtu? Fellini? Lorenzo? Don't you see how it all fits so perfectly now? Me, the Valley of the Skull, the key, you, Lasky, the being of light, us together? It's got to be us."

"And you really think all this matters, that it really makes a difference who lets the hellish thing out."

"How can we take a chance? On something like that when everything might be up to us? The cosmos, good people, the being of light? Tell me you won't take a chance. Tell me with all your heart you won't.

That no matter what happens, even to me, you'll be the one to set it free."

He turned to the porthole. "So they were right all along. It really is possible for one of them to get its power, or at least share in its dark kingdom."

"All I know is the being of light called you, called both of us. Promise me, Blake. That no matter what happens to us, you won't let him down."

Blake faced her. "What does happen to us? If we make it inside that derelict and free the thing? I've felt its evil on the desert with Lasky. What do you think something that awful would do to us?"

"Even if it's a terrible death, even if we never get to be together, what choice do we have? Compared to spending forever, tortured by the most evil thing that ever was?"

For a long while, he stayed silent, emotion rising in his eyes, and she wondered if he dwelled on the events in Violeshan pit. Finally, quiet words passed his trembling lips.

"I promised the being of light I'd do whatever had to be done." He reached for her, his touch buoying her courage even as his voice choked. "I felt his love, Rhonda. He went back up in the sky and I reached for him and begged him to come back and never go away again. There's no way I could turn my back on someone like that. No matter what, I swear I'll do my part, even if I have to do it alone."

She forced a smile, but she knew that her welling eyes betrayed what was inside her. "You won't be alone, darling." She pulled him close, comforting and finding comfort in return. "He'll be with you always, just like my love."

As she rested her cheek on his chest, her headache intensified and she became aware of the rapid flutter of her heart. But no, it was Blake's that she heard, hammering beneath her ear. She pulled free to look into his face, and a fearful realization dawned on her.

"You feel it too, your heart, the way you breathe."

He smiled weakly. "You're in my arms. What do you expect?"

She disengaged herself, impatient with him. "It's happening just like before. We won't make it there. Oh Blake, tell me."

He breathed deeply, as if stoically accepting that they were to be cheated of life together. "Even if we do, we'll never make it back to a colony alive."

Her chin quaked, and all she could do was fall again into his solacing arms.

***

As the ship plunged onward through the skull cloud's gloom, Fellini brooded and searched. He ransacked the supply deck, the empty officers' cabins, the larboard barracks, the cargo bay, all in a futile quest for a Banning. But Lorenzo, despite his mental shortcomings, evidently had jettisoned even the spare parts, evoking silent but vehement curses from Fellini. If he could just gain the upper hand, it would be his. Not just the ship and the woman, but the Leijan in all its power.

Fellini finally resorted to shattering lemstel bottles in the cargo bay until one broke to his satisfaction, an intact neck extending to a sword of glass. Wrapping the deadly end in cloth, he slipped it inside his boot and paused to grin malevolently. Now he would wreak vengeance on those who had denied him a weapon on Violesha Two and pushed the ship inside this horrid cloud. If a black hole or raging sun didn't get them first, he'd make them pay, every last one of them.

And finally he would make his father proud.

Chapter Twenty-Five

Determined to share the episodes of lost breaths and lightheadedness, Blake remained with Rhonda constantly the succeeding seventy-two hours, for he knew the next gulp of air could be his last, and where else should it come but alongside her? He clung to every moment, reaping it to its fullest, avoiding sleep until his body demanded rest and urged him to join her on the air bunk. Every time her head found the pillow of his shoulder and he stroked her hair, he couldn't believe she was the same woman he had called such vile names and mistreated. He knew now that she was the epitome of everything he had ever longed for in a woman, yet, because of that womanhood, he had wasted so much of the short, precious time together that the being of light had granted them.

On the chronometer "morning" that brought the ship to within hours of the derelict, Blake slipped from Rhonda's arms without awakening her and eased out of the air bunk to study the red glow through the porthole. His movement made his head swim and his lungs labor, and he steadied himself and sighted along the fuselage toward the bow. He found the approaching star a fuzzy, hanging disc, the dust coloring it orange and red like a sun setting through a sandstorm. It captivated him, and he wasn't aware that Rhonda had risen until her hand on his shoulder brought him turning.

"The air," she said weakly. "So thin . . . so out of breath . . . just these few steps."

He nodded to the porthole. "Lasky's solar system."

The star glow colored her face as she looked. "Can we make it?"

"Got to hold on just a little longer." The warmth of her fingers sent sudden rage at the unfairness of life surging through him, and he pulled away and slammed his fist into the porthole.

"No!" he exclaimed. "It's not enough!" He whirled to her. "The Lei-jan's not enough if I can't ever have you." For long seconds his chest heaved, and when he could finally utter words again, they were quiet and emotional. "Got to have air just to make it there. Got to get past the others, keep them from killing us. I know we've got to get to the Leijan, turn it loose, but is it so wrong to want to be together?"

He pulled her close, feeling twinges of bitterness because he finally had given himself to another, only to be denied once more ever having her.

Then memories of the pit overwhelmed him again and he withdrew, keeping hands on her shoulders as he stared into her eyes. "Today, for the being of light, we'll do it today."

She smiled even as her chin quivered. "Today," she whispered.

He glanced at the door. "The star-key, make sure you have it. Go to the forward control deck. Get there and don't leave, no matter what."

"What are you—"

"Hurry!"

Then he was across the room and through the door.

Frantically making his way to the upper deck, he shut down the life-support system to all but the forward control deck and air lock, and the route in-between. Readouts showed a steady decrease in the production of oxygen, replaced by a deadly gas, and he could only hope that by reducing the system's load he could prolong its life. He realized the sudden cessation of air to other parts of the ship would threaten anyone caught there, but Rhonda was safe, and who else mattered?

***

Deluged with concern for Blake, Rhonda burst into the forward control deck to find the star looming mysterious through the bow porthole.

She started, for somehow it conjured images of a great, red skull adrift in a pocket of emptiness, even though its size and shape were consistent with a billion other stars in the galaxy.

"That's it, isn't it?" Fellini's demanding voice came from her right. "I can tell by your eyes."

Rhonda turned and went to the larboard porthole. While she was relieved to find the air not as thin on the bridge, she was weak with worry and wanted nothing to do with Fellini, or with Sahtu, who rasped his scimitar across a whetstone at the weapons control.

At the porthole, a hand brought her about. Fellini grinned. "Feels good, don't it, having somebody besides that lemstel scum touch you for a change."

"Even if he were addicted, I'd prefer his touch to a coward's." The moment she said it, she was disgusted with herself for thinking she had to defend Blake to him.

"There's a difference between being a coward and counting your life highly enough to want to hang on to it." He nodded to the corridor. "You think Sharrel was all so brave back in that city? Stick him out there without a Banning and see how fast he runs."

"He hasn't needed much of a weapon to put you in your place."

Fellini flushed and seemed ready to explode, but then his facial muscles relaxed. "We were friends once, Miss Gregory. I don't see why we can't be again."

"We were never friends. A friend doesn't come in my quarters and force himself on me."

"Yeah, and I guess all he's been doing in there is standing at the porthole counting stars."

Rhonda's face grew hot. "You're out of line," she said angrily, and turned her back on him.

A hand clutched her shoulder and spun her around. "When I talk, you look at me." Fellini glanced at Sahtu and his voice dropped to a whisper. "Listen, I'd like us to be friends again. I'm taking this ship over. You can count on it. You get me the Leijan and I'll share it with you. You're a desirable woman, and I know a woman's needs, not like Sharrel. You know what that slut of his from the Academy told me? That she'd never known what a man was like till she crawled in my tent."

"You'd say anything to get the Leijan for yourself. Get away from me!"

The door slid open just as Rhonda recoiled, and she looked over Fellini's shoulder to see Blake scanning the bridge. Fellini turned as well, and withdrew when he found himself the target of Blake's gaze. As Fellini drifted starboard, Blake came to her, anger flaring in his face as he glanced at the European.

"Blake!" She pressed near. "Where have you been?"

"What did he say to you?" he demanded.

"I've been worried about you."

"I asked you what he said."

"Nothing."

"Don't lie to me!"

She clung to him. "Can't you just let it pass? Isn't it all coming to a head soon enough?"

He disengaged her arms. "Tell me."

Hurt clouded her eyes because he had pushed her away. "Her. He was talking about her."

"What about Lyra?"

Her chin began to quiver. "Do we have to talk about it? Don't you care it hurts me to hear you talk about her?"

"I'm with you, aren't I? And it was Fellini talking about her, not me. Now tell me what he said."

Emotion wrenched her, for she knew that the incident had provoked a far greater reaction in him simply because it had concerned Lyra. "He was just trying to get me to go in with him, claiming she told him that she'd never known what a man was like till they crawled in a tent together."

Terrible hatred masked Blake's face as he whirled to Fellini, but he stayed his ground at Rhonda's touch.

"Does it really matter anymore?" she pressed. "After all this time? After us?"

He wouldn't look at her, and she feared that the pressures had set too many bitter memories racing through him.

"I didn't think so," he replied through gritted teeth, "but maybe it does."

Rhonda never would have believed that mere words could have cut so deeply, and she turned away to face a misty world that never had seemed so callous and cruel. But she had only moments for self-pity, for sudden wheezing at the entrance seized her attention.

"Barracks, no air," gasped Lorenzo as he staggered in.

Across the deck, the color rushed from Fellini's face. "It's going out. The backup's going out!"

"It's been going out for days," snapped Blake, and suddenly all eyes were on him. "If any of you had any sense, you'd've known it long before now. We had one chance and I took it. I shut down the system to all but this deck and the route to the air lock. We'll be needing the module."

Rage filled Lorenzo's eyes and he went for his Banning. "You try to kill Lorenzo!"

"No, Lorenzo!" said Sahtu, leaping up. "We need him for the Lei-jan."

The Spaniard directed his Banning to the Asian. "You order Lorenzo?"

"I thought Lorenzo was captain," said Sahtu, lowering his scimitar. "Then he oughta know that nobody orders the captain to do *nothin'*. They all take his orders. Anybody that don't, gets his stinkin' neck slit." He grinned sinisterly. "Sooner or later."

The dimwitted Spaniard failed to grasp the implication that seemed so obvious to Rhonda. He relaxed his grip on the Banning. "Lorenzo captain. Everybody do what he say, else die."

"Then I suggest," said Blake, nodding to the forward porthole, "you give orders to bring us into orbit around the third planet from that star, because that's where we'll find the Leijan."

"We can't. We'll die!" said Fellini. "We've got to check every planet, find one that's habitable."

"Okay," said Blake, "let's all pick one out so we can strand ourselves there and look up every night and see that third planet, and think about coming all this way and not having guts enough to go ahead and take it."

"Even if we got it, we'd die before we could make it back!"

Blake laughed caustically. "I thought gods didn't die."

"Cowards do," growled Sahtu, and with scimitar clenched tightly, he took a menacing step toward Fellini.

"Lorenzo want Leijan," grunted the Spaniard. "He want woman to love, lemstel." He pointed to the solar system. "We go, take Leijan, kill cowards."

***

Reality, fantasy. Where did one end, and the other begin? Or was there any difference anymore?

As they came into orbit about a mysterious world that seemed so far removed from the harsh truths of the Ohiloan desert and Lasky's choking gasps, Blake tried to balance the things his senses and logic told him were real with the undeniable intrusion of forces beyond nature. The planet below was disturbing enough, with its surface so non-reflective that, even when torched by the sun, it held only a glow, while nightfall plunged it into a gloom as abominable as the Violeshan pits. But what of the being of light and the inexplicable summons to the derelict, both of which he knew as real, yet, when judged by scientific principle and common sense, could only be relegated to hallucination and fancy?

He couldn't reconcile it, but one thing was certain. Delusions didn't show up on detection screens, and a blip had just begin blinking on the grid before him, denoting a ship-sized object hurtling in the exact orbit described by Lasky. He froze, his eyes fixed on instruments. A chill crawled down his spine as he waited for additional information to determine if it were simply a moon or a captive asteroid. Then it came, and with a start he realized it was a vessel, thousands of light years deep in an interstellar wilderness traversed by but a single other ship in recorded history. As he laid in computer commands for a rendezvous with that craft created to imprison the Leijan, he knew that the material and the metaphysical were about to merge once and for all.

With Lasky's wild eyes and trembling words haunting him, Blake rose to seek the forward porthole where he would first glimpse the inexplicable vessel. Rhonda had kept her distance ever since his lapse into bitterness, but now she was suddenly at his side again, supporting in a way that needed no words. Even as Blake anticipated the culmination of so many Sphinx-like threads, he regretted his thoughtless remarks to her, no matter what demons might still trouble him.

Still, he kept his face to the dark for so long that his eyes went out-of-focus and his mind reeled. It was out there. Somewhere, that incredibly intelligent and powerful presence lurked as it had for precisely a thousand years. And it was just waiting to be let out.

"He found it, but he didn't even know what it was," he said discreetly. "Lasky knew it wanted out, that he could've had it for himself, but he didn't have any idea." He glanced at her. "Do we, really? Can either of us stand here as students of science and really believe it's some kind of entity that's been imprisoned in a cosmic war that's been going on since before time began?"

He pressed a hand against the porthole, and his voice dropped to a whisper. "I wonder now if we'll ever know for sure. Even if we make it inside and turn it loose, I wonder if we'll be alive long enough to have any idea what it really is. I just hope that whatever we find's worth all the things we've been through." He turned and put a tender hand on her arm. "At least one good thing's come out of this."

She withdrew just far enough so that his hand slid away.

"What's wrong?" he asked.

"If you really meant that," she half-sobbed, "you still wouldn't be thinking about her all the time."

He supposed he had it coming. "Listen to me," he said, gently taking her by the shoulders. "She's out of my life and you're in it, and I wouldn't have it any other way. All I want to do is close that part of my life, once and for all."

"So what's got to happen for you to do that? Aren't you ever going to forget about her, when you know how I feel about you?"

"I don't want to forget. You learn from your experiences, your mistakes, or at least you ought to. And anyway, earlier, that wasn't so much about her as it was Fellini. I've already dealt with her because of you. But Fellini and that talk about his tent, I haven't."

She stifled a sob. "I don't understand," she said quietly, looking away to stare into the void. "I guess you've got your ghosts and I've got mine." She lowered her head and shuddered. "Langdon, what I had to do. He was an evil man, I know that. But there's still all this guilt inside me I can't get rid of, I'll never get rid of, because I can never give his life back to him."

Blake put a solacing arm around her. "Whatever you did, you did it for the being of light. Don't forget that."

The blip on the detection screen hadn't gone unnoticed by the others. As the distance indicator began to beep with ever-increasing frequency, signaling their approach to the object, Blake found them gravitating to the forward porthole to look for themselves.

"The dust fouled up the instruments like I said," spoke up Fellini. "The screen shows a ship, some kind of artificial satellite. But it can't be anything but a moon, not here where nobody but Lasky and those pirates have ever been."

"There's nothing wrong with the screen," snapped Blake, "just with the incompetent scum reading it."

Lorenzo grunted. "Somebody follow us."

"No," said Blake, looking at the Spaniard. "We've followed *it*, a thousand years later." Then he turned again to the porthole and flinched as if jolted by electricity.

"Look!" he said, pointing. "Right where Lasky said it was."

It was adrift, an ominous, black mass hanging over the planet's rim. At first, it was impossible to discern details, so non-reflective was it, but as they neared, Blake began to distinguish its slowly spinning hull. Dwarfing their own ship, it called to mind the cargo transports that moved like great, rectangular boxes through the void of interstellar space. Yet, it was unlike any vessel he had ever seen, lacking an apparent propulsion system, external detector antennae, or portholes either shielded or open. Even in comparison to artificial satellites, it was an anomaly, resembling more a huge coffin moving against the planet's face.

The computers carried them closer in standard docking maneuver, and the shift in relative position of the derelict to the sun brought it eclipsing and revealing the fireball with each latitudinal revolution. Unlike the paneled hulls of U.S.S. craft and satellites, the derelict's exterior seemed one unbroken piece of unidentifiable metal, heavily pockmarked by meteor impact. A minute more and they were abreast of it, and as they moved along its length to study it from ever-changing angles, Blake suddenly discerned the dark slit of an opening.

"A docking bay!" he said.

Then the roll of the derelict carried the bay out of sight, and Blake went to the controls and laid in a command to initiate a similar rotation for the ship and bring them adjacent to the module-sized breach.

They stood anxious with anticipation as the derelict's spin lessened and the hull grew still at a forty-five degree angle, and slowly they began to crawl along the scarred surface toward the impenetrable dark of the aperture. Blake stepped forward to study it from the porthole with the others, and as the computer brought the ship to a standstill before that mysterious bay now flooded by light from the forward control deck, there wasn't a single one of them who didn't cringe.

Etched into the dock, faint and shadowy, was the unmistakable sign of the Leijan.

"It's true!" said Fellini.

"Power just waitin'!" exclaimed Sahtu. "Look at it, Lorenzo. We'll rule the whole stinkin' universe."

Then the three marketers were bolting for the deck door and module, greed and bloodlust leading the way.

Blake clutched Rhonda's arm. "Let's go!"

Chapter Twenty-Six

Even as they ran for the air lock, Blake knew violence was imminent. The Leijan lay just meters away, yet the small module could accommodate only three people, four at most. That meant at least one of them had to stay behind, and he knew that none of the greed-crazed crewmen would willingly relinquish his place when power beyond their wildest imaginings was at stake.

They trailed the crewmen through the mad dash and overtook them at the air lock hatch. Fellini whirled the access wheel and they spilled inside to the hangar deck. Sahtu and Lorenzo immediately made for the module, their moving images distorted in its bubble, but Fellini pivoted toward an adjacent hatch.

"Pressure suits!" he reminded everyone.

Sahtu and Lorenzo stopped at the cry, dully watching as Blake ushered Rhonda past them to the module.

"Get in!" Blake yelled, lifting and pushing as she clambered up to fall inside.

"The derelict!" Sahtu shouted after him. "Pressurized?"

Blake stopped with his elbow against the bubble and turned, hoping to incite trouble. "Lasky said oxygen-nitrogen. For those there's room for."

Sahtu glanced at Fellini, several meters away, and then studied the module before finding Lorenzo's eyes. "How many places you see in there, Lorenzo? Three? Four?"

Lorenzo grunted.

"Way I see it," Sahtu continued, "somebody gets left behind. Which one you think you don't have no use for?"

Fellini wheeled, his face blanching. "Then leave Sharrel!" he pleaded, starting toward Lorenzo. "The liar said Lasky told him it was on Violesha Two. Now he talks like Lasky was here. We're supposed to share it, Lorenzo. You and me and Sahtu."

The Spaniard sneered. "Lorenzo no share nothing with filthy coward. Go devil, Academy scum." He turned to squeeze past Sahtu and seek the module.

Fellini's eyes went wild and he drew something from his boot. Cloth unraveled from jagged glass as he lunged for Lorenzo's shoulders.

"You're dead!" said Fellini.

The brilliance of deck lights flashed in Sahtu's scimitar. The blade swept down powerfully against the side of Fellini's neck, a penetrating force that dropped him and almost decapitated. The jag of glass shattered and Fellini's head bounced on the deck, his eyes seeing but not understanding.

He lay writhing at Blake's feet, his blood spewing as Sahtu's moist scimitar hovered above. For a moment everyone seemed stunned, and then Lorenzo confronted Sahtu.

The Asian grinned. "You and me, Lorenzo, just like always. Ain't no stinkin' coward *ever* turns on the captain without gettin' his throat slit."

As Blake stared down at his last link to the past, Lyra's face deluged him, summoning up bitterness and hatred at all the unanswered questions. He knelt and seized Fellini by the collar, the head dangling back as he jerked the eyes close to his own.

"What happened in that tent?" he demanded, feeling the blood spurt hot against his fists. "Tell me!"

But Fellini could only thrash to the gurgle of blood and air through his bared throat, and Blake, suddenly feeling the compassion of the being of light, laid the head back almost tenderly. Guiltily, he leaned close to clasp the hand of a fellow human being and feel the writhing grow weaker, hear the pitiful gasps grow quieter, until one last spasm stilled him forever.

Blake stood, the blood running down his hands, and without lifting his gaze to any of them, entered the module. He felt Rhonda's shoulder as he squeezed close, but for long seconds he only stared at the instrument panel, feeling again the convulsions through those fingers that had tightened against his own. Finally he turned, finding her eyes penetrating him.

"I had to know," he said quietly. Then he lowered his gaze to the blood on his hands. "Now it's over."

Blake was almost oblivious as the others squeezed in and someone neutralized the artificial gravity and initiated decompression to the air lock. He didn't look up until he caught peripheral movement beyond the marketers. Outside, Fellini's body rose with droplets of blood to hang suspended against the module, the ashen face frozen in a horrible grimace.

Rhonda buried her face in Blake's shoulder. Sahtu cringed and struck at the dead eyes with his bloody scimitar, the blade clanging against bubble.

"Get away from me!" exclaimed the Asian.

But throughout the long minute it took to decompress the lock, Fellini's face clung there, the lifeless eyes staring in, the slashed neck smearing the bubble with blood.

Then Sahtu, obviously impatient to escape those eyes, blew the lock's outer hatch a little too soon. With a great rush of air, the module burst into the blackness beyond, and with it went Fellini's body, bouncing off the bubble to paint it with his macabre visage.

Sahtu recoiled. "Get away!"

Blake's stomach churned; even Fellini deserved better. Nevertheless, he seized the chance to gain a psychological edge over the Asian and forced a quiet laugh. "You didn't leave him behind after all, did you, Sahtu?"

Scimitar clanged against bubble. "Get him away from me. Get him away!"

But Blake was alert enough now to see their imminent danger. Clutching the controls, he veered the module with a small burst of rockets, seconds before they would have crashed into the derelict's looming hull. His actions left the protoplasm hurtling past to slam against metal and drift away into oblivion.

As Blake turned the module to skim back portside along the massive hull that blocked the sun, Rhonda voiced a concern that he shared. "Hard to breathe, like before."

"A small craft. The lifeline's not designed to feed in oxygen for this many."

"It's going out," she said simply, as if accepting the inevitable.

He nodded to the derelict. "Just so we get in there."

Except for their increasingly labored breathing, a tomb-like silence reigned as Blake maneuvered the module in-between starship and derelict, two floating hulls locked in an unholy dance. His head spun with questions as he piloted it on toward the narrow bay entrance splashed by starship light. Soon they came abreast of it, to stare in at the sign of the Leijan in an enormous hangar deck thick with shadows.

He glanced one last time at the starship, remembering the scientific principles governing not only spaceflight but the entire cosmos, and then guided the craft into the bay and the unknown. Instantly he felt the tug of artificial gravity, and despite the bubble's supposed protection against the extremes of space, he had the distinct sensation of intense cold.

As the module reached the end of its tether line forty meters deep and settled toward the deck with a half-turn, Blake heard a whisper pass Rhonda's lips.

"Oh, Dad . . ."

Blake listened, already understanding.

". . . Your life, to get me here."

A moment later, Blake felt the gentle impact of landing pods on metal, a reassuring reminder of the laws of physics. But when he looked back at the drifting lifeline framed in the bay cleft, he twitched in alarm. As if triggered by contact of module against deck, the breach had begun to contract, the upper hull sliding down.

"It's closing!" said Rhonda.

"It'll cut our lifeline!" screamed Sahtu.

Blake reached for a lever at his knee. "I'm jettisoning it!" he said, employing a standard procedure to extend a module's range. He knew that normally a bubble would retain enough oxygen to last its pilot an hour, but here were four sets of lungs, already fighting for air through a failing system.

The line popped free. With the module floodlights, Blake searched the adjacent shadows for manual controls with which to pressurize the bay, but he distinguished only a sealed hatch in an inner bulkhead thirty meters deeper. All he could do was hope that the same automated system that had engaged the bay door would also pressurize the deck, or they were as good as dead.

Rhonda emitted a sudden gasp, and he found her eyes wide with the red reflection of the instrument panel.

"What devil?" grunted Lorenzo.

Then Blake looked and saw too, a silhouette moving against the light of the starship portholes, squeezing inside the bay doors at the last possible instant, settling to the deck just inside. Then the cleft in the hull closed, sealing them together in dark broken only by the module lights.

"What is it?" asked Sahtu.

"Quiet." Blake killed the floodlights and instrument panel and sat stunned, staring at the point in the dark where he knew it rested. As his eyes dilated, Blake saw it take shape in the eerie luminescence of the surrounding bulkheads: a sleek, black craft, ten meters in length, resting on the sign of the Leijan.

"A starship." Blake's cracked voice reflected his disbelief. "They followed us all this way to take it for themselves." His temple pounded with memories of the being of light. "The devil they will."

He flicked on a console readout light just long enough to find the bay pressurized, and then seized Rhonda's hand and lunged across Sahtu and Lorenzo for the module hatch. "Out before they see to shoot!"

Then the hatch was open and all of them spilled madly to the landing pods. As Blake dived away, dragging Rhonda with him, he hoped this revolutionary ship with obvious stealth capability was armed with only standard weapons, for a grounded U.S.S. fighter was unable to redirect its target system more than a few degrees.

Thunder boomed and brightness exploded against the bubble to hurl mangled sections in all directions. Blake cried out, rolling with Rhonda to the shock wave as shrapnel whizzed by. His skull banged against the deck, half-stunning him, but then Rhonda's arms were under his shoulders as she dragged him toward module debris ten meters larboard. A point of brilliance burst from the bow of the craft, an energy bolt blitzing by so close that it scorched Blake's face. With the quick return of his senses, he craned to see it detonate against the inner bulkhead, gouging a three-meter hole where the hatch had been.

To the shriek of more flying shrapnel, the two of them scrambled over twisted metal to sprawl prone. The fumes of melted plastic were unbearable in Blake's face, but they could only lie there as yet another bolt surged past, a full three meters off course.

"They can't do it!" he said. "They can't shoot this far off line!"

"Kill 'em. Kill 'em all!" Not until Sahtu yelled did Blake realize that the Asian lay beside him, and that Lorenzo stretched out just beyond, grunting and clutching a bloody wrist.

"They'll come out!" warned Blake, finding the craft's hatch through twisted metal at his brow. "They can't get us with the ship's Bannings, so they'll come at us with their own." He spun to Lorenzo. "You better be able to use that thing."

Lorenzo grunted and glanced at his wrist. "Hand hit, Banning fall."

Blake's cheek twitched, and he checked the debris-strewn deck where the initial blast had thrown them. In direct line of fire lay the Banning, their only real hope. Still, the realization didn't keep him from spinning to the inner bulkhead's jagged hole and studying all that it revealed: a shadowy foyer that gave way to a corridor glowing like distant brew fires of witches.

But there was more.

Over the corridor entrance was an engraving, and for a moment Blake froze before the haunting images that loomed side by side. One was an ordinary hand, the other, three spikes that joined at a sphere crawling with an unholy trinity of serpents, the sign of the Leijan. The fingers held a three-pointed star, extending it as if it were a key toward a perfectly matching slot in the sphere's heart.

Then the craft's hatch blew, and Blake pivoted amid a hail of energy bolts and saw a form drop to the deck and roll to the cover of a landing pod. Almost simultaneously, the hatch framed a second form that fired a quick salvo before withdrawing.

From the ship's underbelly came a gruff cry. "Gregory! Rhonda Gregory! You're mine!"

Blake whirled to see Rhonda's jaw drop.

"You hear me?" came the voice with its staccato-like inflection. "I chased you clear across the galaxy and now you're mine!"

"Who is it?" Blake demanded of her.

She brought trembling fingers to her cheek.

"You know who this is, don't you?" the voice rasped. "I want you to know. I'm makin' you pay for ever' minute of it."

"*Pierce*," she gasped quietly. Then she shouted. "What do you want?"

A laugh reverberated through the bay. "I'll start with breakin' your neck."

"I left you food and water. I could've let you die, but I didn't."

"You're gonna wish you had, you slut."

As Pierce followed up with invectives, Blake considered their desperate plight. The Banning lay tantalizingly close, eight meters at most. Within seconds, he could dive for it and come up firing. How long could he expect their assailants to withhold an all-out charge, thinking they were armed?

He turned to Rhonda and whispered. "Keep him distracted."

She glanced at him and seemed to understand. "Captain Pierce! Or is it captain anymore, after you let a woman skyjack your ship?"

The man cursed vehemently.

"You let a woman walk right up and take over your ship, hold you at Banning point for dozens of light years!"

An energy bolt cracked to find the wreckage before her and intensify the odor of gaseous plastic.

"I just walked away in that desert with the secret of the Leijan, and all you could do was lie there and know a girl had gotten the best of you!"

"That's all you're gonna say, you slut!"

"I guess you made that elderly woman in the picture awfully proud, the way you let a girl bluff you clear across the colonies!"

"You're dead, I tell you. Dead!"

Blake leaped into the open, hugging the deck, all senses fixed on the weapon before him. He dug a boot into metal, and then another that threw him prone through the air, his arms extended, the fingers straining in anticipation. A blue bolt of energy surged by his head. His hand came down on the Banning, and as his shoulder and pelvic bone slammed against deck, his fingers closed on the grip. His momentum carried him on over, rolling him away from a second bolt. Then he was flat on his stomach, the weapon extended in both hands as he pumped shot after shot at the landing pod.

Instantly, the Banning grew hot in his hands and he knew that shrapnel had damaged it. But he kept his grip through the searing pain and fired repeatedly, momentarily stifling any return volleys. Then came a sudden cry from Rhonda, and he looked around to see Sahtu strike her in the mouth and relinquish her to Lorenzo's powerful hold. Still, all Blake could do was keep up his fire on the intruders, and when he risked another glance back, he saw the Spaniard dragging Rhonda after Sahtu across the open deck and through the twisted breach.

The animals. They'd taken her. They'd taken her and they were going after the Leijan.

He took fire from the landing pod, and he glimpsed a rising silhouette in the craft's hatch.

"Take him out!" ordered a new voice. "You hear me?"

"Nobody's armed but the one on deck!" yelled Pierce.

"Kill him. You've got to kill him!"

But Blake, for the next few seconds, kept up such a barrage that neither of them could squeeze off a shot. With each *crack* his weapon grew hotter, its firepower weaker. In the name of the being of light, it was *failing*, and with it, perhaps, would go the hopes of mankind.

He scrambled up and retreated, shooting as he did. Pierce must have seen the diminishing brightness of bolts suddenly off-target, for he edged out and raked the deck. Lightning exploded at Blake's feet, at his side, against the inner bulkhead, and then from Blake's own weapon surged one final bolt and it was dead.

"His Banning's failed!"

Simultaneous with Pierce's cry, Blake dived through a storm of energy bolts for the jagged hole.

"Then nobody's armed!" shouted the second voice.

Blake felt searing pain as he fell headlong through the breach, jags of casting cutting his leg. He rolled behind mangled metal and looked back. There were only two of them, the nearer man peppering the breach with energy bolts and the farther one only now exiting the craft.

"Let's go!" said Pierce. "That slut's all mine."

The arm of his confederate rose quickly. "I've got better plans."

Fatal blue lightning from a Banning muzzle exploded against Pierce's back, and then Blake was up, the astonishing images above the corridor guiding him into the witch-fire.

Chapter Twenty-Seven

Dragged at Sahtu's heels, Rhonda tried to shed Lorenzo's club-like arm, but the Spaniard was too powerful, even with one hand dangling bloody. The corridor grew increasingly murky, testing the limits of her vision as they went deeper into a creeping cold with Lorenzo's every grunting step. Within ninety seconds they reached a fork, where the faint glow revealed engravings over each passage.

Lorenzo tightened his grip as Rhonda redoubled her struggles. "Which way go?"

Sahtu went wide-eyed as he stretched his scimitar to the sketch of a three-pointed star over the starboard corridor.

"There!" he directed.

The next instant, they were angling down it, Sahtu surging ahead as Rhonda worked a disrupting foot between Lorenzo's striding boots. They had managed only twenty meters when another crossroad slowed them, but this time it was only long enough for the Asian to distinguish the passage marked by the star-key, and they were off again.

For long minutes they snaked through the maze, the marker guiding them into the bowels of the derelict. With each frantic turn, Rhonda saw Sahtu grow more crazed with greed and Lorenzo more wild-eyed with lust. Still, she retained the presence of mind to note a heightened lumi-nescence and intensifying cold as they rounded a final corner to face a forty-meter stretch that ended at a sealed hatch.

Sahtu halted, clearly reeling with excitement. Through the vapor of her breaths, Rhonda saw what captivated him. Over the hatch's access wheel was another etching: the hand, the star-key, the spiked sphere bearing the Leijan's sign. But this time the key rested in the sphere's slot, and something—man, beast, or devil—exploded from it.

"Why us stop?" demanded Lorenzo, shaking the blood from his hand.

A scimitar flashed up to prick Rhonda's neck.

"So all I had to do was give you a stinkin' ship and you'd lead me to the Leijan," Sahtu snarled. "You wanted it all for yourself, you and that filthy scum." He spat in her face, the spittle dribbling down to catch the blade. "Nobody does me wrong." His eyes shifted to Lorenzo. "Nobody."

He withdrew the blade and struck the flat side against her boot. "The heel," he told the Spaniard. "Rip it off and ever' wench in the colonies is yours, and you can start with this lyin' slut."

Lorenzo grunted and threw her down, and as he fell upon her, he seemed to forget everything but his own primitive desires. "Maybe you learn to love Lorenzo."

"The heel, you fool!" yelled Sahtu, kicking him in the ribs.

Lorenzo twisted around with threatening eyes. "When finish, Lorenzo kill you, wicked-eyed devil." But in appeasement, he clutched Rhonda's lower leg and wrenched her boot heel free, spilling the starkey to the deck.

Its similarity to the etching didn't escape even the slow-witted Spaniard. Sahtu lunged for it, but Lorenzo already was throwing Rhonda aside and scooping it up in a bloody hand.

"Give it here," demanded Sahtu.

Lorenzo sealed it in his hairy fist.

Sahtu nodded to Rhonda. "You been wantin' her ever since you laid eyes on her. Take her."

Lorenzo stood to stare past Sahtu at the hatch and etching. "Lorenzo want Leijan more. You do what Lorenzo say."

Sahtu smiled grimly. "Then let's go get it," he snapped, and he moved aside to let the Spaniard by.

Rhonda saw Sahtu's eyes betray his intent the instant Lorenzo brushed past. But while she watched, she dragged herself up and retreated, her boots sticky against the Spaniard's blood trail. Meanwhile, the Asian's blade rose red and gleaming across his chest, until the hilt was at his opposite ear and Lorenzo's back was exposed.

"Nobody turns on me!" said Sahtu.

The blade fell, swift and deadly, and Rhonda wheeled and fled.

She turned the corner and ran thirty meters before halting in sudden realization. She, and she alone, stood between Sahtu and the Leijan, between that horrid power waiting to be unleashed and mankind's hopes for a future. Whirling, she rushed headlong in pursuit, determined that, at the least, she would die knowing she had given her all for the being of light.

Rounding the corner, she looked past Lorenzo's bloody corpse and saw the Asian spinning the hatch wheel.

"No!" she shouted.

But Sahtu already was throwing open the gate to a thousand-year-old prison and lunging inside.

***

Blake ran through the corridor desperately, conscious of all he faced: the Banning of a ruthless killer behind, the scimitar of a bloodthirsty pirate ahead, and a chronometer inexorably ticking away the last seconds of this day of days. It was more than a man could cope with, yet on his shoulders he also carried the hopes of the entire cosmos.

Even now, Sahtu and Lorenzo might be standing on the brink of eternity with key in hand. He could smell their stench in the musty air, and it carried him into a sudden passage veering right. Beyond, he found a brooding labyrinth hollow with the sound of his boots. He plunged on wildly, chasing that sickening odor through a bewildering maze growing ever colder.

He looked back after extended minutes and caught the reflected beam of an illuminator, and he knew that the armed man navigated the passages with the same surety as he. Negotiating a final bend, he met Rhonda as she spun to him in front of a blood-splattered body that he recognized as Lorenzo's. He read alarm in her face and dug fingers into her shoulders, his momentum wheeling them about in the sticky pool.

"Where is he?" he exclaimed.

She slung a hand down a straightaway. "He's got the star-key!"

Turning, he saw an open hatch ahead and felt a frigid rush of air, and he knew it for the same evil cold that had gripped him in the desert. For an instant he found her eyes again, and then he was away, hurdling Lorenzo's body in chase.

As he ran, he found the hatch framing a man, strangely suspended inside against a backdrop of deepest black. Each succeeding meter widened Blake's field of vision, and he saw that it was Sahtu, swimming through a weightless environment, his arms clawing and legs kicking in uncoordinated effort. Then Blake reached the hatch to seize the rim and thrust himself through, and the world inside exploded into vision.

He looked past a meter-wide ledge into a three-dimensional sea of black that seemed to roll away forever. His logic told him it was finite, confined by the derelict, but he was stunned by the sensation that he stared upon a rent in the cosmos where gravity ended and bitterly cold swirls of gloom prevailed. From the hatch spilled the glow of the corridor, eerily illuminating Sahtu's crazed struggles as he took the key deeper into the gulf with every stroke.

Beyond the Asian loomed something else, a form indistinct in the shadows, yet possessing definite mass. Although never before in history had time been such a factor, Blake hesitated a moment, his gaze frozen on that mysterious object that seemed the source of all the sinister cold.

Spinning slowly in that awful abyss, it resembled at once an old-style ocean mine and a morning star, the spiked weapon of medieval times, but he knew that this thing shackled something infinitely deadlier. The corridor's twilight revealing its ancient, pockmarked features in stages: a fierce spike of metal coming to a needle-like point, and then a second spike, a third. Symmetrically positioned, the three jutted the height of a man from a sphere of like diameter, its surface like corroded chain mail. Just as Lasky had sworn, the sphere emitted cries of torment that seemed to transcend the auditory and rake his mind.

Already, Sahtu's hands were almost upon it, and Blake dug a boot into the ledge still subject to gravity and dived into the weightless night.

Chapter Twenty-Eight

Swimming frantic with desperation through surging waves of cold, Blake saw Sahtu seize a spinning spike and bring his body and clanging scimitar in revolution with it. Through motes of frost from his breath, Blake watched the Asian drag himself toward the armored base and the three-pronged rift that marked it. He saw Sahtu reach out with quaking star-key and grope for that matching cleft, bringing all good men's hopes to the brink of hell. And with a fierce, primal yell, Blake drew strength from deep inside and made one last lunge.

Sahtu whirled at the cry and Blake seized him by the heel, dragging him from the sphere. The star-key slipped free to hang between them in synchronous revolution. With an oath, the Asian kicked him in the face, but Blake held on and threw out a hand to meet the sweeping sword arm. His fingers caught flesh just above hilt, but the snap of Sahtu's wrist carried the blade forward to sear Blake's cheek. Then the two were fighting for the scimitar, there between the spikes of an icy sphere that had fettered a great, evil power for a thousand years.

By images that flashed and tossed, Blake knew that Rhonda had gained the ledge, only to yield to a bruising shoulder as Pierce's confederate burst through the hatch. Blake caught the glint of his illuminator, and then the confederate's Banning cracked and a deadly blue arc singed Blake's hair and set the star-key tumbling wildly.

There was a pause followed by a babble of words from the confederate, a quick oath and more, something about the etchings and star-key and how close he had come to destroying it with so distant a shot. But the scimitar was such a deadly presence that Blake couldn't turn, even as he glimpsed Rhonda falling upon the man and taking a vicious pistol-whipping. Dazed, she sank to the ledge, and then the intruder cast aside his illuminator and dived with extended Banning into the void.

Blake suddenly gained a tenuous joint hold on the scimitar and a grip at Sahtu's throat. He hooked a heel over a spike, allowing him to maneuver their bodies so he could see the oncoming intruder. Time was running out, and yet he was locked in a death struggle, taking blow after blow to the cheek and eye. Summoning up the kind of hatred he had known only for Fellini, he remembered Sahtu's anxiety in the module.

"Behind you!" he said. "The dead eyes, the cut throat. Fellini come to get you!"

He felt the Asian shudder and saw his eyes bulge, and he knew that he had pricked the one nerve of flesh-crawling fear that Sahtu had.

"Dead eyes and blood, just like the bubble!"

"I'll kill you!" the Asian gurgled.

"You've got to see. You know you've got to see!"

"Shut up. Shut up!"

The confederate was almost upon them. It was now or never.

"The dead eyes, cut throat. Fellini come to get you!"

The Asian looked. Blake slammed a forearm down and crushed Sahtu's hand against the hilt. The force of the blow spun them half-around, and suddenly Blake's fingers alone were loose on the scimitar.

"Look out!" warned Rhonda.

Blake found the confederate a body-length away with a Banning leveled on him. He came around with a backhand sweep of the scimitar and caught muzzle and confederate with a flat, stunning blow as an errant stream of energy discharged. The clang of steel sent the Banning flying toward the ledge and tore the scimitar from Blake's hold. The confederate went limp as the blade drifted away, glinting in the abrupt light of an illuminator directed by Rhonda. Then something grasped Blake's neck from behind and a maniacal voice rang out.

"Die!" said Sahtu.

The Asian clamped a second hand against the vise-like arm already at Blake's throat and locked legs around his thighs. Simultaneously, Blake saw a dazed Rhonda crawling for the Banning as it plummeted to the ledge not a dozen meters from her.

The eerie dark swam before Blake as he writhed and clutched at the forearm crushing his throat. He clawed at that sweaty arm, sinking nails into flesh, but Sahtu now seemed possessed by the strength of ten. Blake seized the stringy hair, gouged the eyes, drove an elbow into a kidney, and still the vise stayed at his neck, squeezing the life from him. The world whirled and Blake felt that indefinable part that made him alive and gave him self-identity drifting away. As if from a deep, Stygian well, he heard the hollow cry of Sahtu's curses. Then something snapped and he seemed a step removed from his body, aware of, but not subject to, the crushing of his larynx, the ache of his lungs, the futile search for oxygen by his arteries, even the stirring confederate's hand reaching for scimitar.

All the events of Blake's life bombarded him in waves, and he remembered what had changed him, made him care again, given him the will to live. It had been love, that of a woman, that of the being of light. Together, they had created in him something that wouldn't die, that *couldn't* die.

In death throes, Blake flailed his arm at the Asian's back and felt the prick of something sharp. Hanging on to a thread of consciousness, he reached for it, his fingers closing on a spike and drawing Sahtu up against its rapier point. His mind reeled with the brilliance of the being of light. He heard through an ever-lengthening tunnel the words "Mine! Mine!" And with a final burst of strength he impaled the Asian.

Sahtu convulsed, a visceral groan crawling up through his diaphragm. But Blake only increased his leverage, burying the spike ever deeper in the pirate's back, until finally one last breath passed those lungs and the pinioning arms and legs relaxed.

Blake drifted away, clutching his throat and wheezing, leaving Sahtu's lifeless body nailed to the spike to revolve with eyes bulging and mouth agape. Blake seemed to hurtle through a cold, dark vortex alive with the torments of many. But there were also images, distant and vague: the confederate with a blood-stained blade and Rhonda with a rising Banning, a hand ready to butcher and a hand ready to save. He knew he should do something, that he *had* to do something, but he was too lost in a never-never land to care about anything but the love of the being of light and of Rhonda, and his love for them.

The blast of a Banning and heat of its bolt reached Blake's senses even in his maelstrom, slowing his plummet, suspending him in limbo, drawing him up toward a light bearing all the wonder and promise of the one that had summoned him from the pit in the City of the Skull. Yes, there was a light above, growing brighter, and a sound that echoed through the hollowness of his purgatory. As he grew nearer, he recognized his name, carried on the voice of one he had once hated. She was calling, and he couldn't answer; she was pleading, and he couldn't respond.

The flash of an illuminator finally stirred him, and he floated there for long seconds and stared at its rays glinting in something spinning minuscule and fuzzy before his eyes. He shook away the cobwebs and it came into focus, one point at a time, until finally he realized he looked upon the star-key. It lay on a direct line with the scimitar blade, frozen in a hand two meters beyond, and with the charred wound breaching the torso of the confederate who would never kill again.

Blake rolled to find Sahtu's dead eyes staring blankly, his transfixed body still spinning with every revolution of the sphere. Then he turned once more and clutched the star-key, warm and life-giving, and struck out in easy strokes for Rhonda. Her eyes bared so many thoughts as she waited with lowered Banning, but Blake's gaze wandered also to the oval of twilight marking the open hatch. From above it, Lasky had ripped a plaque bearing a haunting promise that had launched many on a long, cruel quest. And now it was over.

Where weightlessness became gravity, Blake took Rhonda's hand and gained the ledge. Rising, he sought reassurance and found it in her embrace and the caress of her fingers on his bloody face.

"Nobody left, just you and me," said Blake. Then he felt her shudder.

"My shot. Blake, it was *Langdon*."

He pulled away, startled. "But—"

"Just hold me."

Even as he complied, he shot a confused look at the shadowy body floating beside the sphere. "How?"

"All I know is I was praying for the being of light to guide my aim. I've wanted to give Langdon's life back a thousand times, but . . ."

He glanced again at the charred corpse and tried to process it all. "You sorry you didn't?"

All kinds of conflicting emotions were in her face as she turned to stare into the abyss, but when she focused on him again, a smile had won out. "You know the answer to that."

Once more, she pulled him close, and when they separated he opened a bloody hand to display the star-key. For a while Blake joined her in staring at it, mesmerized by the implications, and then he nodded to the entrance.

"Lasky. It all started with him tearing that plaque away."

As Rhonda cast an illuminator beam to the bulkhead above the hatch, Blake discerned not only a rectangle of discoloration, evidencing a one-time marker, but etched letters. He exchanged a look of surprise with her, and then together they sought it out to the hollow sound of their steps.

Rhonda halted in the splashing twilight to study the markings from close range.

"Greek?" pressed Blake. "Like Lasky found?"

"Ancient," she verified. Then she translated. "'What is your name, you unclean spirit?' 'My name is legion, for we are many.'"

She spun. "The Leijan, Blake. *A legion.*" Her voice dropped to a whisper imbued with all the awe befitting a glimpse into cosmic truths. "He, his fallen cohorts, the people from the Valley of the Skull, from hell."

She lowered the illuminator and Blake went silent, dwelling on what she had read and considering all that had happened.

"What now?" he finally posed, and his eyes fell again to the key in his palm. He nodded to the hatch. "There's a ship in the docking bay, just you and me to man it. It could take us out of here." He glanced at the armored sphere twirling in the endless night. "We don't know what will happen to us if we let that thing out."

He looked at her and found her staring back, a man and woman suddenly aware that two lives never before had been so intertwined in common destiny.

"Don't you know what we've got a chance to do?" she asked. "Don't you realize that we can set in motion the final chain of events to rid the universe of everything evil? That we can see to it that all the pain and grief gets swept away so good people can finally have a destiny with the being of light? Doesn't that make my life and yours, our life together, unimportant by comparison?"

"By comparison maybe, but it still means something to me."

Her eyes began to well. "I love you, Blake. I love you so much I can't even begin to tell you. One way, I feel so cheated in maybe not ever having the chance to be with you, have a life together. I realize we don't know what it'll do to us, but do we have any choice?"

He took a deep breath. "Did we ever?" he asked quietly, the promise he had made in the pit vivid in his mind. "The being of light called me, brought you and me together, meant for us to be together." Intense emotion gripped him. "Where would I be now if he hadn't?"

Her hands stole up across his shoulders and they melted into one another's arms, and for long moments his mouth was tender on hers. Then he withdrew to caress her cheek, and he suddenly felt the kind of assurance and happiness that only the being of light could bring.

"He brought us all this way, didn't he, Rhonda?" he asked softly. "He brought us this far because he loves us, and I know he won't turn his back on us now."

She smiled and he took her hand, and together they turned and swam toward the sphere of the Leijan.

About the Author

A member of the Texas Literary Hall of Fame, Patrick Dearen is the author of twenty-six books. As a nonfiction writer, Dearen has produced books such as *A Cowboy of the Pecos*; *Saddling Up Anyway: The Dangerous Lives of Old-Time Cowboys*; and *Castle Gap and the Pecos Frontier, Revisited*. His research has led to sixteen novels, including *The Big Drift*, winner of the Spur Award of Western Writers of America and the Peacemaker Award of Western Fictioneers. His other western-themed novels include *When Cowboys Die* (a Spur Award finalist); *The End of Nowhere; Haunted Border; The Illegal Man; To Hell or the Pecos; Perseverance; Apache Lament;* and *Dead Man's Boot*. His three science-fiction novels include *Starflight to Eternity,* a follow-up to *Starflight to Destiny.*

A ragtime pianist and wilderness enthusiast, Dearen lives with his wife in Texas.

Coming Soon!

PATRICK DEAREN'S

STARFLIGHT TO ETERNITY
(a.k.a. Starflight to Faroul)

**"I held the secret of creation in my hands,
but I lost it and can never have it again!"**

In this follow-up to *Starflight to Destiny*, a wizened old man named Kasterfayette has returned from deep space, bearing a strange tale of the planet Faroul. This legendary world is said to be a place where time began and ends, and where a man may gain the power to create. But Faroul is much more, for it holds the destiny of the universe…

**For more information
visit: www.SpeakingVolumes.us**